Unmasking the

Wayward in Wessex

Earl

Elizabeth Keysian

Entangled Publishing, LLC
2614 South Timberline Road
Suite 109
Fort Collins, CO 80525
Visit our website at www.entangledpublishing.com.

Scandalous is an imprint of Entangled Publishing, LLC.

Edited by Nina Bruhns
Cover design by Erin Dameron-Hill
Cover art from Period Images

Manufactured in the United States of America

First Edition May 2017

SCANDALOUS

To my long-suffering best friend and partner, Tim Robey. Your encouragement has been indispensible, your support unswerving, and your ability to answer my questions without resorting to Google has impressed me beyond words!

Chapter One

Oxfordshire, England
May 1821

"To love and not be loved in return is the worst torment of all."

Cassandra Blythe turned and looked into the sympathetic eyes of her cousin, Rebecca.

"Well, yes, indeed," Cassie replied, plying her fan and trying to appear unconcerned as she gazed around the crowded ballroom. "But don't worry about me. My dance card is quite full. See? I have no reason to repine."

Becca examined the small piece of ivory dangling from Cassie's wrist. "How odd," she said. "I see Julian's name down for dances which have already happened, but I don't recall seeing the two of you together."

Cassie sighed and ignored the fist of pain that struck at her heart. "True. Mr. Carnforth has been distracted tonight. He's confused me with Lady Lucy Dyer twice. Look here," she said, jabbing a finger at the finely penciled letters. "He marked himself down for the cotillion and the quadrille with me, but ended up dancing with her on both occasions."

Becca gave a tinkling laugh. "I can't imagine how! Our hosts have bought up every chandelier and candelabrum in Wessex and installed them in their ballroom. I declare I can see a good deal more than I wish to! Julian should have had no difficulty recognizing you, despite the crush."

Cassie looked down at the clump of violets wilting at her breast. She felt like wilting, too, but said brightly, "Anyway, I don't see why you should single out Julian for mention. There are plenty of extremely eligible gentlemen here."

"Ah, but only one who has made you stammer in his presence since you were thirteen," said Becca sagely.

"Oh, Becca, don't tease. I'm too hot and weary to dispute with you. In fact, I think I'll go upstairs and try to cool down a little. Had you better check on Papa? I don't want him getting overtired."

"I have been given my congé," her cousin said cheerfully, and disappeared back into the throng.

Casting a dark look in the direction of Mr. Julian Carnforth, Cassie swept through the crowd of dancers, head held high, and made her way up the grand staircase of Highmore House and into the ladies' powdering room.

It was a relief to find it unoccupied. She swiftly undid the catch on the shutters, pulled them back, lifted the sash window, and leaned out, desperate for the touch of cooler air on her face.

Oh, Julian. What a disappointment! She'd done her best to look beautiful tonight for their old family friend. She'd pushed up her bosom, pinched her cheeks, curled her hair to within an inch of its life, and practiced fluttering her eyelashes in front of a mirror—all to no avail. He just couldn't see past the fact that they were childhood friends. Recently, he'd even remarked that she was like a sister to him.

A sister!

The man she'd loved for years thought of her as no more than that. The pain she experienced whenever she heard him use that word cut like a blade.

Her vision blurred as she gazed out across the Duke and Duchess of Paxton's vast gardens and grounds. She gave a little hiccup of distress, then blinked rapidly as a dark shape came into view on the gravel below the window.

It would have been sensible to withdraw her head immediately and close the shutters, rather than submit herself to the impertinent gaze of the man looking up at her. But good sense hardly seemed important compared to a broken heart. She stiffened, tilted her chin, and glared right back.

When their eyes locked and held, an involuntary shiver shot up her spine. Not a gentleman. This was a servant, simply clad, with shadowed eyes and a frowning brow.

That any such fellow should appraise her so brazenly was disgraceful. She'd a good mind to find out who his master or mistress was and complain. She could, of course, just call down and admonish him, but that would be lowering herself to his level. Besides which, he looked a rough and powerful man, the sort who could very easily scale the nearest drainpipe, throw her over his shoulder, and make off with her into the night if the fancy took him.

The image of him doing just that made her flush and wish her corset were less tight.

By Juno! It must be hotter than she thought. She couldn't possibly be affected by the insolent appraisal of a manservant. Could she? Her frustration over Julian was getting the better of her. If only *he* would throw her over his shoulder and make off with her…

Suddenly, a giggling couple burst forth from the house and scurried down the steps to the gravel drive. Arm in arm, they set off, swaying slightly, along a double line of flickering flambeaux which led toward the formal gardens.

Whatever spell had held the handsome servant transfixed was broken. He was already striding off.

Releasing a pent-up breath, Cassie was about to turn away when something struck her about the laughing couple. She looked again. *Sweet Venus.* Surely that was Julian's slender figure, his particular way of walking, that way he had of tilting his head to listen to one as if one were the only person in the room?

Good Lord. Julian Carnforth was sneaking away from the ball with Lady Lucy Dyer.

The air crashed out of Cassie's lungs, then returned with a great gush…which brought with it a blast of righteous fury.

How *dare* that woman toy with Julian!

And how could *he* behave with such lack of honor?

Cassie folded her arms across her chest and caught sight of the wilting violets. With a growl of anger, she tore them from her bosom, flung them through the window, and slammed it closed.

"Damn you, Julian Carnforth," she spluttered indignantly. "I'm not letting you ruin your reputation with a light-skirt like that!"

Pausing only to grab an abandoned shawl from a chair, she hurried out of the room and cantered down the staircase in pursuit of Julian and his new ladybird.

Clenching her fists, she vowed, "I'll work out a way to stop you, just see if I don't!"

Chapter Two

Something flew out of the window.

Catching sight of it as it fell to earth, Ned Ganstridge turned on his heel and strode back to where he'd seen the girl on the upper floor of Highmore House. What could she have thrown, and why?

Scouting around on the gravel in the shifting shadows was a difficult task, but he found the object eventually and examined it.

A bunch of violets. One that was overdue a watering. Foolish girl. Had no one told her violets were far too delicate for a corsage, especially while dancing?

He twirled the limp stems between his fingers, stroked the silk ribbon binding, and pressed his lips together.

Had his sister done the same with *her* lover, he wondered. Had Georgiana dropped letters, love tokens, even keys from her bedroom window as she carried on her clandestine affair? No one had any proof, of course, just suspicion and hearsay— there was no way of knowing for certain what vile twist of Fate had overtaken her. But Georgiana was gone, and Ned was no longer fully himself.

A soft chuckle made him spin round, just in time to see a couple of Paxton's guests hurrying away from the mansion. They were headed for the hot houses, or perhaps the maze, but wherever they were going, they were surely up to no good. In fact, wasn't the female Lady Lucy, his master's latest fancy piece?

Well, it certainly wasn't Captain Francis Wycherley who was with her now.

Ned's lip curled up in grim satisfaction. Wycherley would be furious, but it was about time that devil got a taste of his own medicine. A man who tangled with the demimonde must expect to be given the runaround.

Ned didn't give a fake farthing. He very much doubted Captain Wycherley's fickle heart—if he had a heart at all—would feel the pain for long.

"I hope she gets thrown on her back by that lusty beanpole she's with and returns to you with an unwelcome gift," he said vehemently, glaring after the departing pair. A good dose of the clap or the pox—now, *that* would be much more painful.

And fitting.

His fingers started to curl into a fist but were halted by the small bunch of flowers in his hand. He peered down at them. Had the bronze-haired beauty thrown them to *him?* No one had ever done that before. No one back home would ever have dared such a thing.

Tucking the limp blooms into the pocket of his nankeen waistcoat, he sauntered back along the line of carriages to join the straggling throng of coachmen and flunkeys. Matthews, Wycherley's footman, gave him an appraising look, then reached into the pocket of his caped coat and produced a flask.

"It's about time, Mr. Ganstridge," he said, "to lighten your spirits. Have a sip of my mountain dew. That'll warm up your gizzard and wipe the scowl off your face."

"Thankin' you," replied Ned briefly, accepting the flask.

He took a sip. Huh! Call this mountain dew? It was weak as maid's piss. Pretending enjoyment, he said casually, "I see our master's been cuckolded by Lady Lucy."

"Has he, now?" inquired Matthews. "Who's she gone off with?"

"No idea. A skinny longshanks, by the look of it. Good-looking, from what little I could see."

"Master won't mind," commented Matthews, retrieving the flask. "He were never going to marry her, anyway."

"She don't seem the kind to care about marriage," Ned observed, matching his accent to the coarse dialect of the other servants.

"Isn't that what they all want, women? Get their fambles on some poor unsuspecting cove, dig their claws in—"

The flask was offered again, but Ned gestured to Matthews to keep drinking. If the liquor loosened his tongue, it could be extremely useful.

"How d'ye know he wouldn't want to marry her?" Ned asked. "She's comely enough."

"Aye. But he won't marry nobody. Not now."

"He's told you this, has he?" he inquired, raising a mocking brow. Masters didn't generally confide such things to their footmen, coachmen, or menservants. But Matthews was more likely to talk if he thought he wasn't being taken seriously.

"He has, Mr. Ganstridge," was the reply. "Though I can't see as it's any business of your'n. But I'll tell you this. He can't wed the one he wants, so he'll not wed at all."

No, he can't, thought Ned grimly, *as the woman he wants may be dead. Or ruined and hiding in some godforsaken hovel.*

"Will he take Lady Lucy back if she comes running, d'ye think?" he inquired.

"Mayhap. He's soft-hearted underneath, our master. If he likes her well enough, she'll be forgiven."

"Pah!" Ned pretended to spit, though he detested the habit. "She'll not get away with going off with another man, I wager."

"Like I said, if she talks to him pretty-like, and promises not to do it again, he'll let her off and take her back. But only if he likes her enough."

Then the man's a fool, Ned thought, but didn't say it out loud. *He* could never care for a woman who couldn't make up her mind between two paramours…

Matthews tucked the flask away and stood up straight. He leaned across and hissed into Ned's ear, "Happen he won't need to forgive her for cheatin', as he's about to do the exact same thing 'imself!"

Ned turned and saw the unmistakable form of Captain Wycherley descending the steps from the main doors of Highmore House. He was not alone.

Clinging to his arm and looking every inch a fellow conspirator was the bronze-haired beauty who'd thrown down the flowers.

Chapter Three

As Cassie stepped out onto the terrace with Captain Francis Wycherley, she felt a thrill of mixed fear and excitement. If it was grossly improper for an unmarried lady to leave a ballroom without her chaperone, it was even more so to do it in the company of a notorious rake.

But running into the captain at the precise moment she'd decided to chase after Lady Lucy and Julian had been fortuitous.

Because they both had exactly the same purpose in mind.

"I don't wish to seem cruel," she said as Wycherley offered his arm to guide her down the sweeping steps at the front of Paxton House. "But I think it very shallow of Lady Lucy to accompany *you* to the ball and then run off into the night with another gentleman."

The captain inclined his handsome head toward hers and said good-humoredly, "Lady Lucy has her faults, I agree, but she has many…advantages, too. Enough to win my forgiveness."

Assuming you don't find her draped around Julian

Carnforth with her back to a tree, Cassie thought bitterly, then shook the unwelcome image from her mind. Julian wouldn't do that. He was being foolish, perhaps because he'd had too much punch. He couldn't *seriously* be interested in that flirt, could he?

Cassie's feet crunched on the gravel of the drive, and she and her accomplice paused a moment, gazing out into the flame-speckled darkness. There was a gaggle of servants and coachmen lounging nearby, smoking pipes and swigging back tankards of ale, while the grooms and tigers walked the horses so they'd be fresh for the homeward journey.

Of Julian and Lady Lucy there was no sign.

"Any idea what direction they took?" Wycherley asked.

"They were heading that way," Cassie said, pointing her fan toward a distant ornamental lake. "But more to the left. They could be heading for the hot houses. Or the maze."

As soon as the words were out of her mouth, she knew it had to be the maze. She'd no idea if Julian knew the key to mastering it, but it didn't matter. What better place for a tryst?

Her heart thudded painfully. She couldn't bear the thought of Julian with another woman. Especially one so completely undeserving of his attentions.

"Is there a shortcut?" Wycherley asked. "If our aim is to separate them, it would be best to head them off before they reach the maze. Otherwise, we're going to need reinforcements."

There *was* a shortcut, but it would be awkward to navigate in the dark.

"There is, sir, but those paths are unlit."

"My man can bring a light for us. Here, Ganstridge," Wycherley shouted in the direction of the coaches. "I know you're over there lurking. Stop swigging ale and fetch a lantern for us. We're undertaking a quest for a damsel in distress."

In response to Wycherley's shout, a tall, strapping man

separated himself from the throng of coachmen. Cassie felt a twinge of uncertainty as he plucked a lit flambeau from its sconce and strode toward them.

As he came closer, the hairs rose on the back of her neck.

It was *him*! The man who'd been gazing up at her in that intensely intimate way. She gulped and dipped her head, hoping he wouldn't recognize her in the looming darkness.

Oh. My. Goodness. Up close, the fellow was practically a giant, with the shoulders of an ox and a chest to match. It had been impossible to tell when looking down on him just what an impressive figure he made. She gulped again and clung tightly to Wycherley's sleeve.

"Don't look so dour, man," said her noble knight. "You can return to your ale presently. Pray, walk beside us so Miss Blythe can see her way."

Cassie cringed. Now the manservant knew her name. He would have a juicy tale to tell about her when he returned to his cronies, and who knew where her name would end up? On the gossiping tongues of the tabbies? At the gentlemen's card tables? In the conversation beneath the church porch?

She bit her lip anxiously. Now would be the time to return to the ballroom, before her reputation was put at any further risk.

Then she thought of Julian dallying in the darkness with the flirtatious Lady Lucy and steeled her nerve. She would risk anything to save him from such an unsuitable companion.

Anything.

"Lead on," Wycherley said encouragingly, patting her hand.

She lifted her chin and stared straight ahead, trying to look as if it were the most natural thing in the world for a young lady to be stepping out into the night with two men.

As they set off, Cassie became aware of a kind of restless energy about Wycherley, which communicated itself to her through the silk of his sleeve. He was fit, he was fast, and his sense of urgency spurred her on as she went over in her mind the paths they must follow to overtake their quarry.

The servant, Ganstridge, on the other hand, seemed in no hurry at all. Indeed, his heavy tread suggested he'd been called out on this errand much against his will. He was close enough for her to feel the heat emanating from his body, and despite Wycherley having a terrible reputation, she couldn't help but feel this Ganstridge was the more dangerous of the two.

"So tell me, Miss Blythe," said the captain, "now that we are fellow adventurers, might I call you by your first name?"

Ganstridge's flambeau jerked up violently, creating a well of darkness in front of them. "Keep it steady, man," snapped Wycherley. "You don't want us to trip and break our necks!"

The light steadied, but the lack of apology from Wycherley's servant made Cassie wonder if he perhaps wouldn't mind if his master actually *did* break his neck.

Wycherley's voice regained its velvety tone. "Am I too bold, Miss Blythe?"

Very aware that the servant was hanging on their every word, Cassie replied, "No more than anticipated, sir, for though we've not been properly introduced, your reputation precedes you."

"Ah." He pressed a hand to his chest in a gesture of woe. "I can guess what you've heard. Though, some of the stories are too wicked for your youthful ears."

"I'm not a child, sir. I'm very nearly twenty, and I've read many books and journals. I have no illusions about men such as yourself."

A snort erupted from her right side, which was quickly turned into a sneeze. "I beg your pardon, miss, zurr."

Cassie gave the servant a sideways look. What an odd way of talking! He rolled his *R*s and dragged out his *S*s in a most exaggerated way. Not Oxfordshire. Somerset, perhaps? And…had he been *laughing* at her?

She turned her head away and discovered that Wycherley was treating her to a dazzling smile.

Cassie knew, in that instant, why he was a reputed Casanova. That lazy, tempting smile and those eyes with their wicked glint offered a gateway to pleasure of a most indecent sort.

She licked her lips and hoped she wasn't blushing.

"You read a lot, do you?" he asked. "I can't imagine such a charming young woman as a bluestocking. I'll try to behave, but if I forget myself and call you Cassandra, please slap me for my insolence. Indeed, I urge you to do so, should I overstep the mark in *any* way."

"*Somebody* needs to slap him."

"Pardon?" Cassie snapped her head round—and up—to glare at Ganstridge. Surely, she hadn't heard him correctly? His face remained impassive, thrown into stark planes of light and shadow by the dancing flame he carried. Small particles of soot had settled on his collar, and the smoke was blowing into his eyes, but he made no attempt to wipe them.

Wycherley's free hand came up and caressed her fingers, instantly distracting her. "Ignore him, Cassandra," he advised. "He ofttimes utters deprecations beneath his breath, but usually sets to his tasks with alacrity, so I put up with it. There is no one stronger in the world than Ganstridge. Is there, sirrah? I would have left him at home, but my groom's sprained his wrist, and I can't cosset Lady Lucy and drive a chaise at the same time. I say, those look like glasshouses ahead. Does that mean the maze is near?"

"Yes, we're almost there."

"You're an angel," he declared, pressing her hand to his mouth. "Not only beautiful, but clever, too. I truly admire such qualities in a woman. You must have a line of suitors as long as Paxton's drive."

"Not quite so long. But there have been a few," she admitted, feeling somewhat uncomfortable with the direction of the conversation.

Wycherley gave her all his attention. "So, whom have you accepted?"

"None."

His brow rose. "Not one? You must have very exacting standards, my dear Cassandra. I suppose you would not even consider someone like me?"

Cassie missed a step, but an iron hand caught her as she stumbled and set her back on her feet. Wycherley was correct. The manservant wasn't only strong, but quick, as well.

She laughed uneasily. "No, I don't think my standards are too high, but I'm afraid not even you would be acceptable. I'm devoted to the care of my father, who, since his riding accident, has not yet regained full use of his legs. Any prospective husband would have to please both Papa *and* me since he will be spending a good deal of time in our company. I think I'm happy to wait, for now. If any of my suitors is still unmarried by the time I feel ready, I may reconsider my answer."

She hoped her lightness of tone would not betray the fact that she was lying. There was room for only one man in her heart besides Papa.

Julian.

Oh, Julian! Why could he not love her back?

The familiar pain clawed at her heart, and she gazed up at the moon-silvered night through a mist of tears.

"This appears to be the maze, zurr," said Ganstridge in his peculiar drawl. They stopped walking. Oh, pray God they hadn't noticed her moment of weakness. She must concentrate now and put Julian from her thoughts.

"Ah, the duke has illuminated his maze."

Not such a good place for stolen kisses, then. Excellent.

She said brightly, "Do you see the platform there, with the wooden steps? That's the center."

"Splendid." Wycherley looked around, and when Cassie started to speak, he put a finger to his lips. After a moment, he said, "I do believe we have beaten the lovebirds to it. I suggest, lest we risk your reputation any further, that I remain here to deal with the situation, and you return to the ball with Ganstridge as your guide. I'll come back with Lucy, and your friend Mister, er…"

"Carnforth."

"Your friend, Mr. Carnforth, can do as he pleases. If he returns to the ball without his prize and his nose severely out of joint, I am certain you will be able to give him whatever comfort he needs. How does that sound, Miss Blythe?"

It sounded rather good. Julian would return to the main house heartbroken, and she would be on hand to cheer him up, dance with him, and distract him until the fickle Lady Lucy was just a distant memory.

"I shall give you Ganstridge for the rest of the evening," Wycherley said, bowing over her hand. "He will do whatever you wish, and please do not be put off by his odd behavior and his whispered asides. I believe," he added, his voice falling to a whisper, "that he may be a little touched in the head. But he is quite harmless, I assure you."

She doubted *that* very much.

Looking sideways at the stony-faced giant who stood at the entrance to the maze with his torch held in front of him like a weapon, she would never have dared call him harmless. Perhaps she would do better to wait here with Wycherley and observe the outcome of tonight's adventure, much as it would pain her to see Julian with another woman. Wycherley's confidence that he could separate Lady Lucy from Julian might be foolhardy. There might be something more she could do to help.

"Captain Wycherley—"

"Shh! I hear them. Go now, go quickly!"

Before she could utter a protest, Ganstridge had taken her by the elbow and half-lifted, half-dragged her back the way they had come, not slowing until they were completely out of sight of the maze.

The odd thing was, he seemed…angry.

Whatever could have infuriated him so?

Chapter Four

As soon as the maze was out of sight, Ned slowed and accommodated his pace to Miss Blythe's, as any good manservant or footman should.

He wondered if he should offer her his arm then thought better of it. He was no gentleman now, and he needed to remember that.

Cassandra Blythe was stunningly beautiful, but so young and vulnerable. Her figure was superb, with those softly molded breasts pushing against the neckline of her gown, that slender waist, and those shapely hips.

His mouth twisted with bitterness. It was not his place to have such thoughts about any young female at this time. It was wholly inappropriate. But his self-imposed celibacy had taken its toll, it seemed.

He cast another glance at Miss Blythe and wondered how she would look in daylight. What exact shade of bronze was her hair, and was it light or dark? What color were her eyes?

Why had Wycherley picked *her* to show him the way to the maze? Did the blackguard have designs on her? Was she to be the replacement for Lady Lucy if he couldn't prize her away from Mr. Carnforth?

Miss Blythe didn't fit the captain's usual choice of women. She was too fresh, too unsullied, and apt to blush at the tiniest thing. His employer's preferences tended toward women with more gloss and experience, mature but still beautiful. Women eager to taste forbidden fruit.

Cassandra Blythe was more like Ned's sister, Georgiana. She, too, had been fresh out of the schoolroom, innocent and untouched, but with a heart both great and giving.

His throat tightened. Where on earth *was* she? How could Georgiana have vanished so completely, like a bauble in a conjuror's trick? She wasn't dead. She couldn't be. He'd feel it if she were. No, that very same Captain Wycherley, for whom he was now working, had surely dishonored her, ruined her, and hidden her away so he could carry on his whoring and gambling with impunity.

But Ned would make him pay. When he had the proof, Captain Wycherley would pay dearly for what he'd done.

"Mr. Ganstridge?"

The lady's voice was soft, like falling leaves in autumn, caressing the air. "Hmm? I mean, yes, Miss Blythe?"

"Could you slow down a little? I am in no particular hurry."

Well, she should be, he thought grimly. Tongues were probably already wagging at her prolonged absence, and if it were known that she had departed in the company of the notorious Captain Wycherley, she could find herself in very deep water.

"I believe we must, miss," he said. "My master would wish you returned to the ball posthaste."

And Ned wanted to get her back there, too. She was far too tempting a morsel, and having just escaped the jaws of the leopard, she wouldn't want to find herself in the clutches of the lion.

"Mr. Ganstridge, what amuses you so?"

He shook his head. "I beg your pardon, miss. Foolish thoughts. I do but laugh at myself."

"A servant who laughs at himself? How very intriguing. Is it a jest you can share?"

It most certainly wasn't. How much farther until they reached the damned house? This delectable young woman, with her voice of honey, made his body react in a way that staggered him.

He asked gruffly, "Did you throw those violets at me?"

Now it was her turn to laugh. "Of course not! Why ever would you think so?"

Because, clearly, he was an idiot with too much imagination and a soft spot for a pretty face.

"I didn't, really," he said. "But I couldn't tell from your face what you were thinking. You might have confused me with somebody you knew."

She gave him a sidelong glance. "You really shouldn't have stared up at me like that. It was unutterably rude."

"I am often told I forget my place."

"I can well believe that. And you forget it now."

He realized they had slowed their pace to nothing during this sparring, which wouldn't do at all. He needed to get Miss Blythe back to the house quickly, before he said—or, God forbid, *did*—more than he ought. For if he took advantage of their situation, he would be no better than Wycherley.

"I really think we must hurry, miss."

"It's too hot to rush about, Mr. Ganstridge. When you saw me at the window, I was trying to cool down. And the violets were wilted, so I was just throwing them away. I don't see the point in getting all hot again by hurrying."

He ran a finger around the inside of his rough collar. He was feeling the heat, too, but for a very different reason.

He must get her back *now*. It was imperative. He racked his brains for a way to speed her up.

"Miss Blythe, please mind your skirts."

Her eyes widened. "I beg your pardon?"

"A rat just scurried toward your feet. They are attracted to muslin, you see, and use it to line their nests, I believe."

"Oh!"

He hid a grin as she picked up her pace, as well as her skirts. In moments, they had reached the steps leading up to Highmore's front entrance.

An older lady, respectably dressed, hastened down the steps as soon as she saw them. "What are you doing out here, Cassie? You've been gone an age! And who is that with you?"

"No one. Just a servant. I needed some air and picked the first one I could find as an escort so I could walk about a bit."

Ned had long since ceased to wince every time someone said, "just a servant." He was certainly more than "just" anything. But hearing Miss Blythe say it made a dent in his pride's armor, especially as he was applauding her quick thinking in explaining his presence.

The older woman barely acknowledged his existence as Miss Blythe took her arm and they made their way back into the cheerful brilliance of Highmore House. Neither of them looked back. Miss Blythe didn't even bother to nod her head or thank him.

Well, good. In his servant's garb, Ned Ganstridge was invisible to those he wished not to see him, and easy to forget.

And that was exactly the way he wanted it.

Chapter Five

As she sat down to a late breakfast the following morning, Cassie's mind hummed with the events of the previous night. Trying to act as if nothing out of the ordinary had happened promised to be an ordeal.

"Ah, what a splendid evening," proclaimed her papa, glancing up from his newspaper. "Old Paxton certainly did us proud."

"I'm so glad you enjoyed yourself. Your legs aren't plaguing you too much?"

"Fortunately not. I didn't need to do much walking or standing. Now don't fret, daughter, you know Dr. Franks said I needed to continue using my pins, or else they would atrophy."

"It was a long night, though. You must be weary."

"I'm fine. Better than you, I think, with those blue patches beneath your eyes. Anyone would think you had barely slept."

"Uncle Hector!" came an admonishment from the door.

"What is it, girl?" Papa said as Becca swept into the room. Her cousin was staying with them for the Season. "Can't I comment on the looks of my own daughter?"

Cassie smiled. Becca could probably guess why she'd spent a sleepless night, even if Papa could not.

"I was afraid you might have a touch of dyspepsia, Papa," Cassie said. "You ate an inordinate amount of very rich fowl last night."

"I happen to be particularly partial to peacock," her father responded, unabashed. "It's not the kind of thing one would ever have at home, so one must make the best of every occasion on which it is served."

"I'm sure the king does exactly the same, and look what it has done to his figure," Becca countered, taking a seat and pouring her tea.

Papa frowned. "What you see in the pamphlets and journals is the work of lampooners. I'm sure he is much thinner in actuality. Think of all the exercise he gets."

Cassie tried hard not to think of the kind of exercise preferred by the new king. It made her blush…and try to imagine Julian engaged in similar exercise with her…that was to say, naked.

"I didn't see much of Carnforth last night," her father added, stabbing a devilled kidney and conveying it to his mouth.

Cassie nearly choked. Was he reading her thoughts?

"You were too involved in your cards to notice," she gasped from behind her napkin.

Becca leaned forward and said earnestly, "It was very bad of him to keep forgetting when he was meant to be dancing with you."

Cassie resisted the urge to kick her cousin beneath the table. She didn't need to be reminded of that particular blow, thank you very much. People needed to stop talking about Julian.

"I felt sorry for Captain Wycherley," she said. "It seems

he came with Lady Lucy, but she was more than happy to dance with every other gentleman under the age of forty."

"Oh, I wouldn't feel sorry for him," Becca replied. "He had his heart broken once and has been punishing women ever since, I hear."

"Now, Becca, surely that's just gossip," Cassie admonished.

"Oh, but it's true," her cousin said firmly. "I wouldn't say it, otherwise. I wager the girl who threw him over must be kicking herself now, for Captain Wycherley distinguished himself at Waterloo and became quite the war hero."

"Ah. Is that why women set their caps at him?" Cassie asked.

"Part of it, I'm sure."

And he really did have a cherubic look, with golden curls to match. A sinful Cupid. How could women resist?

Cassie trawled her spoon thoughtfully through her porridge. "So, how did he get his reprobate reputation?"

"That came later. He —"

"He does extremely well on the stock market," interrupted Papa, peering at them briefly over the top of his newspaper.

"Yes, Uncle. His investments have made him very wealthy," Becca agreed. "I've heard," she added, leaning in conspiratorially, "that he regularly journeys out of town, but no one knows where he goes, as he has no country estate, only his house in Oxford and his London house."

It was a bit odd that Becca should know all that. But as Cassie was interested to find out all she could about Wycherley — without alerting her father's suspicions — she suggested to her cousin, "As soon as we've breakfasted, shall we go for a walk? I'd love a breath of air."

Becca finished her tea with alacrity. "What a splendid idea. I'll just dash upstairs and fetch my reticule."

Waiting by the open front door a few minutes later, Cassie gazed down at the raised scallop shells that edged the path and steeled herself against the unpleasant memories they always invoked. She had set them there herself as a child, to please her sickly mama. Mama had been wheeled out in her Bath chair to admire them, but all too soon, the pain had driven her back inside again.

Death had been a blessed release when it finally came.

No one could be unaffected by the loss of a parent at so young an age. Julian had been a tower of strength to Cassie as a lonely, uncertain eleven-year-old. That was when her affection for him had blossomed into true love—a love so deep, so enduring, she could barely cope with the burden of it.

A bee buzzed past her, laden with pollen. That was just how she felt, weighed down by a love that was only returned in the smallest part…as friendly affection.

Becca's cheerful voice broke in on her thoughts. "Here I am. Shall we take the footpath toward Oxford? Or would you rather head into the countryside?"

"Oxford, I think."

The way Cassie was feeling, she needed distraction, and the sight of people going about their daily business, riders out enjoying the clement weather, and laden wagons rattling into town bearing fresh produce for sale, would be just the tonic she needed.

"If we go far enough," Becca said, "I can point out Wycherley's house to you. Did you notice that he and Lady Lucy arrived together last night, but departed separately? I saw her give Julian the cold shoulder, too, when he approached. I wonder which man was the cause of her ill temper?"

Lucy gave Julian the brush-off? Better and better, thought Cassie.

She glanced up at the sky and watched a pair of swifts skirting above her. She ought to feel bad about helping Wycherley intercept Lady Lucy at the Highmore maze. But it had all worked out too well.

Becca continued, "There was a rumor of some connection between Wycherley and Lord Edmund Stranraer's sister a year or so ago."

"The lady who died in that dreadful fire?" Cassie asked, casting her mind back a few months.

"Her body was never found. It must have hit him hard."

"Who, Wycherley or Stranraer?"

"Both, I imagine," said Becca gravely. "I know nothing of Lord Stranraer, save that he, too, has vanished from the face of the earth. It's all very peculiar. There are rumors he may have been kidnapped for ransom, or been done away with—"

"We were speaking of Wycherley," Cassie interrupted before Becca could get sidetracked.

"Who has been wilder than ever lately, I hear, changing his women like other men change their cravats. Whatever it is Wycherley has to offer, there are plenty of ladies keen to partake of it."

"I'd have thought he'd be keen to fix his interest with Lady Lucy, as she's very rich." Which would, thankfully, cut Julian out of the picture.

"I'm not sure he cares about a woman's wealth. Why, here's Captain Wycherley's front door." Becca paused and stared off into the distance. "I wonder if Sampson's is open yet? Shall we walk right into town and see?"

Cassie gazed at the sun-warmed steps, the fresh paint, the shiny door knocker, and her cheeks grew hot as a plan began to form in her head. A plan so bold, so wicked, she could hardly believe her own mind had conjured it up.

She would pay a call on Captain Wycherley. He could explain to her what it was about Lady Lucy that attracted both himself and Julian. Then he could teach her to be an even more accomplished flirt than Lady Lucy so that Cassie could blind Julian with her new charms. Wycherley was bound to agree, for it would take Julian Carnforth out of the running.

She began to tremble at the audacity of her plan.

"Cassie my dear, you look extremely flushed. And your eyes are too bright. I think we must return at once. We've been walking far too quickly after last night's exertions."

Cassie grasped her cousin's shoulder then swayed alarmingly. "Oh dear. Becca, I do believe I am overcome with the heat. I think I am…about to…"

Chapter Six

Pavements were extremely hard and decidedly dirty.

Cassie had collapsed as gently as she could. Nonetheless, it took a considerable amount of fortitude to stay still with the gutter and a heap of fresh horse dung so close to her nose.

"Oh! Oh!" Becca flapped her skirts at Cassie's head.

Sweet Venus! Why didn't the woman knock on Wycherley's door before someone came out of the wrong house and ruined her plan?

"I need...fetch...water," Cassie croaked. "Wycherley... closest."

Taking the hint, Becca scurried off to knock on the door.

After what seemed no time at all, she heard heavy footsteps hurrying toward her, after which a pair of strong hands thrust themselves beneath her knees and shoulders and lifted her up. The horse dung fell out of view as she was hoisted high in the air and held against a man's chest.

It felt...oddly comforting and secure.

"Put your arms about my neck."

The comfort evaporated. What poor luck! It wasn't

Wycherley at all, but his servant, Ganstridge. She'd know his strange accent anywhere. Confound it!

The hands eased their grip a little, and she found herself nestled against a powerfully muscled chest as Ganstridge turned toward the house.

The fact that he was a servant faded away, and she became startlingly aware of him as a man. The hand which supported her back was curled round and pressed against her ribs, dangerously close to her breast. She held her breath, suspended between shock and curiosity. Was this what it felt like to enjoy a man's touch?

The brief, chaste touch of Julian's fingers always thrilled and delighted her. But this—this was something altogether different.

She had no idea what this ruffian really looked like, not having seen him in daylight. Not that it mattered in the least.

Still, she peeped up at him through lowered lashes. His face was softer than she remembered. Although the hard planes and angles were still there, they were no longer thrown into stark contrast by torchlight and shadow. The hair which brushed against his stiff collar was medium brown, as were his nicely shaped eyebrows, but she could not tell the color of his eyes without him knowing he was being examined.

A comfortable warmth emanated from him, along with formidable strength—just the right sort of man to have around. As a servant, of course. He would be good for Papa, would easily be able to lift him from his Bath chair when he was tired, or carry him into the carriage.

But *comfortable* warmth? No, that was the wrong word. The heat emanating from Ganstridge's body and melting into hers was not making her feel the least bit comfortable. She was feeling…shamefully stimulated.

"Oh, Cassandra! Oh, this is terrible!" Becca's voice interrupted the shocking thought.

"Pray calm yourself, miss," Ganstridge said, and Cassie felt his voice rumble intriguingly through his chest into hers. "Miss Blythe has merely fainted. Do you have salts? There are none in the house, I'm afraid."

"No, I never thought to bring any."

"We are very close to the market. Shall I run and get some?" he offered.

"No, no, take poor Miss Blythe indoors and lay her down. I'll go myself."

Cassie quivered nervously as she was carried through the door, feeling as she imagined Caesar had when he crossed the Rubicon.

From here, there was no going back.

The sunlight was cut off, and the noises of the passing traffic dimmed as she was brought inside the elegant, but very masculine, house. It was tastefully decorated with dark woods and marbling, the whole suffused with the smell of beeswax and leather.

Ganstridge elbowed open a door and lowered her gently onto a chaise longue. He removed her shoes, then tackled the ribbons of her bonnet. She was very aware of the touch of his fingers on her feet and chin.

Fingers, she noted, that seemed unable to undo the bow. Well, a man of his size might be expected to be clumsy. But... surely his hands weren't shaking?

Grimacing in defeat, Ganstridge left her, calling for water and snapping at another servant to fetch their master.

Thank goodness! Captain Wycherley *was* at home.

Moments later, he was at her side, concern written across his handsome features. Relief trickled through her. Her ruse hadn't been for naught.

Not yet, anyway.

"It's all right," she whispered conspiratorially as Ganstridge excused himself from the room and Wycherley knelt beside her. "I am perfectly well. I just needed an excuse to talk to you."

He looked stunned for a moment, then let out a guffaw of laughter. "My dear Miss Blythe, there are far easier ways of making contact with a gentleman. Sending a servant with a note is a popular method, or promenading around the town where one is sure to meet anybody and everybody sooner or later. I hope you didn't hurt yourself when you collapsed?"

She pursed her lips at his mild scolding. "Only my pride and my bonnet, but a little steam and a hot iron will soon put that right."

"Won't you sit up, now the need for deception is past?"

"Best not. My cousin has gone for smelling salts and could return any moment. I don't want to seem recovered too quickly."

Still grinning, Wycherley took her hand. "Very well. Why did you wish to see me?"

Being in close proximity to Wycherley—especially in a reclining pose—was an unsettling experience. Not as unsettling as being held tightly in Ganstridge's arms, however. It was going to take her a little while to recover from *that* dizzying sensation.

"You said you were in my debt after last night," she replied.

"I am, indeed. Thanks to you, Lucy was caught wrong-footed, and my rival was seriously embarrassed. She and I did not leave together."

Alarm stabbed through Cassie. Wycherley and Lady Lucy *had* to be together so Julian would be available. She asked hopefully, "Will you amend your quarrel?"

"I shall certainly attempt it. So long as she's not decided to choose that beanpole of a man over myself."

Cassie smiled to herself. There spoke a jealous man. Julian was tall and slim, but no beanpole. "If I could drive a wedge between the vacillating Lady Lucy and Mr. Carnforth, would that please you?" she asked.

"It would." Wycherley sat back on his haunches and eyed her speculatively. "What exactly did you have in mind?"

Cassie looked around the room to ensure they were still alone. The door to the hallway was ajar, but there was no sound or movement beyond it.

"I want Mr. Carnforth's heart to beat for me alone. We are already great friends, but he has watched me grow up, and he simply can't see beyond that."

Wycherley slowly nodded. "He's blind to the fact that you're a lovely young woman with needs and desires, not a child."

"Precisely."

"But…how can *I* possibly help?"

"Tell me what makes a man attracted to a woman. How does she get him to notice *her* instead of a dozen beauties in the same room? Tell me how to speak, how to act, how to entice him."

A lazy grin curved Wycherley's mouth. "Telling is one method, certainly. But when it comes to lessons in flirtation or love, an actual demonstration is infinitely preferable. I would also have to show you how to receive the attentions of the gentleman when they are given."

There was something feral in his gaze that unnerved her. What did he mean by "demonstration?"

There was only one way to find out. "You'll do it, then?" she asked.

"An intriguing plan. But how would we go about it? I imagine your chaperone guards you well. Is there any way you can escape her?"

"I had an idea," said Cassie, embarrassed by a slight tremor in her voice. "I could pretend to come here for French lessons. From, say, a Parisian cousin of yours—female, of course—who could teach me once a week. I'll bring my maid as chaperone. She can continue into town and go to the market, then collect me on her way back."

He smiled at her, the expression in his deep blue eyes inscrutable. "That could work."

"I trust your staff can be discreet?"

The smile didn't waver. "I pay them well enough. They're used to my ways…and the kind of relationships I pursue."

A welter of wicked imaginings romped through Cassie's mind, but she crushed them mercilessly. It was *love* she wanted to have, soul-deep, searing, eternal love, not this other thing she wished to learn about. That was just a means to an end.

The thought of deep love brought to mind what Becca had mentioned about Wycherley, and before Cassie could stop herself, she nodded and said, "Yes, I heard somebody broke your heart when you were young, and you've sworn never to fall in love again, or to marry."

His grin vanished. "Don't listen to idle talk," he said. "It rarely reflects the truth. Shall we say I've had more than one disappointment, despite my best efforts, and leave it at that?"

"Quite. Now, quickly, before my cousin returns, what say you of my plan?"

The predatory look was back again. "I think I shall enjoy it immensely. Life would be most dull without such amatory adventures. Once you've hooked the beanpole, I'll have Lucy to myself," he concluded. Then his handsome face took on a more serious expression. "You're sure Mr. Carnforth is good enough for you? I'd hate to see you marry a man who can't make you happy."

Captain Wycherley couldn't be *all* bad. A true rake wouldn't give a farthing about such a thing.

She assumed.

She waved off his concern. "He can, and he will," she answered. "He's so generous and kind. Intelligent, too. I'm sure you'd like him if you got to know him."

Was that a derisive snort? Cassie gave Wycherley a hard look.

"Your cousin will be back at any moment," he said, the picture of innocence. "As you're supposed to have fainted, I'd better loosen your clothing and remove your bonnet."

As his fingers reached for the buttons of her walking dress, a peculiar noise from the doorway made them both jump.

"Who's there?" he barked, leaping to his feet. The door opened wider, and Ganstridge appeared, holding a large red handkerchief to his face. Had the snort come from *him?*

"Well, man? Has someone been trying to strangle you?" Wycherley snapped.

"No, zurr. I felt a tickle and didn't wish to cough. I didn't want to disturb you."

"Why are you lurking outside the door like a skulking thief?"

"I beg your pardon, zurr," the man said, tucking the handkerchief into his waistcoat pocket. "I was waiting in the hallway to delay Miss Blythe's companion if she returned...at an inconvenient moment."

"Ah, good idea. Thank you, Ganstridge. Return to your post. Now then, where were we, Miss Blythe?"

He returned to untying her bonnet, then tugged out a few strands of hair. "It wouldn't do to look too tidy," he said, stepping back to admire his handiwork. "Now, does your gown fasten at the back or the front?"

There was another strangulated noise from the doorway. Wycherley looked so put out, Cassie found it hard not to laugh...despite her alarm at his shocking query.

He growled at his servant, "Undo your stock if it's choking you, man. You're no use to me if you suffocate yourself."

"I heard a lady coming up the steps," Ganstridge said, red-faced. "Shall I keep her occupied?"

"Who is it?" Wycherley demanded.

"I don't know, zurr, begging your pardon."

The captain patted Cassie's hand. "I'd better go and see for myself. We don't want any awkward situations arising, do we? Ganstridge, stay here. And if you hear my signal, spirit Miss Blythe out of sight. You take my meaning?"

The servant nodded, and Cassie sat up, perplexed, as the door closed behind Wycherley.

"What signal? What did he mean?"

Ganstridge pulled her to her feet and subjected her to a dark, disapproving look. She felt her cheeks grow warm under his scrutiny.

He said, "You already know that man's a rake, one of the worst. You shouldn't be surprised if he has ruses in place to stop his lady friends bumping into one another."

Cassie glared. "You were listening!" she exclaimed in acute mortification. "How dare you?"

He gazed down at her, a mocking eyebrow raised. "I overheard, Miss Blythe. *Overheard.* Shall I take your pelisse?"

Dumbfounded, she let him remove the garment and fold it neatly on a chair next to her bonnet. Wycherley had better watch out. It appeared his servants weren't all as loyal—or discreet—as he believed.

She wasn't used to being gainsaid by one of the lower orders, but when she turned to confront him, Ganstridge put a finger to his lips.

"As we don't know who's at the door, you'd better not ring a peal over me. Or if you must, do it quietly. But I warn you, Miss Blythe, you are playing with fire here. Do *not* get involved with Captain Wycherley. He will ruin you."

This stark statement left Cassie reeling. Of course she knew about Wycherley's somewhat tarnished reputation. Coming to him for help was not a decision she'd made lightly. But why should she justify herself to a jumped-up servant?

"Mr. Ganstridge—" she began.

"If that's your cousin come to collect you," he said, ignoring her outraged expression, "we'd better do what the captain suggested. I see you fasten at the back. Forgive me."

The next moment, Cassie was gasping with indignation. The man turned her about and was about to unhook the back of her gown. There was nothing clumsy about his fingers now, she thought—anyone would think *he* was the rake, and not his master!

She jerked away. "Mr. Ganstridge! Sirrah!"

"Yes, miss?"

Oh, but he was insolent beyond belief! She spun round to face him, her hands on her hips, her voice shaking with annoyance. "What do you think you are doing?"

He tilted his head to one side and gazed down at her with a look of studied innocence. "It's far less shocking for a servant to tend to your, er…needs, than for a gentleman to have done it. I use the term gentleman loosely."

Ah. He was, annoyingly, correct in this. It *was* better for a servant to attend to her, rather than Wycherley himself.

But Ganstridge didn't behave like someone in service. There was nothing at all submissive about him at this moment, when he seemed intent on lecturing her. Before she could think of a suitable riposte, he placed his hands on her shoulders, bent his head, and looked deep into her eyes.

She gaped back at him.

And suddenly felt an intense pull of physical attraction.

Her stomach clenched as she fought against the feeling. Attracted to a servant? Impossible! She blinked, praying the rush of heat and awareness hadn't shown in her face.

"Apart from the risk of ruin," he told her softly, "you are not in any way increasing your chances of winning the man with whom you're infatuated. No, don't shake your head at me," he added, as she tried to pull out of his grasp. "Hear me out. Flirtation is a meaningless game. It might lead to a bedding, but it's less likely to lead to love. The same can be said of seduction, which is exactly what Captain Wycherley plans to do with you. If the man who has captured your heart cared for you, he'd have shown it by now. Love is not something which can be won by trickery."

His hands, warm but heavy, held her prisoner. Once again, she had a sudden vision of him throwing her over his powerful shoulder and making off with her. After which he would do unspeakable things to her body…

Sweet Venus! Her throat went dry. What was she *thinking*?

"Mr. Ganstridge," she rasped, "your advice is neither sound nor welcome. You don't know Julian, and you certainly don't know me, and even if you had a right to speak to me thus—which you don't—there is no reason why I should listen to you."

He pulled her closer, until she had to crane her neck to see his face.

"Wycherley is no better a tutor in the ways of love than the next man," he growled. "You could learn just as much from *me*. But *I* value a lady's honor. He does not. In fact, if you insist on going on with this ludicrous plan, why not learn from a woman? Wouldn't it be better to let Lady Lucy herself teach you how to attract a man's attention? She's damned good at it, from what I've seen."

Cassie's gaze slid to Ganstridge's mouth. A firm, masculine mouth. Very determined, just like its owner. A mouth she could imagine pressed against hers, kissing her with all the force and passion of this man's rebellious soul.

Dazed and breathless, she shook her head, tore out of his grasp, and seized her bonnet and pelisse from the chair.

Her fingers trembled as she thrust her bonnet back on her head. She could learn as much from *him?* Never! It didn't matter if he was a lackey or the Emperor of China—she could never allow him such a liberty.

He was too strong, too charismatic. Too…tempting. A man like him would consume her like a blazing inferno, until there was nothing left but a pitiful pile of ash.

Wycherley might be a rake, but at least a woman knew where she stood with him. With Ganstridge, she had no idea at all.

The sound of raised voices in the corridor outside flooded her with relief.

Wycherley and Becca.

Rescue!

Her hands were shaking too much to do up the ribbons of her bonnet, and she was only half inside her pelisse as she exploded through the door, exclaiming, "Ah, Becca, I'm so sorry to put you out! I'm much recovered now, thank you. No need for the salts! I just need to get home and rest, and then I'll be perfectly well again."

"My dear Miss Blythe," Wycherley said, looking at her in some alarm, "you are definitely *not* recovered. Please, may I offer you some refreshment before you go? There is a cold ham, some wafers, and a bull's tongue in aspic. I'm sure we have cheese, as well, and some excellent German sausage."

Cassie's stomach contracted at the thought of so much meat, and contracted again when she thought of how she had reacted to that disrespectfully bold Ganstridge. How would she ever find the courage to go through with her plan now? If it meant she had to see *him* again?

Chapter Seven

It took Cassie nearly a week to forget the indignities piled upon her by Wycherley's insolent servant, not to mention rationalize the effect he had on her body, firing her imagination in a way she could only describe as wanton.

In the end, she told herself she'd simply been on edge due to the daring nature of her plan. So, she decided to make another attempt to carry it out. A note was penned to Wycherley, the butcher's boy was bribed to deliver it discreetly, and by the time market day came round again, Cassie had once more embarked on a course of action that was highly improper and had the potential to ruin her reputation forever.

But to be united with Julian was surely worth the risk.

He was generous, thoughtful, and calm, and so very good-looking. There was rarely a cross word spoken between them, which would make for a splendid marriage. So many couples she knew seemed to fight all the time. They became tired of one another, took lovers or mistresses, embarrassed each other in public. Why, you only had to look at the travesty of a marriage that existed between the new king, soon to be crowned George IV, and Princess Caroline!

Thankfully, Cassie would not be forced into marriage for dynastic reasons. Nor did she need to marry for money, due to a handsome settlement due to her when she came of age. Papa was not the kind of man to impose those things. Indeed, he would be happy to see her wed to their close family friend.

But neither Papa nor Julian would be at all impressed by her current wicked enterprise. She would simply have to be very, *very* careful not to be caught.

As luck would have it, on the day she was to put her scheme into action, a bout of rain almost ruined everything.

Papa decided that their servant, Ella, should not go to the market until the weather had dried up a little and that Becca must accompany Cassie with a pair of umbrellas to get her to her French class. Becca could wait in Captain Wycherley's kitchen with a book until the lesson was over, if no more suitable room for a lady was available.

By Juno! It was a sore test of Cassie's frayed nerves. If she hated deceiving her relations, she hated still more the thought of her true enterprise being discovered.

Standing by her father's window in an agony of indecision, she eventually said, "I'm sure Madame Dupont won't mind if I'm a little *en retard*. I would hate to put you out unnecessarily, Becca, and I cannot vouch for the comforts of the Captain's kitchen, or any of the other rooms in his house. From the amount of meat being offered to us the other day, the kitchen is probably knee-deep in animal carcasses and not a suitable place for any gentlewoman. Let's wait a quarter of an hour before we decide what to do. The rain may ease off."

She couldn't bear the thought of her scheme being delayed, now that it was in motion. She'd been imagining the expression on Julian's face when he finally saw her, *truly* saw her, and all that she had to offer him...

He would grasp her arm and spirit her off to a rose-garlanded summer house. There he would kneel before her, kiss her hand, and press it to his cheek amidst declarations of eternal adoration. Then he would chastise himself as a fool for wasting so much of the time they could have spent together if only he had not been so blind.

The vivid vision drifted in front of her. He would propose. Blushing charmingly, she would accept, and then he would stand, crush her to his chest, and press his heated lips upon hers.

"Cassandra, do be careful, please. You will quite ruin the look of the drape if you keep clutching at it like that. Poor Ella will have to take it down and iron it."

Cassie's cheeks flamed. "Oh no, Becca, I was merely trying to rub away a sooty mark." She smoothed down the drape and made her way to the chair, where she could watch both the clock and the scudding clouds.

The delightful fantasy reclaimed her mind but...stalled. What would happen *after* that heated embrace, *after* that first impassioned kiss? She knew about animals, but surely humans didn't rut in the same bestial fashion? She'd tried to imagine what she and Julian might share when they were married... but there were infuriating gaps in the picture, things she had no knowledge of.

Things too deliciously wicked even to contemplate.

Oh, but it must stop raining! If she couldn't begin her illicit lessons right now, she would burst! Where would she find the courage again to risk everything? Would Wycherley even be interested next week? They'd agreed on a trial today but had not planned beyond that.

And what if the annoyingly intriguing Mr. Ganstridge answered the door? He had been so insolent, so rude to her, yet their argument had somehow excited her.

No, not excited. *Diverted*. He had tempted her with his strong hands and his powerful body, confused and appalled her with his lack of gallantry and finesse. She'd no idea what to make of him, or what to do about him.

What if Ganstridge spread gossip about her?

By Juno! Was she mad? Calling at Captain Wycherley's home in broad daylight was very public, making it far too easy for her flimsy subterfuge to be discovered. Maybe instead she should creep out at night and be whisked away in a covered carriage to a secluded spot where Wycherley could teach her all she needed to know about the art of seduction.

She shivered. Secluded spot? With a renowned rake?

No, that would be complete folly. Too fraught with danger…of all kinds.

Day or night, this whole thing was *not* a good idea.

"I say, Cassandra, it has stopped raining," her papa informed her, folding up his newspaper. "You can now go to your French lesson without trouble."

"Oh. Um, splendid."

Just when she'd nearly made up her mind *not* to go.

Confound it!

A shaft of sunlight slanted across the cobbles outside, rendering them a blinding river of silver. She blinked, teetering with indecision.

"If my experience is anything to go by," warned her papa, "you'd best not keep Madame Dupont waiting. They can be very emotional, these foreigners, and you don't want to give her any excuse to send a stiff letter and a bill for a lesson you didn't have."

Trapped! Like Eurydice in the Underworld.

To Captain Wycherley's house she must go. She only hoped it didn't go as badly for *her* as it had for poor Eurydice.

Chapter Eight

Half an hour later, Cassie was seated once more on Captain Wycherley's chaise longue in his darkly masculine withdrawing room, striving not to be distracted by salacious prints of a young Emma Hamilton, apparently wearing nothing but a flimsy shawl. She felt all fingers and thumbs as she attempted to drink the glass of claret she'd been given.

"So, to our first lesson," Wycherley declared. "How to drive a man to distraction."

She swallowed nervously and assumed what she hoped was the mien of a diligent student of Aristotle.

"I won't touch you, but I want you to make me wish to do so. You must test my resolve to the utmost," Wycherley instructed. "Please stand up."

Her heart shifted to beat high in her throat as she gulped a deep draught of the wine and placed the glass clumsily onto a nearby table. This could, if she wasn't careful, turn into a complete disaster. There was no one to save her reputation, no one to rescue her should Wycherley become…over-amorous. She was entering Terra Incognita, and the risk she was taking suddenly worried her.

"Make you want to touch me? How do I do that?"

He gazed at her critically. "Start by looking alluring."

Her mind went blank.

When he just continued to gaze at her expectantly, she took a deep breath, tilted her head, and batted her eyelashes like an actress she'd once seen playing Sheridan's Lady Teazle.

He cringed. "No, that won't do at all. You look as if you've got a cinder in your eye. No need to pull such faces. Just glance at me from beneath your lashes, then look away, as if you have no interest in me at all."

She schooled her expression to one of studied disinterest and tried again, this time with no batting.

He looked at her critically, then nodded. "That's better. Also—and I'm sure you must have been taught this—deploy your fan. Show just your eyes over the top of it. Look at me as if you desire me, but are too shy to do anything about it."

The man was handsome as Apollo, but she'd have to fake the desire. Oddly, if it were Mr. Ganstridge in front of her, it would have been far easier. Even after the passage of a week, she could still recall the feel of his hands on her, and the way his mere presence charged the atmosphere around him like a bolt of lightning.

Perhaps if she imagined it was Ganstridge, not Wycherley...

"That's exactly it. Very good. Now, I am going to turn away and inspect a picture on the wall. Look at me as if I was a plate of honey cakes, and you a starving pauper. Examine me closely without moving and see if you can make me aware of you."

Not Wycherley. The Herculean Ganstridge, with his bulging muscles and compelling presence...

Wait, what on earth was wrong with her? She should be imagining *Julian*, not a manservant, however darkly handsome.

Phew. That felt much better. The thought of Julian was familiar and safe.

"Hold your breath," Wycherley said. "I need to *feel* your gaze on me."

She gazed intently at Wycherley's profile and tried to imagine he was Julian. But, surely, it wasn't possible to make a man turn round just by looking at him.

Evidently, it was. Wycherley turned to her with a smile and said, "Excellent."

She let out a sigh of relief…until he said, "Now, lower your fan and run your tongue lightly over your lips."

She faltered. She'd seen Lady Lucy do that very thing at the Duke of Paxton's refreshment table, but thought her rival was just gathering in a stray cake crumb or drop of wine. The insight into what the woman had *really* been up to staggered Cassie. Well, if Lady Lucy could do it, so could she.

"Hmm, not bad," Wycherley remarked. "But you need to look less like you're eating a water ice."

She tried again.

"Better. I'm going to look you in the eye now and show you that I welcome your regard. And that I *want* you. See if you can return my gaze without blushing."

Wycherley proceeded to scrutinize both her face and her figure, top to bottom and back again, and his expression conveyed there was no doubt he liked what he saw.

Good Lord.

This was so embarrassing! She felt an overwhelming urge to sit down again and fold her arms across her bosom.

Flustered, she jerked her fan back and forth to cool her burning cheeks.

He chuckled. "See what can be done with merely a look? Get it right, and I promise, Mr. Carnforth will come running."

She shook her head fitfully. "But I couldn't possibly ogle a gentleman like that! It would put him off, surely?"

"Believe me, most men enjoy such flirtation. But beware of being too obvious. A woman should always retain a certain air of mystery, keep a gentleman guessing. Slowly reel him in…and then let the line out again."

She frowned, thoroughly puzzled. "That's not what it says in my etiquette books."

He smiled and lightly touched her chin with his finger. "Learn your lessons from life, my dear, not from books. Only actual experience brings real knowledge."

She thought about that for a moment. It made a lot of sense.

"Let us imagine the question of mutual attraction is in the air," he continued. "How will you act upon it?"

"I'm not sure I know what you mean…"

"You've flirted, and he has given you a look that says you have his attention. What next?"

She considered for a moment. "Well, there's not much I can do unless we're alone, which is unlikely to happen."

He cocked an eyebrow at her. "Like now, for instance? One may need to be a little devious to grasp that moment of privacy, but it's possible. However, much can be done in public, too, with subtlety. Dancing, for example. A man can do a number of things while you're dancing to signal his interest."

She was aghast. "In front of everyone? But that's scandalous!"

"He may take a lady's hand thus."

Cassie had never had a gentleman press his fingers between hers in quite so suggestive a way. Nor had anyone rubbed their thumb softly over the back of her hand, or stroked that particularly sensitive point on her wrist. She tried to imagine Julian doing it, and couldn't.

A vision of Mr. Ganstridge thundered unbidden into her mind. No, *he* was definitely not up to such subtlety. And he wouldn't know anything more refined than those clod-hopping country dances where the women got tossed up into the air or swung around vigorously with their skirts flying and their ankles showing.

Wycherley was looking at her questioningly, so she quickly banished all thought of Ganstridge.

"But how am I to respond?" she asked. "And how can I make Julian want to do such things in the first place?" When he never had before…

The captain continued to caress her wrist. "If the magnetic attraction is not there to start with, it's hard to cultivate. But I can see no reason why Mr. Carnforth wouldn't be attracted to you. He just needs a bit of encouragement to see you as a woman, rather than a childhood friend. You must endeavor to seem less innocent, more knowing. That will intrigue him."

She nodded, trying in vain to extract her hand from his.

"Make him feel jealous about another man. Myself, perhaps? That should capture his eye and his interest."

Wycherley stepped closer, and his free hand brushed over the curve of her waist. With a soft gasp, she pulled back.

It was one thing to experience a man's hand on your body during the heady excitement of a ball, quite another when alone with a single gentleman in his drawing room.

"Don't be coy, Cassandra. You must get used to a man's touch. If all you do is withdraw— Damn it, man, I gave orders not to be disturbed!"

Oh thank God.

She took several more steps backward as Wycherley released her, then glanced in horrified embarrassment at the man who'd just burst in upon them.

Ganstridge, naturally.

He hadn't knocked, nor did he wait for his master's nod before striding to the middle of the room, interposing his sturdy frame between her and her…tutor.

"I'm sorry, zurr. I didn't know you were busy. I came to… check the fire irons. I was told one of them was…damaged by the maid this morning while cleaning."

"A pitiful pretext, Ganstridge," Wycherley snapped. "I've a good mind to send you packing. When I ask not to be disturbed, I *mean* not to be disturbed, except in the direst of emergencies. *Not* for a blasted bent poker."

"My apologies, zurr. I really didn't know you were in. I beg your pardon, miss," he added, turning to Cassie with an awkward bow.

"Idiot."

Cassie winced as Wycherley spat out the word.

"Get out of my sight before I terminate your employment with immediate effect."

"Surely, there's no harm done," Cassie said in Ganstridge's defense. She gave a forced laugh. "It's not as though he interrupted anything." She choked out another laugh, tried to catch Ganstridge's eye, and added loudly, "The very idea."

He paid her no heed. He narrowed his eyes at Wycherley and seemed to grow taller, until he towered over him. When he clasped his hands behind his back, every sinew of his arms stiff, she saw the knuckles were white. There was a moment, just a fraction of a moment, when it seemed terrifyingly possible he would strike his master.

She didn't give much for Wycherley's chances.

Summoning up all her courage, she stepped between the two men, forcing them apart, then twirled toward the door, saying brightly, "Oh goodness, it's later than I thought. Ella will be back at any moment to collect me. Ganstridge, I'd be much obliged if you could fetch my bonnet and pelisse. I shall wait in the hall until she comes."

Tight-jawed, the man turned on his heel and inclined his head toward her, took a deep breath and apologized again to Wycherley for the misunderstanding, then stalked out of the room like an angry guardsman.

Wycherley scowled after him. "That man is infuriating, much harder to manage than the other servants. He's always in places he shouldn't be and interrupts when I have company. I've never met anyone with such a poor sense of timing. Fire irons, indeed! Hurtling in as if his life depended upon it."

"Perhaps he's not too clever," Cassie suggested, although she was sure this was not the case. She was quite certain Ganstridge had burst in to rescue her from a situation he feared she couldn't handle. Even though he was mistaken, she ought to feel grateful, so she added, "I'm sure he means well. Has he been with you long?"

"Just above a month. He rescued me from a minor carriage accident, which is why I put up with him, I suppose. He came very well recommended. I had a note from the Duke of Paxton himself. Couldn't sing his praises highly enough."

Ganstridge, a hero? Cassie was startled by a mental image of him, stripped to the waist, exercising his Herculean muscles by heaving a carriage out of a ditch.

Lord, she was feeling hot!

Hoping Wycherley wouldn't think himself responsible for the heightened color in her cheeks, she said, "He'll settle in time. Well, sir, I really had better go. I don't want Ella peeping through the window and catching me alone with you. You don't look at all like a dignified French *émigrée*. Papa would be outraged to discover my deception, and the poor man's had enough to contend with since his riding injury."

"Then go, sweet lady. But not without my blessing."

Which turned out to be a kiss.

Directly on her lips.

It lasted a mere moment, but the shock of feeling his mouth on hers lingered long after he had stepped away.

By Juno, the man had a nerve! He'd given her no warning. And there was no reason why a kiss from him would help her become more attractive to Julian.

Or did Wycherley have a different purpose in mind?

Still reeling from his boldness, she made her swift escape into the hallway—and walked directly into something tall, warm, and depressingly familiar.

Ganstridge's hands fastened around her arms, and before she could draw breath, she was dragged into a dingy little closet filled with boots, coats, and a pungent smell of pipe smoke.

Her pulse rocketed when the door closed behind her with an ominous *click*.

Chapter Nine

Ned's heart pounded like a steam hammer, instantly regretting the audacity of his impulsive action. An insane risk.

Even as he released his grip on Miss Blythe's arms, he feared it could cost him everything he'd worked so hard for.

With unsteady hands, he struck a sulfur match and lit a horn lantern, which filled the small space with yellow light. He turned to face his captive, who was gaping at him like an outraged fish, her pretty, peach-colored lips taut with fury.

Christ, she was lovely, even in her anger.

Especially in her anger.

Not that he had any business noticing.

"Miss Blythe," he hissed, taking her by the shoulders. "What in God's name do you think you're doing? I warned you not to trust Wycherley. Did my words mean nothing to you?"

The bones of her shoulders were so fine, so delicate. It took an enormous effort not to explore their fascinating dips and rises, to trace his fingers along her collarbone to the slender column of her neck.

But that would make him no better than his enemy.

After a few fluttering breaths, she seemed to recover herself, and hissed back, "It is no concern of yours, sir. Let me go this instant, or I'll scream and set the whole household about your ears!"

Her eyes were locked with his, attempting to stare him down, but he was a man not easily moved from his purpose. He said firmly, "Miss Blythe, I know who you are, and I know all about your family. Not one word of scandal has touched the Blythes down the centuries, not one blot on the escutcheon. Yet here you are, about to risk it all, regardless of my warning."

"I don't know why I should listen to the opinion of a servant," she snapped, her chin hitching up a fraction.

He ground his teeth. "Because, despite appearances, I know about Society. Why should you, who have every privilege, every advantage in looks, in character, and in prospects, dally with a notorious rake? Think of the shame your actions will bring on your family. Forget Wycherley and never come here again." He gave her a little shake to plant his words more firmly.

She wriggled in his grasp. "Unhand me! This is unforgivable. I'll have Captain Wycherley dismiss you at once!"

"You will not," he growled back. "Or I shall take myself straight to your house and inform your father exactly what you've been up to today."

Her shoulders sagged, and her gaze dropped from his face to his chest. Could she hear the thundering of his heart? To him, it was almost deafening.

For a moment he thought he had pierced her armor, but she leaned closer and demanded accusingly, "How do you know what I've been up to? Have you been listening at doors again, Mr. Ganstridge? That is reprehensible, even for a servant."

In this small space, it was impossible to ignore the sweet, rose-fragrance of her perfume and the lure of her warm femininity. But he had to try. It was for her own good.

"You criticize *my* behavior?" he queried sharply. "When you have behaved like the veriest light-skirt, you dare to ring a peal over *me?*"

The mounting fury on her face warned him he might have gone too far. Damnation, he'd never been good with words.

"*Mr.* Ganstridge," she seethed. "You have *no* right to interfere in the affairs of your betters. My father would be appalled to be approached by a mere minion with such gossip. You would be horsewhipped from the door."

Ned's spine went rigid. "Horsewhipped? *Me?*"

"Yes, and I could do it myself, I'm so angry. Now, let go of me before I decide to make good on my threat."

She jerked out of his grasp and regarded him as if he were something that had just crawled out from under a stone. Ungrateful hussy! Had she no idea of her own stupidity? Clearly not.

Although she was now free of him, she made no effort to escape. An astounding thought struck him. Was she, perhaps, *enjoying* their battle? Because to his surprise, under his supreme exasperation, he found he quite liked crossing swords with this lively, intriguing woman. The indignation, however, was real.

He forced himself to calm down. His warning would never be heeded if both of them were angry. And arguing without being able to raise one's voice was frustrating beyond endurance.

He stepped back as far as he could in the enclosed space and modulated his voice. "I only have your best interests at heart, Miss Blythe. If you knew what I suspect about Captain Wycherley—"

She cut him off with a wave of her hand. "I've heard the rumors. Whatever people have said, it does not affect me."

His ire returned in force. "It damned well should. Forgive my vehemence, but it *really* should. And I sincerely doubt a gently bred young lady like yourself has heard the worst of the rumors."

She regarded him icily. "I'm surprised you remain in Captain Wycherley's employ if you think so little of him."

He met her hard stare, trying to read her. Was he getting anywhere at all? If only he could keep his temper in check— and his burgeoning, highly inappropriate lust.

He said, as evenly as he could, "Good positions are hard to find, and this one suits me well. However, I say again, this is no place for a young lady of your obvious quality."

When her glare eased a fraction, he berated himself inwardly. He hadn't intended to flatter her.

"What does a servant know about such matters, anyway?" she asked with a huff.

"My dear Miss Blythe," he said, striving for patience. "Nothing pleasant can ever come of your association with Wycherley. He has a history of ruining young women such as yourself and simply can't be trusted. That you should come to his home, chaperoned or not, is highly improper. Does your reputation mean nothing to you?"

Her shoulders notched down, and an unreadable look flashed through her eyes. "I understand your concern, Mr. Ganstridge, and I do appreciate it. But you can't stop me coming again. My purpose here is not yet accomplished."

He narrowed his eyes in frustration and suspicion. "I dread to think what that purpose may be," he said darkly.

She shook a finger at him. "That's my concern alone. The sooner you accept *that*, sirrah, the better. You cannot go about accosting your master's visitors, however noble you believe your reasons to be. One word from me and you'll be demoted to boot boy."

Boot boy? He was barely able to restrain himself from grabbing her and teaching her a lesson.

A lesson she so richly deserved. And one which Ned was itching to administer—to show her what happened to innocent young ladies who found themselves alone with unscrupulous, lack-moral men. Men who desired them. Who craved the taste of their soft lips and the touch of their silken skin. Who wanted nothing more than to take what was so naively offered and revel in the thrill of conquest. Men like Captain Francis Wycherley.

But *not* Ned.

Ned was not without honor, regardless of his current lowly status.

If she only knew who she was actually dealing with.

If he told her, would she be any more likely to heed his warning?

No, it wasn't worth the risk.

A sudden knocking at the front door made her jerk back. She tore her gaze from…his lips?…and looked up at him in alarm.

"That will be Ella," she said in a breathy whisper. "I cannot be seen coming out of a cupboard with you!"

He shook off the powerful, unbidden arousal his wayward thoughts had wrought. "Move quickly. No one will be any the wiser."

She made to go, but he caught her elbow again. "Promise me you'll say nothing of this."

Her eyes widened at his grip on her. "Is that a threat?"

"There's much at stake."

"For me? Or for you?" she bit out.

For a moment, he was distracted by the way the anger sparked in her dark eyes, bringing them to life. Their promise of passion taunted him and aroused him further.

With great effort, he forced himself to loosen his hold. "We are in each other's power, it seems. If I reveal your secret, you will expose mine, and vice versa. An impasse, Miss Blythe. I'm sure you're intelligent enough to appreciate that."

Her shapely lips thinned. "Oh, well done, sirrah. You manage to make a compliment sound like an insult. Just let me out of here, you odious oaf! I promise I won't say anything if you don't. For the time being."

There. He had what he wanted. So, why this wash of regret as he opened the closet door and watched her scurry out into the hallway?

She was misguided but had a strong spirit. He had to admire that. And she'd been prepared to stand up to him… even though she was a head shorter, with a fraction of his strength.

He blew out the lamp and stepped from the cupboard, pretending to dust off an old apron, just as the front door was opened to Miss Blythe's maid. Miss Blythe hurriedly donned her pelisse and bonnet, keen to make a hasty escape. If she had any idea he was standing there watching her, she gave no sign of it.

Would she come back, even after his warning? Did she not realize the threat to her reputation from visiting Wycherley?

Worse, did she have any idea—and he sincerely hoped she did *not*—how close he had come to kissing her in that closet?

Chapter Ten

Ned swilled platters around in the lead-lined sink and mopped at them irritably.

Wycherley had been right. Ned *was* an idiot. The amatory adventures of foolish young females like Miss Cassandra Blythe were as nothing compared to his quest. He should never have risked revealing his true identity by interfering.

If he *had* stormed out and gone to see her father, it would definitely have raised eyebrows. Not at all the kind of thing a genuine servant would do. And with the raised eyebrows would come questions, and descriptions of that servant. Memories would be stimulated, and he would be found out.

Gone would be his best chance of ever finding his sister Georgiana again. And he *must* find her, whatever her fate.

He propped a pewter dish on the wooden drainer and stared out at the bright spring day. The second week of May and it had been quite promising so far, with only a little light rain, enough to nurture the plants. It was damnably warm down here in the South, though. The cow parsley, ox-eye daisies, campion, and vetch were out in profusion in the hedgerows on the edge of town. In the North, back home, spring would just be on its way, and the wind that blew across the stone walls and feathered the backs of the sheep would still be chilly. How he missed it!

He supposed he might get used to the South, eventually. But he much preferred the wild landscape of Yorkshire, with its romantic ruined abbeys and dark, rain-fed skies, and the lonely cries of the buzzards over the jagged outcrops.

He held a glass with a twisted stem up to the light and polished it with a thick cotton cloth. Undeniably, Wycherley had good taste, but that was the only good thing Ned could think of to say about him. The number of different women he entertained—including Lady Lucy and the Blythe girl— was quite shocking. At least Miss Blythe had not yet been in Wycherley's bed, while he knew for certain Lady Lucy had. But with a man like his master, it was only a matter of time.

Which would be a shame, for Miss Blythe was a charming girl with a healthy pink in her cheeks. Her bronze-colored hair shone in both sunshine and candlelight, and she had the most delightfully peach-colored lips. How infuriating that all these appealing attributes should conceal such a stubborn and determined—and very misguided—character!

But Miss Blythe was not Ned's problem. There was no need to wonder if and when she would be back again, how she might react to him, or what she might say.

It was Georgiana he wanted to save, needed to save. Not Cassandra Blythe.

He rested his hands on the edge of the sink, the knuckles whitening as he revisited the tragedy of six months previously. It seemed like only yesterday—he could still see, with vivid clarity, the grim sight of his aunt's house after the fire—a blackened, smoking ruin, with the servants standing about in tears and pale with shock. The fire assurance machine stood to one side, the men gamely pumping its wooden handles, first one side, then the other, damping down the ashes to make sure the greedy flames could not consume another dwelling or ruin another life.

On his arrival, Aunt Claudette had run to him and flung herself, weeping uncontrollably, into his arms. When she'd looked up, the tracks of her tears were like white scars through the soot on her face. He would never forget her expression.

Lamps had been brought and lit all around them, and spectators stood in hushed groups, some still clutching their water buckets, waiting to see if the crisis was over.

It was not.

"Ned! Ned, is Georgiana not with you?" Aunt Claudette had asked him breathlessly.

"No. Should she be?"

"We have asked all the neighbors, and none have seen her."

He recalled the first trickle of unease. "But…surely, she was here at home with you? It's after midnight."

He had looked at his aunt's desperate face, and gradually the awful truth had begun to sink in.

"You're saying she is *missing*?" He dreaded the answer, but the question had to be asked. "She has not been…found?"

"Not a sign. Perhaps she's wandering about somewhere, too shocked to find her way back to us. She went up to her room at the usual time. We all did. In fact, she went early. I had to chide her because she was yawning so much." His aunt had gazed up at him with overflowing eyes. "You look exhausted. You must have ridden like a demon from Highmore House."

He had, as soon as word had reached him of the disaster at his aunt's home, all the while fearing the worst—that they had all been killed, or severely injured.

During that entire, never-ending, terrible ride through the darkness, he had cursed himself for allowing Georgiana to stay with Claudette. The Duke of Paxton had invited them

Ned had persuaded his aunt to move back to Yorkshire with him. Eventually, racked with grief, he'd followed her northward to bury himself in the business of his Scottish and Yorkshire estates, hoping thus to mend the broken pieces of his life. At length, one of the inquiry agents he'd hired informed him Captain Wycherley had resurfaced in Oxford where he'd commenced a life of dissipation and pleasure, an instant favorite with the ladies.

Ned could have just taken a carriage and traveled down in person to beard the lion in his den. Or he could have instructed his agents to make more thorough inquiries. But a part of his mind had urged him that it would be better to use subtlety.

So he had come down to Oxford wearing a Rifleman's tattered jacket, in hopes of gaining Wycherley's sympathy for a fellow veteran down on his luck.

Ned had engineered a minor carriage accident, making sure he was there to rescue the captain from the wreckage, then asked if he knew anyone who could use a strong back and a firm pair of hands. A grateful Wycherley had employed him on the spot, Ned's friend, the Duke of Paxton, having supplied references to support his subterfuge.

Which was how Lord Edmund Talbot, Earl of Stranraer, had come to be working at Captain Francis Wycherley's residence, disguised as a domestic servant.

Chapter Eleven

The ruse had meant considerable sacrifice on Ned's part over the past few months, as well as an inordinate amount of self-restraint.

But he was convinced the captain knew something about Georgiana's sudden disappearance. It was too much of a coincidence that, having raised the alarm about the fire, he then vanished completely for several weeks. An innocent man would have stayed to give his version of events to the investigating authorities.

As much as he despised the man, Ned could not, however, believe the captain had done Georgiana deliberate harm. Abducted her, abused her, or outright killed her? No. Wycherley was a rogue and a philanderer, but he had never been violent in any way that Ned had uncovered, not to any woman.

Therefore, Georgiana and Wycherley *must* have had some kind of understanding. The man must have persuaded her to run away with him, and set the fire to delay any pursuit. But the conflagration had become more serious than the lovers intended, so Wycherley had raised the alarm before they fled, lest anyone get hurt. It made sense, if terribly inconsiderate and risky.

Unfortunately, it was turning out to be devilishly difficult for Ned to prove any of his suspicions.

Once he had the proof, though, he would use his fists on Wycherley's handsome face in a way that would make the blackguard confess Georgiana's fate. He intended to render the man unrecognizable. Bereft of his good looks, the bastard would never be able to seduce another woman the way he had Georgiana. For good measure, Ned would announce to the *ton* that Wycherley was a cheat and a liar. His comfortable income from gambling would evaporate, and his shares and investments would lose their value as the honest investors withdrew their support. He would be thrown into debtor's prison, left to eke out the rest of his days in misery.

Which was better than the villain deserved.

Ned was determined to find Georgiana and to utterly ruin Wycherley for what he'd done to her.

The sound of the door knocker crashed through his thoughts, and he dragged his mind back to the present.

It was Wednesday, the day appointed for Miss Blythe's next visit, if she was foolish enough to come despite his warnings. Drying his cold hands quickly on his apron, he strode to the door. If it *was* her, he was honor bound to warn her away again.

Damn, too late! Matthews had already answered.

Ned withdrew into the shadows and watched as someone was let inside.

A shapely young woman with bronze-colored hair.

Miss Blythe. Back again, despite all he'd said.

He ground his teeth in frustration. The little fool was walking right into the wolf's lair.

She glanced about as Matthews divested her of her

outdoor clothing. When she saw Ned, color rose in her cheeks. Well, she *should* be embarrassed, coming back for more love-play with Wycherley.

He gave her his sternest, most disapproving look, the one that made even his own family back away from him. She blinked at him a few times, then turned her back and sailed into the drawing room while Matthews went to fetch Wycherley.

The minx!

Despite his firm intention not to interfere again, Ned strode to the door and paused outside, taking a deep, calming breath.

He *had* to make one last effort to deter her, lest she end up like his sister. Though he had yet to find proof, he believed Wycherley had deposited Georgiana—most certainly with child—in some obscure place, out of sight, out of mind. Ruined, and too ashamed to contact her family, she was now raising Wycherley's by-blow in poverty somewhere. God forbid she was in a poorhouse, or even abroad, where he might never find her.

Meanwhile, the captain had happily returned to his former bachelor lifestyle, flirting with women, enticing them with his fine looks and his reputation for being an exceptional lover.

Miss Cassandra Blythe, with that bright, fresh face and those sparkling hazel eyes, would soon go the same way as his sister if no one exposed Wycherley for what he was. And soon.

Ned *had* to stop her.

He stepped into the room. Miss Blythe turned sharply and glared at him.

Before he could speak, the sound of rapid footsteps announced the arrival of Wycherley, and he was obliged to back away and make his bow.

"Ah, Miss Blythe," the captain exclaimed. "How lovely to see you again. Ganstridge, what are you thinking, greeting visitors in your apron? Begone. I'll ring if we need anything."

So Ned was forced to leave with not a word exchanged between himself and Miss Blythe. Maybe his eyes had conveyed the message his tongue had not been able to. But he couldn't afford to press his point in any other way.

If Wycherley dismissed him, the time for subtlety would be over. He would be forced to drag the whoreson through the courts—if his fists couldn't get the truth out of him first.

One way or another, the world would know of that blackguard's villainy.

Chapter Twelve

Cassie dredged up a smile as Captain Wycherley came to greet her with hands outstretched.

Really, that Ganstridge! He had just barged into the room, still wearing his damp apron and shooting her a look of such disdain she could have shouted at him, she really could! Yet, just as he turned to go, his expression had changed, leaving her more perplexed than angry. He'd seemed almost…sad.

"So, are you ready for your next lesson in how to seduce a man?" Wycherley's smile was unnerving.

She must remember why she was here—to win the heart of Julian Carnforth.

Bolstering her courage, she replied, "Yes. Of course. What would you like me to do?"

Wycherley gazed at her speculatively for a moment, then said, "I would think twice, my dear, before saying anything like that to a renowned rake."

"But you're my *tutor*," she said, forcing confidence into her voice. "I should be able to trust you."

The corner of his lip curved. "Clearly, you're new to this

age-old game. But, yes, we made an agreement, and I intend to hold to it. Now, to the first lesson of the day."

"Which is?" She hoped it wouldn't involve anything too intimate. Like a kiss.

To her surprise, he said, "Lower your voice."

She frowned. "Like this?"

Wycherley chuckled. "No, I don't mean whisper, I mean lower your tone. Men are more attracted to a deeper voice, a slower way of speaking. Make your potential lover hang on your every word."

She made a sound in her throat like a low growl. "Like this?"

He laughed. "Perhaps you can go a little higher. You don't want him to think you have dyspepsia."

This brought a genuine smile to her face. She liked Wycherley, despite his notorious reputation. He was engaging, as well as exceedingly handsome, and she could see why so many ladies were attracted to him, even if she was not.

"Now, we need to talk about your appearance." He indicated the chaise longue, then sat beside her and tugged at a wisp of her hair.

Alarm sang through her. "If you knew how long it took Ella to create this style for me, you would not dare interfere with it," she said, resisting the urge to pull away.

"It's much too severe. There needs to be at least one wayward lock, just to make a man imagine what it would look like if every lock were set free. Your hair is brilliant, warm, and glossy. What man would not wish to see it loose about your shoulders?"

"I suppose I can cope with one stray strand," she said hesitantly.

He teased out the curl and laid it against her neck, his warm fingers just brushing her skin. She shivered. Surely, he could have told her what to do instead of doing it himself?

Was that wretched Ganstridge right, after all?

Now so close she could feel his breath upon her neck, Wycherley asked, "When you're at a ball, you will, presumably, wear an off-the-shoulder gown?"

She nodded mutely, all senses alert, hoping he wouldn't touch her again.

Her hope was in vain. His hands smoothed her dress down over her shoulders. She swallowed hard. If any other man—excepting Julian of course—had taken such a liberty, he'd have received a hearty slap. But this man was *teaching* her, she reminded herself.

She needed to concentrate. If Wycherley helped make Julian her husband, if he united her with the one man she knew could give her a lifetime of happiness, it was all worth it.

"Would you say this was a respectable depth?" Wycherley inquired, his voice languid and warm.

She nodded. He pushed the sleeves down farther, exposing the tops of her breasts where they nestled, supposedly safely, beneath her shallow corset. "And what about this?"

"No longer respectable," she whispered, and her gaze shot toward the door. She could only hope the disapproving Ganstridge wasn't listening at the crack, or peering through the keyhole. She made to pull the sleeves up again, but Wycherley stopped her.

"No, not yet. Now that you've gained the man's attention with the wayward lock of hair, you need to move your head slightly so the stray curl caresses your neck, or your breast, everywhere his fingers long to go. But you must take his thoughts just a little further. You have to stoke his need, fan the flames of his desire." He frowned. "Just a moment."

As he disappeared through the door, she perched on the edge of her seat, her heart beating wildly, wondering just how far the captain was thinking of going…and whether or not she could swallow her pride enough to call Ganstridge to her rescue.

Wycherley returned and stood behind her. "Here," he murmured.

Something cold touched her neck, and a small, heavy cabochon cradled itself in her exposed décolletage.

"Obtain a ruby necklace just like this one," he advised her. "I chose the pale stone especially. It can sit tantalizingly between your breasts, the same color and size as the two rosy jewels which are hidden from the gentleman's gaze. This will get his imagination working feverishly."

By Juno, this was madness! Cassie leaped to her feet, tugged up the shoulders of her dress, and opened the door so abruptly she almost hit herself with it.

"Miss Blythe! Cassandra!" he called after her.

"I thought I saw Ella outside," she lied. "I must hurry. You'd better not see me out, in case she gets suspicious."

Ready to just grab her things and race out the door, Cassie's heart dropped like a stone when she saw the looming form of Ganstridge right next to the coat stand.

For a second she saw alarm on his face, but then his expression turned grim, and he strode toward her.

Damnation! He wasn't going to drag her into a cupboard again, was he?

When he took her by the elbow, she feared the worst. Then why wasn't she screaming and shouting for Wycherley or one of the footmen to rescue her?

She barely had time to register where she was going as the brute dragged her to the end of the corridor, through the kitchen, and into a tiny scullery with a lead-lined sink at one end.

When he closed the door behind them, she readied herself for another tirade.

But it didn't come.

Instead, he held her by the shoulders and captured her

gaze with his. "What has that damned libertine done now? Just say the word, and I'll teach him a lesson he'll never forget."

Cassie gaped up at him, struck with sudden insight. He wasn't angry with *her*. He was angry at Wycherley.

She swallowed hard. Now they were in close proximity, she once again felt the lure of this man's powerful body. And the fact that he was prepared to champion her made him almost...admirable. The urge to cling to him and accept the comfort of his arms was close to overwhelming her.

She shook the thought away. *Julian*. This was all about Julian. Soon, if all went according to plan, it would be *his* arms that were offered in comfort, *his* fists that were prepared to do battle for her—although she sincerely hoped the need would never arise.

The idea of Ganstridge chasing into the parlor and spilling Wycherley's blood on the rug was not a pleasant one. Even though the captain had won honor at Waterloo, he had not the muscle to best his strapping servant.

She forced a smile, saying, "Oh, it was nothing. I'm being foolish."

"This whole enterprise of yours is foolish," Ganstridge replied. "But I've already told you that. Perhaps now you realize how dangerous being alone with a man can be?"

She blinked, uncertain for a moment if he was referring to himself, or to Wycherley. Both of them had managed to set her heart pounding, but for very different reasons.

"I know I'm taking a risk," she said, looking away. His gaze was far too penetrating. And disturbing.

"Then stop doing it," he said simply. "Put it all behind you and hope no one ever finds out. If you use Wycherley's idea of courtship to win your ideal man, you'll end up with a lover, but *not* with a husband."

Her heart fluttered on hearing the word "lover" on his lips. He was certainly very blunt. And completely out of order.

It was a mystery why she wasn't more furious with him. And why the feel of his hands on her shoulders was so… distracting.

"I appreciate your concern," she said. "I think you mean well, despite the abominable way you've behaved toward me. But don't worry. I'm learning how to handle Wycherley."

She'd learned a lot about men in general in the process. Although, this one was still an enigma.

His fingers tightened on her. "You really think this man, the one you deem perfect for you, is worth ruining your reputation for? Could you not simply forget him and look elsewhere for a husband?"

She bit her lip. Of course Julian was worth it. She hadn't spent most of her teenage years crying into her pillow over him to let a silly little thing like modesty get in the way.

"There's no need to look elsewhere for a husband when I've already found the man I love," she said firmly. "I've received offers from others, but none of those men were superior to Julian."

Ganstridge's hands slid to her elbows, and he pulled her toward him. Speaking softly with his head close to hers, he said, "I think you'll find the world is full of men superior to Mr. Julian Carnforth, if only you were prepared to open your eyes."

She stared up at him, puzzled. His face had softened, and there was an appeal in his look she'd never seen before. His eyes bored into her, soul-deep, questioning, stunned and— surely not—vulnerable?

His closeness was making her insides knot up, and her nerves were completely on edge. It was a struggle to tear her eyes from his firm, masculine mouth and to stop herself from wondering how a kiss from Mr. Ganstridge would compare to that kiss from Captain Wycherley.

Totally lacking refinement, no doubt. Rough and raw,

but…possibly all-consuming. Something beat in this man's breast which she had not experienced with Wycherley, nor yet seen evidence of in Julian.

Passion.

"*I* could teach you," he said, so quietly she could barely hear him. "But with me, it would be real."

Her heart spurred to a gallop. She sucked in a breath in an effort to calm herself.

His chest heaved as he did the same.

Her head spun as his lips drew closer to hers.

No, this was completely wrong! Time to end it.

She tipped her head back and regarded him with disdain she somehow managed to summon. "Once again, Mr. Ganstridge, you overstep the mark." She wrenched herself out of his grasp, out of the seductive spell he had woven about her. "You clearly have some terrible grudge against Captain Wycherley and will do whatever you can to frustrate him. You've done your utmost to turn me against him, but you have failed, sirrah. Now, get out of my way. I'm going home."

She pushed against his chest, and just for an instant she feared he'd refuse to budge. But at the very same moment, a knock came on the front door, which jarred him into movement.

She could feel his presence close behind her as she marched toward the front entry, expecting to see Ella come to collect her.

But when one of the footmen opened it, an elegant female in a satin dress and elaborately feathered turban stepped into the hallway.

It was Lady Lucy.

Chapter Thirteen

A full week had passed since Cassie's agonizingly embarrassing visit to Wycherley's house. Lady Lucy had stormed past her down the hallway and, as soon as Wycherley appeared, launched into a jealous tirade about fickle beaux and loose, scheming females, which had made Cassie's ears turn pink.

Ganstridge had been the saving of her. Again. He'd stepped between her and the irate woman, not giving Lady Lucy the opportunity to get a good look at her face. While Wycherley had begun the courageous process of explaining away the presence of a pretty young woman in his house, Ganstridge had hurried her out the door and up to the top of the street.

Naturally, he'd given her another unwelcome lecture about her highly improper behavior, which had distressed and infuriated her so much her eyes had been moist by the time Ella hove into sight and rescued her.

Why the man had the power to unsettle her so, she couldn't explain, but it was becoming increasingly difficult to stand up to him. And he was impossible to ignore.

Finally, partly because of, the obstacle of Mr. Ganstridge,

she had decided to make only one more visit to Wycherley's house.

Then she would start her campaign of Getting Noticed By Julian Carnforth.

Unfortunately, the following week when she and Ella were on their way to her final "French lesson," they had walked barely halfway when the gray sky resolved into a dreary downpour. They huddled together under a shared umbrella, eyes to the ground as they picked their way around the puddles. Lifting their skirts as much as was decent, they struggled on, keeping close to the railings to avoid the wash being sent up by carriage wheels as they clattered over the glistening cobbles.

"I hope you appreciate what I'm doing for you, Julian Carnforth," Cassie muttered under her breath. "Getting soaked and risking my reputation. All because you are too blind to see the diamond that has been glittering beneath your very nose!"

But never mind. He was such a perfect gentleman, obliging, very rarely out of temper, and so handsome, too. He was less lithe than Wycherley, and no Atlas like Mr. Ganstridge, despite being strong. He'd often given her piggybacks when they were children, and could carry her at a run all the way across the rear lawn and back without getting out of breath. He was capable of dancing every dance at an assembly and still having enough energy to hoist her, laughing, straight up into the carriage so her gown wouldn't catch on the steps.

The sunny memory of such moments brought a smile to her lips, and she urged Ella to greater speed. The sooner her lessons in seduction were over, the sooner she could reap the rewards.

When they reached Wycherley's door and Cassie was safely sheltered beneath the portico, Ella took the umbrella and scurried off to the market.

Cassie knocked and waited. The door was opened by one

of the footmen, Matthews, who gave a jerk of surprise.

"Miss Blythe? Didn't you get the master's note?"

Now what? "No, I received no note."

He bowed. "My apologies, but Captain Wycherley is not at home. He sent a note with Ganstridge to inform you he was going away. It never reached you?"

It certainly hadn't. That pompous, interfering Ganstridge! No doubt, he'd done that quite deliberately, to put her nose out of joint and make her waste her time.

"Aren't you going to invite Miss Blythe in?" came the voice of Wycherley's other footman, Baxter. "Don't keep her standing there in the rain. I'm sure she could use a warming cup of tea."

Matthews stood back and ushered her inside. Well, she would have had to wait, anyway, as Ella wouldn't be back for at least half an hour. Cassie stepped past the footman and into the drawing room. "When do you expect your master back?"

"Not today, I fear," stated Matthews. "The roads will be awash if this rain keeps up."

She settled into a chair near the empty fireplace, feeling like an intruder in Wycherley's absence. Had something happened between himself and Lady Lucy which had occasioned his unexpected departure?

As Matthews bowed out carrying her damp coat and bonnet, she asked, "And where *is* Ganstridge? I should like a word with him about that note he failed to deliver."

Baxter's voice called from the hallway, "He's gone with the master."

"No, he hasn't," said Matthews. "He told me he was going on an errand for the captain that would keep him away all night."

"That can't be right," countered Baxter. "I definitely heard him say he was following the master with something he had forgotten to take."

Matthews backed out of the room and closed the door.

Cassie could hear the two servants arguing on the other side, sotto voce, about the whereabouts of Ganstridge. It seemed he'd told a different story to each of them and gone off on some nefarious business of his own.

With a sigh, she got up and wandered across to peruse the bookcase, choosing a book of Byron's verses. Smiling at a romantic inscription on the flyleaf that revealed the small volume was a gift from—unsurprisingly—one of the captain's many lovers, she returned to her seat and settled down to enjoy tea, overly sweet fruitcake, and overly dramatic poetry.

Not long afterward she heard the opening and closing of the front door. Eyeing the clock, she realized it couldn't be Ella—it was too soon. Maybe it was Wycherley returning. She stood, the book open in her hands, ready to greet him.

There were muffled male voices in the corridor, but when the drawing room door opened, it was to admit not the captain, but a rather damp Ganstridge, stamping his feet and pushing his dripping hair out of his eyes.

Her stomach flipped over at the sight of his tall figure, the multi-caped coat he wore accentuating the breadth of his shoulders, blocking the doorway so there was no means of escape.

For a moment his face lit up, but she had barely registered this expression before it was replaced by his more customary one of total disapproval.

"Mr. Ganstridge," she said coolly. "We've all been debating your whereabouts. I understand you have a note for me which should have been delivered two days ago."

The door closed behind him, and again she was trapped with this stranger who affected her right to the very core. From the grimness of his face, she half expected him to lock the door and remove the key.

"You took no heed of my warnings then," he said stiffly.

Honestly, did the man have no manners, at all? She

snapped, "Why should I care for the opinions of a servant?"

That made him wince, but he moved forward until he was towering over her. "Aren't you ashamed that a *servant* has more concern for propriety than you?" he ground out.

Why did he always fail to keep at a respectable distance? She was struggling to catch her breath, and the memories of being closeted in close proximity to him returned in force.

As did the troubling pull of attraction. She was drawn to him like a compass needle to the pole. Yet, he'd not even touched her.

It seemed it was not just Julian she could have vivid imaginings about…

"You're dripping on me," she complained, mortified that her body was reacting so uncontrollably to his nearness.

He took a deep breath. "My apologies," he said. He shrugged off his coat and flung it across the back of the chaise longue, followed by his broad-brimmed hat. Indicating a chair, he waited until she'd seated herself and then joined her at the tea table.

"Damned awful weather. These clouds have been following me since Westbury. I'm soaked right through my hat." He reached for a slice of cake. "Is there any tea left in the pot? Baxter and Matthews are idiots. They should have made up a fire in here. You must be freezing."

Struck dumb by the man's cavalier use of his master's furniture and tea things, Cassie just stared at him. Water trickled slowly from the damp curls of his hair into the white folds of his surprisingly neat neck-cloth, and small droplets clung to the lashes of his dark, sensual eyes. His handsome face was ruddy with the cold, his breathing deep from the exertions of his errand, whatever it had been.

What *had* he been up to that forced him to lie to the other servants?

Wait a moment. Westbury? Wasn't that in Wiltshire?

Before she could ask what reason he had to travel so far, he said, "So, you couldn't resist returning for another taste of the deplorable Captain Wycherley's lovemaking skills."

Did she detect a hint of bitterness in his tone?

She found her voice at last. "You make it sound so sordid! I have the best of reasons for my actions."

"Hah! It would take a great deal to convince me of that. I know he has a gift for bringing women under his spell."

"Why are we even having this conversation? I don't wish to speak to you, Mr. Ganstridge. Haven't you duties to attend to?"

His brown eyes met and held her gaze for a long moment, and there was something indefinable in them that stole her breath. But all he said was, "This is excellent cake—though a little on the sweet side. What's that you're reading?"

"Nothing." She balanced the book on the arm of her chair then stood up, needing the advantage of height. "Please explain to me what you were doing in Westbury, and why you are sitting here now, doing your best to ruin my day?"

"Isn't it obvious? I meant, once my other business was concluded, to get you alone and make one last effort to deter you from your purpose."

"You mean, you deliberately concealed Wycherley's note so I would come here, only so you might ring a peal over me?"

"I don't give up easily," he said. "As it seems I've failed—at least temporarily—in one venture, I am doubly determined to succeed in the other."

"In what have you failed?" she asked, looking down at him, and was instantly distracted. What wonderfully thick hair he had! Rich and waving, sculpted across his high forehead by the rain. A pity all she wanted to do was pull it until he yelped.

His brows drew together. "Maybe one day I'll let you in on my scandalous secret, since I already know yours. All I will say for now is that I followed Wycherley, but he didn't lead me where I'd hoped."

"To Westbury?" she asked, puzzled.

"To Westbury."

She waited for him to explain, but he just picked up the teapot and offered her more tea before pouring some for himself.

She said, "You do realize I'll have to speak to your master about this."

"Then I will have to speak to your papa about *him*," he replied, gesturing to a military portrait of Captain Wycherley hanging above the fireplace.

"You wouldn't dare!"

He raised an eyebrow at her. "Try me," he said.

She should have been infuriated, but when he looked at her like that, she lost the will to fight, and her mind again shot back to how she had felt when confined in the closet with him. Excited and…tempted.

She battled desperately with the inappropriate feelings. She mustn't let this man affect her in *that* way! Only Julian was allowed to do that!

Finishing a mouthful of cake, Ganstridge wiped his lips on a napkin in such a well-bred fashion she narrowed her eyes at him. Suddenly, she realized the usual peculiar burr of his speech had been replaced by a cut-glass accent as crisp as her own.

But…

Her mind raced. And came to the only conclusion possible.

Good Lord! He wasn't a servant at all!

But how could that be?

Who *was* this man?

"You don't strike me as being a completely witless female," he said, oblivious to her shock, "so I'm surprised you can't see what's wrong with your little scheme. Has it not occurred to you that any scandal linking your name with

Wycherley's might result in your being forced to marry *him*?"

No. Because she had no intention of being found out. That would completely scupper her plans to marry Julian.

Would Ganstridge really carry out his threat to tell her father?

"I should refuse to marry him," she said stoutly. "I would say that nothing had happened, that it was a complete misunderstanding. Who would people believe? The servant or the genteel young lady—"

He gave her a wry look. "When it comes to a scandal—"

She took a deep breath and cut him off. "Who are you really, sir? You can't fool me any longer. I know you're no servant!" She drew herself up. "And if you continue to threaten me, I'll tell everyone, and you'll be thrown into a prison cell!"

The color flowed out of his face. "By the devil!" He leaped up and went to the door, opened it, and apparently satisfied there was no one within earshot, he closed and locked it, then came to stand over her.

Her stomach did a somersault. He was furious. No, wait, that wasn't anger. It was fear. Fear, presumably, of what she could do to him, now she'd uncovered his secret.

Which served him right.

A myriad expressions flitted across his face. Clearly, he was wrestling with some internal turmoil. She lifted her chin. No doubt he was trying to bring himself to apologize to her and beg her indulgence.

His eyes narrowed, and he leaned in closer. So close she could smell the rain lingering on his hair and see the darkening of his pupils, feel the subtle change in his emotions.

And suddenly, she was terrified she couldn't have been more wrong.

He didn't intend to apologize…

Sweet Venus.

He intended to kiss her!

Chapter Fourteen

Ganstridge's lips were hard and demanding, overwhelming every part of Cassie's mouth like a cavalry charge. Unprepared for his sudden onslaught, her jaw went slack, and his tongue pressed forward, invading her and taking control of all her senses.

She should push him away, slap him, stamp on his toes, scream for help. But her body refused to cooperate. Everything was focused on the man and the heat of his touch, the powerful hand on the back of her neck holding her steady, the fingers stroking her face, their movements becoming more confident when she didn't resist, working in harmony with his tongue.

A powerful yearning sprang to life in her belly, flooding hotly through the rest of her body, making her breasts ache and her center tingle with anticipation. Was this what desire felt like? That feral, elemental desire which drew male and female together like iron to a magnet?

She tried to tell herself it was disgraceful to allow this man to kiss her, in broad daylight no less, in the middle of

Wycherley's drawing room. No, not just allow it, but *welcome* it. But it was no use. Her body was melting to his touch, her lips and tongue following his lead, exploring him, inciting him, reveling in the heavenly wickedness of mutual desire.

She was drunk on the taste of him, dizzy with the feel of him. Not even the heady excitement of dancing with Julian had awakened feelings like this.

The thought of her beloved washed over her like a bucket of cold water. What was she *doing*?

She placed her hands firmly against Ganstridge's chest and pushed.

For a moment nothing happened, then he stepped backward, breathing hard.

"Good God!" he exclaimed, looking at her as if she had just grown two heads.

"I second that sentiment," she replied, gingerly touching her bruised mouth.

He blinked. "I… Forgive me. That was *not* what I intended."

Her reaction hadn't been what she'd intended, either. But to be perfectly honest…she'd enjoyed it.

A lot.

Who *was* this man, who could bring her to tears with a few well-chosen words and make her want to rip all her clothes off just because he'd kissed her?

She swallowed. "Let us assume," she ventured, trying to get her husky voice back under control, "that we have both made a foolish mistake. I think, perhaps, this evens the score between us, Mr. Ganstridge. You can no longer report my so-called hoydenish behavior to my father, and I would feel a hypocrite were I to report you to your master."

Ganstridge dragged a hand through his hair. "Please sit down, Miss Blythe. There is something I need to tell you."

A trickle of foreboding slithered through her. She sat.

"You were wise to suspect me. My name is not Ganstridge, and I'm no servant. My name is Edmund Talbot, and I am the Earl of Stranraer. My Aunt Claudette lived here in Oxford… until quite recently."

Cassie felt the world spin round. She clutched at the tea table, her jaw dropping. "*You* are Stranraer?" she said incredulously. "The missing earl?"

And yet, the stunning revelation explained a lot. The insubordination, the pomposity, the total confidence that his opinions were the only correct ones.

Well, *really*!

"I see I've shocked you, Miss Blythe," he said. "Unless that is pure disbelief?"

She snapped her mouth shut. *Sweet Venus!* She'd just been kissed by the Earl of Stranraer!

And what a kiss it had been…

"Oh no," she managed. "I can very well believe it. I knew there was something suspicious about you from the very first."

"Indeed?" His lips curved. "I thought I'd been doing rather well."

She ignored his obvious reference and straightened. "With that ridiculous accent? Spare me. Shall I recite all the things that gave you away?"

"Well, I suppose I can congratulate you on being perceptive—except when it comes to judging character. You are quite out of your depth with Captain Wycherley."

"Says the man masquerading as his servant! How can you criticize me when you've had the whole country searching for you? There have been rumors of kidnap, murder, spies, and Bonapartist plots. Your family and friends have worried themselves to death, I wager. I fail to see any honor at all in *your* character."

His expression darkened. "Don't think to judge me, Cassandra, when you don't know the whole."

"Then tell me," she said, exasperated, hating that she might be developing…highly inappropriate feelings…for a deceitful rogue. Her mind and her body were in such conflict she didn't know what to believe. Or to feel. "I'll reserve judgment until I've heard your reasons."

He studied her for a long moment. "Very well. But you must promise me not a word of this will go any farther than this room. My family's honor, and my own, depend upon it."

Intrigued—and relieved at the mention of honor—she nodded. "I promise."

For the next quarter of an hour, she sat listening in amazement as the man she now knew to be the Earl of Stranraer told her the grim tale of his sister's disappearance.

It wasn't until he had brought his story up to date that she suddenly remembered something which might be significant.

"Did you say your sister's name was Georgiana?" she asked with a prickle of excitement.

"It is. Why do you ask?"

"It may be nothing, but…" She rose and looked around for the poetry book she'd been reading. "Here, see?" She showed him the handwritten note on the flyleaf. "To my Dearest Francis, from Georgiana, Easter 1821, Aston."

He leaped to his feet and seized the book, then scanned the inscription, his face as intent as a hound on the scent. He strode to the window and read it again. Was it a trick of the light, or had he suddenly gone very pale?

"It's her handwriting," he said, his voice so quiet she could barely hear him. Then a smile slowly spread across his face, the first genuine smile she'd ever seen there.

She liked it. The softening of his eyes and face made him look even more handsome.

Dropping the book, he strode toward her, radiating a sense of joy so encompassing she couldn't help but smile back at him. Before she knew what was happening, he threw his arms around her and pulled her into a tight embrace, spinning them both round and round until she felt dizzy.

All the breath went out of her—and along with it, all her sense. She reveled in him holding her tight, acutely aware of the strength of his muscular body as he moved around the room. They were dancing, but her feet weren't touching the ground.

"You angel!" he exclaimed, setting her down abruptly and taking her face between his hands. "Georgiana is alive. And now I know where she is!"

Then he kissed her. Again. A long, hard, heated pressure of the lips which made her heart leap and her body tremble with need. When it ceased, it left her fumbling for a chair and collapsing into it, her pulse jumping madly.

Sweet Venus. She couldn't help but adore what the man did to her.

He turned to rummage through the bookcases, scattering books and maps onto the floor. The tea things were moved to sit precariously on a window sill so he could unfold a map onto the table. With an unsteady finger, he traced the lines of roads, prodded the dots of towns. He looked up with a frown and demanded, "Where the deuce is Aston? Is it too small to be on the map?"

Cassie moved around to study it. "Didn't you say you followed Wycherley to Westbury?" she asked.

"Aye. But he'd only gone there to meet up with an army friend of his. One of my agents overheard him saying he meant to return via Bath to fetch some bottles of the health-giving water for a sickly relative."

She regarded him wide-eyed. "You have agents?"

"Of course. I don't do anything by halves."

So I've noticed. She cleared her throat. "Then why disguise yourself and live in Wycherley's household? You could have employed an agent to do it."

He looked up at her, no longer smiling. "I needed to see for myself what manner of man Wycherley is. To see if he is the kind to seduce an innocent young woman, despoil her, and abandon her somewhere with his child in her belly."

Cassie recoiled at the vitriol in his words and tone. "You are very blunt, my lord."

He held her gaze, and she felt a shiver down her spine. "I will not sugarcoat the matter, sweet Cassandra. You know what he's like. The devil nearly had *you* in his clutches."

"I disagree. I feel certain he would have honored our agreement and would not have hurt me."

"Don't be a fool. Men like Wycherley never change. He was a rake before he met my sister, and he's a rake still. I fully intend to put a stop to his behavior before any other innocent gets hurt. Now you've heard my story, you shouldn't even want to give him the time of day."

She shook her head. "You have condemned him without any proof. You must find your sister and speak to her. Hear her side of the story."

He stood and started pacing. "If only I could! She must have been blinded by love. Just as *you* are with that blighted Mr. Carnforth of yours. When I've finished with Wycherley, no woman will look twice at him."

Cassie shuddered in apprehension. "What do you mean? Do you intend to use violence against the poor man?"

"*Poor?*" the earl exclaimed, his voice getting louder. "You *worry* about the blackguard? He's done you no favors. He might easily have ruined you, if I hadn't intervened."

"And you wouldn't?" she shot back, standing up and meeting his gaze full on. "It seems to me, from what has happened between us, that you are hardly better."

She expected heated denials, or even anger. She moved closer to the door, just in case.

He glanced away, but not fast enough to hide the look of

hurt in his eyes. "That was…unintended," he said. "I'm sorry. I forgot myself."

"It wasn't the first time," she reminded him, uncertain whether she was seeking an apology…or a declaration.

She got both.

"No, it wasn't," he said. "Forgive me. I find myself drawn to you, Cassandra—if against my better judgment. But don't worry. It won't happen again. You can get on with it and pursue Carnforth, if that's truly what you want. Just promise me you won't have anything more to do with Wycherley. He's going to get his just deserts."

"Lord Stranraer—"

"Please. Ned is fine. My days as Ganstridge are over, but given the circumstances, it would feel strange for you to start kowtowing to me." He gave her a meaningful smile.

Her cheeks grew warm, but she refused to let him fluster her. "Very well…Ned. You must take no action until you have found and spoken to your sister. If you harm Wycherley with no justification, you could fall foul of the law. Even if you have justification, you are still not above it. And if your sister loves the man, she won't be too pleased if you hurt him."

"I don't mean to kill him," Ned said. "Just to spoil his looks and ruin him."

Cassie's stomach coiled. "Oh, is *that* all?" Could Stranraer really be such a brute? She turned and set about replacing the books he'd scattered around, saying, "Well, if you won't be swayed from such a *vile* plan for vengeance, you can find Aston yourself, without any help from me."

She could hear the menace in his voice as he said, "You know where it is, don't you?"

She turned to face him, lifting her chin. "No."

"You're lying." He was across the room in a couple of strides, catching her by the shoulders. "Tell me, damn it!"

"Not if you growl at me like an angry dog. You *do* have

the most deplorable manners, my lord."

"*Ned*. And I can live with that. Are you going to tell me, or do I have to throw you over my lap and spank it out of you?"

What? How *dare* he? Of all the rude, pompous, ungrateful—

Fighting back her indignation, she inquired icily, "Tell me, is all of Scotland so uncivilized, or just you?"

"Wretched wench. Do you think to tease me? Shall I make good my threat?"

She felt the power of his proximity, the lightning rod of his touch searing through her nerves, igniting her very core. This man had an elemental allure she'd never imagined existed. And clearly, he knew how to use it.

"Ned," she said, keeping her voice as steady as she could, even as her imagination took flight at the images his threat conjured up. "Shall we make a bargain?"

"I'm listening."

"Promise me you will not harm Wycherley, and I will tell you where Aston is. I will even help in your quest to find Georgiana."

He shook his head. "I can't make a promise I may not be able to keep."

"You must temper your anger. Wycherley may not have acted as reprehensibly as you believe. At least wait until we know the truth."

There was a lengthy pause while he scanned her face. Eventually, he released her, saying, "I'll try. I can promise no more than that. Now, have pity on me, Cassandra, and tell me where my sister is to be found."

It probably didn't come easily to this man to beg. How could she ignore such a heartfelt request? She was going to have to trust him. "There's a small village in Wiltshire called Aston Tankerville," she said. "My friend Portia lives there."

His countenance brightened, and she felt the power of his smile. "It's near Westbury, I wager?" he said eagerly.

She could feel his excitement. It positively crackled around him. Smiling back, she replied, "It is."

"Damnation!" he exclaimed, driving his fist into his palm. "I knew I should have stuck with Wycherley. He might have led me straight to her after he'd been to Bath. I wonder if Maxim has any more miles left in him today."

Cassie's wrinkled her brow. "Maxim?"

"My horse."

She was astonished. And alarmed. "But you can't mean to ride there now? You'll never make it before dark. And in this weather—"

The roads would be full of potholes. What if his horse slipped and threw him? He could break his neck.

Not that she should care.

"If I don't go now the roads will be even worse," he said, returning to the chaise longue to grab up his coat. "I've searched for her for six months. I can wait no longer." He pushed his hat onto his head and strode to the door. "Say nothing of this to anyone, I beg you."

But...no! He couldn't just disappear, possibly altogether, from her life! There was still so much to say, to think about, to decide.

About their kisses.

About...*them*.

Except, now she knew he was an *earl*, not a lowly servant. So there could never be a "them." They were too far apart in rank.

"Promise you'll let me know the outcome of this story," she urged as he eased her gently away from the door and unlocked it.

"I will contrive to let you know, one way or another. But swear to me you will *not* call on Wycherley again."

She nodded, her thoughts in a whirl of shocking disappointment. "Very well."

"And if you persist in pursuing a man so clearly undeserving of you as Mr. Carnforth, at least woo him by respectable means, not through…nefarious lessons."

Her face flamed to recall, not her lessons from Wycherley, but instead Ganstridge's—Ned's—arousing kisses…even as Julian's name filled her with a wash of guilt.

And suddenly, she could not imagine enjoying such wicked, sensual kisses with anyone but Ned.

Not even Julian Carnforth.

Which was ridiculous, because *Julian* was the man she loved, not the Earl of Stranraer.

She dipped her head and studied the toes of her shoes so he wouldn't see the chaos of confusion in her eyes. "I promise."

He gave her a very gentlemanly bow. "Thank you," he said gravely, then left the room, closing the door behind him.

She stood for a while in silence, all the things she'd just discovered fizzing around in her head like freshly poured champagne. How was she supposed to deal with the new and worrisome emotions she was feeling over losing a relationship she hadn't even realized she wanted?

Which she *didn't* want.

She only wanted *Julian*. Julian was her perfect match— kind, considerate, sensitive Julian. Not the uncivilized, mercurially passionate, revenge-seeking Ned Ganstridge.

No, Talbot.

Edmund Talbot. The infamous missing Earl of Stranraer.

She pushed out a breath of frustration. And how infuriating she couldn't share *that* discovery with anyone!

Where was Ella? Fresh air and the brisk walk home were exactly what Cassie needed right now. She needed to think.

Spotting the books still scattered all over the floor, she continued to gather them up and return them to their shelves.

When she came to the inscribed book of Byron's poetry, her fingers moved thoughtfully over the cover. And she smiled.

She had promised not to reveal Ned's secrets to anyone. But she *hadn't* promised not to pay a visit to her good friend, Portia. Certainly, the young widow must be in need of some company.

Perfect. She could keep an eye on Ned and make sure his temper didn't land him in jail. She could also ensure no harm came to Captain Wycherley.

And if, when Ned saw her again, he insisted on giving her another kiss or two, well, perhaps she should allow it.

Perhaps he'd been right, and *he* was the man who should be giving her lessons in the art of kissing. He was, after all, very good at it.

Chapter Fifteen

Ned had stabled his stallion Maxim at the Lamb and Flag in St. Giles, well away from the curious eyes of Wycherley's household. He'd walked only half the distance there when the heavens opened.

Blast! His caped coat was still damp from his earlier ride and would give no protection at all. He was forced to find the nearest shop and take shelter in its doorway.

"I'll cut his tongue out," Ned vowed to the rain. Now that his goal was in sight, his emotions ran hot with thoughts of his impending revenge. "I'll blacken his eye and break his nose. No one will ever want to look on his face again. My dear, sweet Georgiana, what has he brought you to?"

His tirade was startled out of him when a gentleman stepped out of the shop, a paper-wrapped package under his arm.

The man waved a hand at Ned and peered out at the skies from beneath the brim of his stylish beaver hat. "I say," he exclaimed. "Not a good day to be out and about. I have my umbrella, but I'd still live in fear of drowning." This last was said with a laugh, but the amused expression faded from the man's face when he saw the expression on Ned's.

"Have we met, sir?" Ned asked suspiciously.

"I don't believe so," the other said equably. "I think I would have remembered you. Julian Carnforth, at your service."

He bowed, and momentarily stunned, Ned bowed back, spilling a quantity of water from his hat brim.

The other man chuckled. "You, I take it, did not think to bring an umbrella."

"Ned Talbot. And, er, no, I didn't," said Ned without thinking, unable to drag his eyes away from the other man's face. *Good Lord.* The longshanks, the beanpole, the one who had nearly wrested the fickle Lady Lucy away from Captain Wycherley.

The very man Cassandra Blythe was prepared to risk everything for.

"Carnforth? Hmm. I believe we have a mutual acquaintance," Ned said carefully, well aware he was no expert at small talk. Or subtlety, for that matter. But he just couldn't help himself.

"We do? How splendid!"

Cassie's beloved was a cheerful gentleman, at any rate. Must be one of his attractions. Ned suddenly wished to know all of them. Why she preferred this man over any other.

Over him, for example.

"Indeed," Ned choked out. "I have recently come to know Miss Cassandra Blythe."

Carnforth's eyes widened. "Hold on. Did you say Ned Talbot? Not the missing Earl of Stranraer, surely?"

Damnation! Why the hell had he given his real name? What an idiot. "The very same, but I'd be in your debt if you would keep that to yourself for now. I am not quite ready to return to the world at large."

Carnforth tapped the side of his nose conspiratorially. "Won't say a word, my lord. I was sorry to hear of your family tragedy. It must be truly terrible to lose a sister. I can't imagine how I'd feel if I lost Cassie."

Bitter gall rose up in Ned's throat. Jealousy? No, of course not. But he was curious. She was gambling her reputation to attract this man. The least Ned could do was make sure Carnforth's intentions were honorable.

"You are very fond of her?" he asked.

"Oh yes. We are the best of friends. We grew up together as near neighbors. While our parents visited, we entertained each other when adult conversation turned boring. She used to love looking at my schoolbooks and my drawings, I recall, and I used to put her up on my pony and lead her around. But naturally, things have changed now."

"How so?"

"She's grown into a proper young lady. No more piggybacks or romps. That wouldn't do. She needs to think about finding a husband soon."

Ned refrained from spluttering at the word "proper." Or laughing out loud. "I can't imagine there'll be any difficulty in that area," he offered.

Carnforth winked at him. Ned wasn't used to being winked at. He wasn't certain he liked it. "Not with her looks," the other man said. "Although bronze hair and hazel eyes are not exactly the fashion. But she is a right out-and-outer, isn't she?"

Of course she was. She was stunningly beautiful, and desirable, too. It was an outrage that she'd had to resort to such lengths to attract this man's attention.

"I couldn't really say," he demurred. "We've barely met. Has she anyone in mind for a husband? Or rather, has her father?"

Carnforth chuckled. "He'd have *me* marry the chit if he

had his way."

Ned shot him a sharp look. "Sounds like you might object."

"Much as I like the old man—and Cassie, of course—it would be like marrying my own sister." Still smiling, he gave a delicate shudder. "All the same," he added, "she does have a huge dowry settled on her. Some distant relation who made his fortune in India. So, there's no lack of suitors after her."

Ned didn't know why that information hit him like a punch to the chest. His emotions teetered between a surge of unbidden relief and pure outrage. Did the lackwit not know how Cassandra felt about him? How in love she was with this obtuse, undeserving creature?

"Has she had offers?" He had to ask the question, even if he didn't like the answer.

"Plenty. But she's holding out for...God knows what. The perfect man? As if there is such a thing." He snorted. "Women, eh? How are we ever to understand them?"

How, indeed? It was quite clear Carnforth hadn't been leading Cassie on. She had decided without any encouragement from him that he was the only man for her. However, as he'd observed last summer at his friend the Duke of Ulvercombe's house party, men preferred it if they did the running, rather than the other way round. Marcus's dogged pursuit of his beautiful quarry had paid off in the end, though it had looked to be a close-run thing at times...

It would do Cassie more harm than good if she continued to chase after Carnforth.

Ned gazed out at the leaden rods of rain and the carriages splashing past, churning up mud from the road that turned the curbstones black. Despite the grim weather and the long journey that lay ahead of him with its uncertain ending, his heart lifted a little.

"You see this?" Carnforth inquired, indicating the parcel

under his arm, "A dozen yards of best Indian cotton, printed with rosebuds. I mean to take it to the mantua-makers and have it made up into a gown for my intended."

Ned froze, then frowned. "Your intended? May I assume that's not Miss Blythe?"

"Heavens, no," Carnforth said, mildly appalled. "Even though both our papas might wish it. She's far too dull for me. No, I'm referring to Lady Lucy Dyer."

Good God. Cassie would not be pleased to hear this news. Nor would Wycherley. Not that Ned cared about the captain's feelings. He deserved every bad thing that came his way. But not Cassandra. She would be devastated.

"Might I suggest, sir," Ned said slowly, "that you are careful how you break this news to Miss Blythe? I fear she may be shocked at it."

"I doubt it. She's my friend, and I expect my friends to congratulate me."

Not all of them, Ned thought. Cassie had risked her reputation for nothing and would certainly not rejoice at this news.

"Have you actually proposed to the lady in question?"

"Well, not *quite* yet," the other replied, toying with the string on his parcel. "My father is dead-set on Cassie, you see. Very venal of him. But Lady Lucy is wealthy, too, so I daresay he'll come round in time. Why on earth do you think Cassie won't like the match?"

Ned was going to have to choose his words very carefully here, or Cassie would never speak to him again. He said, "I'm sure she mentioned a Mr. Julian Carnforth in quite glowing terms. Or someone else said she had."

Damn it. He wasn't good at dissembling.

"Oh, that," said Carnforth. "Just a passing fancy, after her mother died. She was very young."

"And yet, now that she is a woman grown, and has had a

number of suitors, she's rejected them all?"

A dubious expression crossed the man's face. Good. He was getting the message at last.

"I see what you mean. I suppose it's possible she might still carry a torch for me… But it's of no consequence, now I've met Lady Lucy. She's a bit tempestuous, but I have every hope of being able to calm her down. In time."

And Cassie *wasn't* tempestuous? Ned begged to differ.

"But of course, in the light of what you say, I'll let her down gently. Cassie, I mean. I collect you are not from these parts, my lord," Carnforth went on cheerfully. "Scotland, is it?"

Ned gathered his wits. "Yes. But I spend most of my time on my Yorkshire estates. I say, I'd heard—and I hope you won't take this amiss—that Lady Lucy had some connection with another gentleman."

"You mean Captain Wycherley? True, she had a bit of an obsession with him at one time. He's very charming to the fair sex."

Ned gave him a puzzled look. "You seem to bear him no ill will."

"Why on earth should I? The rules of fair play do not apply in love and war, as the poet said. I'm confident she'll get over him. He'll never marry her, it's a fact. But I will."

Ned's head was spinning. The man was an utter fool. How could he even consider marrying someone of Lady Lucy's tattered reputation? Especially when she still had feelings for another man. Quite strong feelings. More than once, Ned had needed to block his ears against the sounds of Lady Lucy screaming her pleasure up in Wycherley's bedchamber. Mr. Carnforth would be getting well-used goods.

Ned asked, "Does that not worry you, at all?"

"I suppose it does, but I'm quite in love, so I won't let that get in my way. I must forgive her peccadilloes if I am to win her."

Ned could only feel wonderment at this peculiar attitude. He would find it impossible to forgive such wanton behavior in someone he loved. Hell, he'd been intensely bothered by much less deplorable actions in a woman he'd only just met.

"You have a great heart, sir," he concluded. But couldn't help adding, "I don't want to interfere in your business, but it concerns me that you might not know all the truth about Lady Lucy."

Carnforth seemed a decent enough chap, if obtuse. It would be a shame if he ended up leg-shackled to a notorious light-skirt for the rest of his life.

"Is there something I should know?" Carnforth asked.

"I have it on good authority," said Ned, "that she was at Captain Wycherley's home very recently. And I don't think they were just taking tea."

"Ah," said the other man, almost philosophically. "She has not got over him yet. But she will, in time."

Ned was astonished. "You're not bothered by that?"

"Of course I am. I shall speak to her about it, yes. But in the end, I will have to forgive her."

The man was too damned forgiving. Or possibly spineless. Anger speared through Ned. How could Cassie have become so besotted with such a sap?

"I could not forgive so easily," he ventured.

"But if I don't forgive her, we will just fight and make each other miserable." Carnforth shrugged, and allowed, "I wager I'd get a bit more cross if she cuckolds me after we're married."

"I should think so!" Ned concurred. He would loathe anyone to cuckold *him*—he'd seen the damage it could do to a man. His former friend, Hal, Lord Ansford, had become a recluse because of his late wife's loose behavior.

Carnforth added, "Until then, I daresay I can live with it.

We're all human, and we all have to compromise in the end, don't we? Being angry, bitter, or full of hate is quite wearing on body and soul. I wouldn't recommend it."

Ned was so taken aback by the entire assertion, he had no response to give.

"I believe it's starting to clear. Are you going my way? We might share my umbrella."

"I am not, but thank you," replied Ned, holding out his hand. Juggling with his umbrella and his parcel, Carnforth shook with him, then put up his umbrella and departed with a bow and a grin.

"I won't forget to keep quiet about meeting you!" he called over his shoulder, then headed off to the other side of the street.

Ned stared after him for some time. What an extraordinary conversation. What very *novel* views on love and forgiveness. If he'd been Carnforth, he'd have wanted to call out Wycherley for continuing to dally with Lady Lucy. And he'd have thought up a suitable punishment for the lady, as well. But would he have forgiven her?

Still pondering the question, he replaced his damp hat on his head and set off for what he very much hoped would be the last phase of his long quest.

When he found Georgiana, along with proof that Wycherley was responsible for whatever fate had taken her from her loving family, there would be no room for forgiveness.

None.

Chapter Sixteen

As another lurch of the coach forced bile into her throat again, Cassie asked herself why in blazes she had embarked on this questionable adventure. The recent rain had made craters of the roads and mudslides of the verges. Now these were drying out and hardening to uneven surfaces so that every jolt of the wheels whisked her stomach up like someone making a meringue.

She was perched uncomfortably between an elderly farmer who smelled of sheep and a parson who smelled of brandy and mildew. Trying to keep from joggling against their unattractive frames took much concentration, and she thoroughly envied Ella riding up on the box, enjoying the elbow room and the fresh spring air.

She picked at a loose thread on her glove and reminded herself this visit *had* to be made. It was too risky to let Ned deal with this business of Wycherley by himself. Ned had a fiery temperament and was apt to turn angry at the smallest infraction. If all his dire suppositions proved correct, he was going to make sure Wycherley was finished.

Yes, it would be truly despicable if the captain had sent an innocent young woman into hiding because he had—possibly—got her with child and refused her marriage. But did he deserve the awful punishment the earl was likely to deal him? What if Ned killed him, even accidentally? It would be a terrible waste of two lives.

Hopefully, if Ned found Georgiana in Aston Tankerville, Wycherley wouldn't be with her. But either way, Cassie needed to warn the captain that the Earl of Stranraer was getting close to the truth about his sister and was out for blood.

Was Wycherley really such a terrible man? Despite his allegedly dissipated lifestyle, he ran a tidy household, had been accepted into respectable clubs, and numbered many peers amongst his acquaintance. He enjoyed culture, poetry, and the pursuit of knowledge. And he was so very good-looking. Not striking like Ned, or handsome like Julian, but she'd hate to see his nose broken by the irate earl's iron fist, or see his bright eyes bruised and blackened from an assault by that angry bear of a man.

Admittedly, she had also hastened to Aston to assuage her own guilt. If Ned killed or maimed Wycherley, it would be entirely her fault. It was she who'd discovered the inscription and told Ned where Aston was located. How could she ever forgive herself if either gentleman were to harm the other?

The creaking of the coach abated, and the ringing sound of horse's hooves on cobblestones reached her ears. The coachman's horn blared out, and there was a significant easing of tension amongst the passengers. They had reached the next stop and could look forward to a stretch and refreshments.

"Aston!" called the driver. "We stop for half an hour, exactly, to change horses. You'll find a ready welcome at the Rose and Crown."

The coach rocked as it gradually emptied of its passengers.

Cassie finally emerged from the crush of the interior, feeling like a butterfly freed from its chrysalis.

A brightly trimmed bonnet atop a mass of curls bobbed up and down amidst the general melee of people on the green before the inn.

"Cassie! Over here!" cried its wearer.

Cassie hurried to her friend and embraced her happily, noting with pleasure how well she looked. After arranging for Cassie's bag to be delivered, they strolled arm in arm to Portia's whitewashed cottage situated close to the center of the village.

"I'm so glad you came to see me!" enthused Portia as she ushered Cassie into her small parlor, which looked out across the village green. "At last a break in the boredom. How I long for something exciting, like a goose fair with games, a traveling lantern show, or a tethered air balloon. You're so lucky to be able to walk into Oxford whenever you want."

Cassie gratefully received a cup of tea. "Then you must come and stay with me one day soon. But let me tell you," she added, feeling the hairs stand up on the back of her neck, "excitement may have already come to Aston."

Portia's eyes sparkled. "Pray *do* tell."

"I can't reveal all, as I've promised not to. But I've come here in hope of saving someone's life. And someone else's honor."

Portia clapped her hands. "An adventure with very high stakes! Please tell me it's not going to be dangerous!"

"Don't worry. I think I can prevail."

Ned liked her. Cassie knew he'd never hurt her. But she wasn't so sure he wouldn't follow through on his threats to seriously injure Captain Wycherley. She prayed she could make Ned listen to reason, but her own safety was the last thing she was worried about. No, it was another thing entirely…

"Have any people of note come to the village recently?" she asked. "A powerfully built gentleman in the last couple of days? Or a lady, about six months ago? Or even a man who looks like an angel with golden hair?"

Portia leaned forward excitedly. "What interesting people you seem to have been consorting with! But none of them sound like your beloved Mr. Carnforth. Is he excluded from this adventure?"

Cassie sat back abruptly at the reminder. "It's best he knows nothing about it."

Portia's eyes widened. "Two gentlemen involved, neither of whom is Julian. How *very* intriguing!"

"No, it's nothing like that," Cassie said quickly. Perhaps a little too quickly, for Portia's gaze sharpened. *She would not blush*, Cassie told herself firmly. Ned—*Lord Stranraer*—meant nothing to her. His kisses had just been…briefly distracting. And she would *not* allow him to take such liberties again.

She loved no one but Julian. And that was that.

"So, how would I know this powerfully built gentleman?" Portia asked. "Apart from that description?"

"He looks like Hercules. Or how I imagine Hercules might look. A tower of strength, sinew, and muscle…" Cassie broke off and gazed out the window, an image of his handsome face in front of her, remembering the searing heat of his last kiss. Her breath condensed in a cloud of hot mist on the window pane.

"Go on," her friend prompted gently. "Does this demigod have a name?"

Cassie forced herself back to the present. "I'm not at liberty to say."

"How irksome! Is he handsome? Dark or fair?"

She smiled. "He's striking-looking, in a very masculine way, with dark hair, deep brown eyes, and long lashes."

Portia gave her a penetrating look. "He sounds splendid.

I'm half in love with him already."

Cassie snorted. "Don't be. He's irascible, interfering, temperamental, and thoroughly annoying. But the point of the matter is, have you seen him?"

Portia smiled. "Sadly, no."

Outside, the strident sound of the coachman's horn called the remaining travelers to heel.

Portia glanced up and asked, "Would he have come by coach or carriage? I usually look out when they go by, but as the road's on the opposite side of the green, I can't always make much out. If he came on horseback, I might not have noticed him. But if he's here, he'll be staying at the Rose and Crown. Unless he's a very important personage, in which case he'd probably stay with one of the local aristocracy."

Portia was obviously digging for information. To deflect her, and to spare her own blushes, Cassie asked, "Have any new tenants arrived in the village of late?"

"How recently?"

"Within the last six months. It would be a young lady."

"Am I allowed to learn *her* name?" Portia asked hopefully.

Cassie grinned. "Better not. You're far too good at working out puzzles."

Portia sighed. "This is the most infuriating thing you've ever done to me, Cassandra Blythe!" She made a face. "And I know for certain you didn't come to see me. You're just using me for a place to stay while you pursue your adventure."

Cassie reached for her friend's hand, aghast. "No! That is only a small part of my reason, believe me. I so miss having someone to confide in. My cousin, Becca, is completely wrapped up in her books and her studies, and I certainly can't talk to Papa about…well, anything but the weather. I promise as soon as I have permission I will tell you as much as I know. And if there is any adventure to be had, you will be included in it."

This seemed to mollify her friend a little, for she smiled and then pondered for a moment. "Well, there is an old lady who's taken a cottage on the Kenville road. It's right on the edge of the village. She doesn't come into Aston at all, but a well-dressed manservant appears sporadically and runs errands for her."

Discouraged, Cassie said, "No, this wouldn't be an old lady."

Ned would be so disappointed. But at least Wycherley's skin would remain whole for a while longer.

She put her cup down and gave a genteel stretch. Her friend immediately said, "You must be stiff from your journey. How about a stroll around the village? We can inquire after the people you're looking for."

That sounded a splendid idea. Although the prospect of meeting Ned again so soon did something strange to her insides.

And definitely, she told herself firmly, there'd be *no* kissing involved.

Chapter Seventeen

Ned sat in simmering fury on a grubby, straw-filled mattress atop a narrow wooden shelf. Something had crawled out of the bedding and bitten him several times before he'd found and crushed it. Now his head was itching, as well as his legs, arms, and torso, but it was exceedingly difficult to scratch where he needed to, due to the manacles fastening his right arm and ankle to the wall.

His jaw clenched as he stared out at a small square of blue sky—broken up by bars—which was all he could see of the outside world. Without the chains, he'd have been able to look out, see how his surroundings appeared in daylight. Not that it mattered. The damned village could go hang, and all the people in it, too, for all he cared. For a person of *his* status to be so manhandled, to be cast into this wretched jail cell for a full twenty-four hours with no hope of release, was the outside of enough.

When he finally got out, he would string that obnoxious constable from the church tower by his bootlaces. He would knock together the heads of the men who'd thrown him into this cell until they forgot their own names, and he would send in a crew of stonemasons to pull apart this ghastly little lock-up, stone by stone, then break the stones and use them to fill in potholes. *That* would show the world exactly what he thought of Aston bloody Tankerville, its residents, and the damned Blind House on the green!

The parish constable, a well-fed oaf with a multitude of keys jangling about his person, had brought Ned a stale loaf and some ale an hour ago. The man had stood just out of reach and rung a righteous peal over him for not being able to control his temper and for causing damage to other people's property.

Him? Not control his temper? Of course he damn well could! Wasn't Francis Wycherley's continued existence in unaltered form proof of his self-restraint? Besides, Ned could easily pay for the blasted damaged door hinge.

In retrospect, it had been a mistake not to change out of his servants' garb before making the journey. The half-baked villagers, seeing him upon a superior horse, immediately suspected he must have stolen it from his master. Now his faithful, exhausted steed was in a stall at the back of the inn, being watched over by a boy who didn't know his fetlock from his forehead. If any harm came to Maxim, Ned would not be responsible for his actions.

Damn the innkeeper, asking to see the color of his coin before offering him the hospitality of the Rose and Crown. That, along with all the hostile faces, when he was already feeling fractious after his grueling ride, had been the straw that broke the camel's back.

Taking up the gritty loaf in his left hand, he took a desultory bite and sat back on the cold, hard plank of a bed, staring up through the bars at the taunting patch of blue.

Beyond the curved walls and dome of his jail, village life continued. He had heard a coach arrive, empty, fill, and leave again. There'd been the heavy hooves of horses pulling wagons, the screeching of jackdaws, and the *clack, clack, clack* of pigeon wings. Now he could hear soft feminine voices, growing louder as they approached.

"I understand some poor wretch was cast into the Blind House last night," one woman said.

Ned ground his teeth. Yes. That would be him. He didn't care for being called a poor wretch.

"Does that happen often?" the other woman enquired.

"Not too often. They are usually let go the following day. It's assumed they've learned their lesson...or sobered up. There's the pillory for repeat offenders, of course," answered the first voice.

"How dreadful," exclaimed the second.

Ned's ears pricked up. That voice. Had he heard it before?

"Achilles Marsh, our constable, is meticulous in carrying out his duties. He owns a full set of *Parish Law* and can quote you chapter and verse."

Ned scowled, distracted by the name of his persecutor. *Achilles Marsh*. He would remember that name.

"If you stand on this stone here, you can peep in," the first woman informed her companion.

"Heavens, no. I don't wish to revel in some stranger's misfortune."

Ned felt as if he had been struck by lightning. He *did* know that voice. All too well.

He leaped up and went as close to the bars as his chains would allow.

"Miss Blythe? I am *quite* certain I ordered you to go home and stay out of trouble," he called.

There was a strangled noise from outside, then, after a bout of scrabbling, a bonneted head appeared silhouetted against the sky.

"My l— er, Ned? Is that really you?"

He ground out, "Miss Blythe. What are you doing here?" *As if he didn't know.*

After a guilt-laden pause, she said, "I'm here to visit my friend, Mrs. Fiennes. I believe I mentioned she lives in Aston."

He was proud of how he kept his temper. *Quod erat demonstrandum.* He *could* control it. "You traveled alone?"

"I came with my maid, Ella. Not Wycherley, if that's what you're asking," she said, with obvious affront.

He heard the first voice ask, "Is this one of the people you were asking about?" A second shadow obscured the opening. "Good afternoon!"

Ned groaned inwardly. As if it wasn't bad enough for Cassie to see him in this mortifying situation.

Both heads disappeared amid a muffled discussion. Ned's chains clanked dismally as he scrubbed his face with his hands. Could this day *get* any worse?

Cassie's voice came again as her head reappeared. "What have you done to deserve your incarceration, sir?"

"Nothing! It's a complete farce, a travesty of justice. The landlord of the inn was rude to me, so I decided to move on, and slammed the door a bit too vigorously, never for a moment expecting to break its hinges. They must have been inferior, or already damaged. The landlord is being unnecessarily vengeful."

Cassie gave an unladylike snort. "You're a fine one to talk. Isn't vengeance exactly what *you* want?"

Minx.

Had she no compassion for his untenable situation? Obviously not. The woman needed a good— She wanted a thorough—

He clamped his lips together in a hard line. Damn it! He would *not* think about that right now.

When he didn't reply, she said softly, "Has your true identity been discovered?"

"Certainly not," he managed.

"I fear if you're not prepared to use your influence, you've no choice but to serve the rest of your time."

"Bring dishonor on my family by revealing my name? What would the tabbies say if they heard about this maddening misunderstanding?"

She tilted her head and peered down at him in a disconcerting way. "I suppose you think it honorable to spy on another gentleman in his own house?"

His chains rattled and clanked with his agitation. "You're enjoying this, aren't you? Now that I can't reach you to silence that mouth of yours."

He could tell from the jerk of her head she knew exactly what he meant. Then she lifted her chin at him, and said stoutly, "I'm not afraid of you. Anyway, Mrs. Fiennes informs me that it's not like the constable to imprison someone for merely breaking a door. Is there any more you wish to divulge?"

She already knew, the little wretch. He could hear it in her tone. Oh, when he got his hands on her again —

"If I tell you," he said, "will you get me out of this damned place?"

Her head tilted the other way. "I'll think about it. But I would ask you to mind your language when talking to a lady."

"You are going to regret your teasing," he muttered. As soon as he was out of here, he'd make her pay. And pay. And pay. In the most pleasurable of —

Damnation.

"Fine," he snapped. "I regret that I…lost my temper a bit further when unfairly taxed with breaking the door."

She pursed her tempting lips. "A *bit* further?"

He pressed his hand against his forehead. "Somebody came bowling out of the inn and attacked me from behind. I swung round and caught the man in the face with my fist."

She inhaled sharply. Ned hoped it was sympathy over his

misadventure, not a laugh at his expense.

"So, you were charged with assault?"

"At the very least, I'm sure. I had the great misfortune to have struck the constable of this wretched place. Although, obviously, it was in self-defense."

There was a pause. Cassie said at last, "You've been most ill-advised in your actions, sir. I wonder that you had the gall to criticize mine when you are so clearly no angel. I've never struck anyone, accidentally *or* on purpose, nor have I ever broken a door."

"How fortunate for you."

"*I* would call it good breeding and the ability to control my temper."

Were they back to that? "Be careful not to tease me too much," he said, his voice dark with warning. "I *will* get out of here eventually. And when I do, woe betide your impertinent mouth." The idea of kissing her senseless and administering other, more wicked punishments, was an exquisite torture. "What would your dear Mr. Carnforth say about *that*?"

His threat was met with so heavy a silence, he feared he'd gone too far. With her, as well as in his own imagination. Aside from feeling a large stab of guilt at invoking the name of a man he knew for a fact wouldn't give a fig if Ned kissed her ten times in front of the whole *ton*.

"Miss Blythe," he called. "I'm sorry. Won't you please talk to me?"

A muted argument erupted just below the tiny barred window of the cell. Minute piled upon minute, and still he waited, until the voices fell ominously silent, and quiet footsteps retreated.

All the anger flooded out of him, and he collapsed back onto the louse-infested mattress. *Damn it all to hell.*

No doubt he'd just ruined his only chance of getting out of here without revealing his true identity—and the whole world learning his family's scandalous secret.

Not to mention rendering impossible his own, more personal, scandalous secret—his insatiable desire to possess the infuriating woman who'd just given him his congé.

Chapter Eighteen

Suddenly the sunlight was cut off as, once again, a head popped up from below the barred window, throwing Ned's jail cell into Stygian darkness.

He lifted his gaze, hope surging through him.

Had Cassandra come back?

"We'll do what we can to have you released quickly," said the one voice that could truly stir his soul. "Portia knows the constable well, so we'll try and talk him round."

Ned jumped to his feet. "Thank you! I shall be forever in both your debts."

"There are, however," Cassie added in a stern tone, "conditions."

Why was he not surprised? "Name them."

"First, you must tell the constable who you are. I'm told his discretion can be relied upon. Second, you must swear you won't attack Wycherley, even if he is guilty of ruining your sister and setting fire to your aunt's house as you believe. Surely, the fire was never intended to be so dangerous. I don't believe he's capable of such deliberate cruelty. Third, you are to promise, on your life, you'll say nothing to anyone about my…lessons with him."

His heart twisted. The last went without saying. But not take revenge on Wycherley? Why did she still champion that rake, the man who ruined Georgiana's life, along with untold other innocents?

"Miss Blythe," he said, "I can agree to some of your terms. The only one I can't be certain of concerns Wycherley. You don't have brothers or sisters, do you?"

"I do not."

"Then you cannot fathom the love a brother may have for his sister. Perhaps not as children, but once they are grown up. Anyone who strikes a blow against a sibling becomes an enemy."

Silence again. He hoped she was starting to understand his position. He needed her to understand it, and how much his sister meant to him.

"I suppose an earl might be more protective of a sister than most," Cassie ventured.

"Particularly when it comes to her reputation," he added.

"More concerned than she is, herself?"

Fury surged through him. He opened his mouth to voice a sharp retort, then closed it again. He dare not speak his mind. He was too angry. She *dared* to blame sweet Georgiana for what had occurred, rather than Wycherley?

He would find a way to convince her to let him even the score with the blackguard. But for now, he must accede to whatever she demanded, no matter how much it galled him.

"I had no idea Georgiana was…involved with a man," Ned said, trying to keep his tone even. "Only the very deepest love—or delusion—would have given rise to such behavior. I could never have expected such a relationship to transpire without my knowledge."

"I can't imagine an innocent sister wishing to disclose

her innermost feelings to you. You can be somewhat…
formidable," Cassie said.

That hurt. Because, obviously, it must have been true.

"Miss Blythe," he snapped defensively, "you clearly do not
have a very high opinion of me. But the fact is, neither of us
will discover what did or did not happen between Wycherley
and my sister while I'm stuck in this stinking hellhole. Have
pity on me, please, before I'm eaten alive by bedbugs, fleas,
and frustration!"

He could dimly make out her face against the bright
square of sky. She was chewing her lip, deciding. He didn't
like that. She had a lovely mouth, which didn't deserve such
treatment…from anyone but *him*.

"I was obliged to tell Portia who you really are," Cassie
confessed. "She wants to know what you'll do when you're
released."

"Apart from shaking you until your head wobbles? Or
kissing you senseless…?" he growled, sotto voce. He cleared his
throat, and in a louder voice said, "I'll seek accommodation."

"At the Rose and Crown? I'm sure if you offer to pay for
the damage—"

"Wild horses couldn't drag me back through that
doorway," he said emphatically. "Though, I'll have to go back
to the yard for Maxim and my saddlebags. Unless they have
all been stolen by now, which wouldn't surprise me."

There was more whispered conferring between Cassandra
and the unseen Mrs. Fiennes.

"Portia invites you to stay with us."

He regarded Cassie's silhouette warily. Unsure if the
experience would be a pleasure or a Purgatory… "How kind
of her," he managed, dousing some vivid imaginings.

"We'll fetch your things. You shall have your own
chamber. Ella can sleep in mine."

Meaning no possibility of having her to himself. Which, at

least for her sake, was probably just as well…

Although, he was no Wycherley, regardless of the demands of his body. He would never take what wasn't freely offered.

"I thank you for your kind consideration," he said, struggling to sound polite.

"I see you've finally remembered your manners. Please continue to do so once you are released."

He took a deep breath and counted to ten. "I shall endeavor to please."

"Very well. We'll do what we can to free you. Can we fetch you anything in the meantime, something that can be pushed through the bars?"

"Don't bother. It would doubtless land on the floor just out of reach."

In spite of his complete and utter frustration over every aspect of his life at that moment, he made up his mind just then, that wherever he had influence, he would see to it that prisoners were not required to wear manacles. Or if it was absolutely necessary, that they would only have one foot or hand bound, but not both. The rough edges of the manacles would also be carefully smoothed so they didn't chafe. And the straw for the mattresses would be regularly changed and washing materials would be provided.

"We will speak to Mr. Marsh," said Cassie, "and return to you directly."

"Before nightfall?" He didn't want to be stuck in this noisome, rat-infested place after dark.

"Well before nighttime. Adieu."

"Adieu," he replied as the head retreated, leaving him to his patch of sky and his loneliness once more.

He couldn't believe she'd forbidden him from punishing Wycherley. She'd probably make him apologize to that little grub of a constable, too. Damn Cassandra Blythe and her infuriating notions of forgiveness! She had not the smallest idea of family honor. Damn her hypocrisy, too! She'd behaved in an utterly scandalous way, but about *that* she had nothing to say.

When he was free, he would have to point out to her that little mistake in judgment.

One way or another.

Chapter Nineteen

Constable Achilles Marsh was eventually tracked down to the Rose and Crown Inn and brought thence into Portia's kitchen. It took Cassie rather longer than expected to convince him to release the Earl of Stranraer, however. The good man had insisted on downing a whole bottle of elderberry wine and a quarter side of bacon before consenting to consider any mitigating circumstances.

Thankfully, he'd heard about the dreadful fire in Oxford which was thought to have claimed Lady Georgiana's life, and he was intrigued to find out where the earl had been hiding all this time. Cassie couldn't divulge that information, though, without risk of exposing her own misdemeanors.

She looked out the window and realized the sky had become very dark.

"Mr. Marsh, do you think Lord Stranraer might be permitted his liberty now? Dusk is already upon us."

Portia's hands flew dramatically to her cheeks. "Oh, my word, I'd no idea we've been conversing for so long. The unlucky man must be freezing. I'll run and put a cauldron on the fire so he can have some hot water to wash if he wants it."

But Mr. Marsh was not to be hurried. He returned his hat to his head, wiped a sleeve over his buttons, tested the weight of his staff, jingled his keys officiously, and tipped up his cup to make sure he'd drained the very last dregs of elderberry wine before rising at last to head for the jail.

Cassie chewed on her lip as the little procession made its way solemnly across the green to where the dark dome of the Blind House was silhouetted against a fading pink sunset. She wasn't worried about Ned—seriously, she wasn't—she was just averse to Portia being on the receiving end of his annoyance because they had taken so long to secure his freedom.

The constable leaned his staff against the limestone wall and unlocked the cell door with a flourish. "These ladies have obtained your early release, my lord," he announced magisterially.

Silence.

Cassie advanced to the open doorway and gripped the lintel. "Ned? Lord Stranraer? Is aught amiss?"

"I should say it is," was the response, clearly uttered through teeth clenched in the very greatest of furies.

"I'm sorry it took a little longer to arrange than we'd planned, but you are still getting out several hours early."

"You could not, I suppose, have returned before the mass departure of patrons from that hellhole I hesitate to accord the title of inn?"

Cassie tilted her head. Why should that matter? She stepped closer and the constable came in behind her, hanging his lantern from a hook on the wall.

"What's that smell?" she asked with a grimace. There was a distinct odor in the chamber, reminiscent of the rough coaching inns she'd stopped at on the journey to Aston. As she moved forward, her feet encountered sticky moisture on the flagstone floor.

Terrible understanding dawned. "Oh no, they didn't!"

"Oh yes, they did. And it seems they're quite experienced at it."

She turned to the constable, who was busying himself sorting out the correct key for the shackles. "Mr. Marsh! Why has the Earl of Stranraer been assaulted in this barbaric fashion?"

"I hope you are going to remain calm, my lord," advised the constable. "You won't find the culprits. They are all gone home to their suppers."

"What's the matter?" Portia was hovering outside, excited about meeting her first earl, no doubt disappointed that he wasn't leaping up in great good humor, delighted to have been released.

"The villagers have been throwing stale beer through the bars," Cassie explained, backing away from the bedraggled and seething Ned. "At least, I hope that's what it was, and nothing worse."

"Oh, great heavens! How very *heathen* of them. I shall rush back and start filling the bathtub."

"I should be much obliged," replied Ned, each word grating like a knife on a grindstone. At last the manacles fell away, and he stood up.

Looking every inch the aristocrat that he was, he seemed to grow distinctly taller and larger as he moved closer to the door of his prison.

In that brief moment while Cassie waited for him to explode, she felt considerable admiration for Achilles Marsh. The constable stepped back, but only to give his prisoner space, then stood his ground, removed his hat, and bowed briefly. "My lord," he said, "you are free to go."

In the flickering light of the lantern and the last embers of the day, Lord Stranraer's face—for this was not Ned, but the earl in all his rank and glory—looked positively demonic. He glared at Marsh, who stood waiting impassively. Then he moved his glare to Cassie.

She dropped her gaze in flustered embarrassment, unused to experiencing the full force of this powerful man directed straight at her.

Although the earl remained stonily silent, she sensed he was plotting his revenge…and while the constable would partake of some, she was fairly certain the brunt of his wrath would fall on *her*.

And the worst was, the thought of that didn't terrify her.

It thrilled her.

Because whenever he was angry with her, he always seemed to end up kissing her.

"Th-thank you, constable. You have been very h-helpful," Cassie stammered, quickly banishing the unbidden yearnings of her body. "Do you think someone from the inn might send the earl's belongings along to Portia's cottage? I mean, *Mr. Ganstridge's* belongings, as that's the name he is known by."

"Miss, are you quite certain you wish to give the gentleman lodging? He could always try Kenville Manor if he wants to be with his own sort."

"Quite certain." She turned to Ned. "And I have some news for you," she said brightly, in hopes of deflecting his mounting emotions. "A mysterious lady came to live in the village about the time your sister disappeared." He didn't need to know she was an *old* woman. Cassie could always claim ignorance later.

Her wrist was seized in a fierce grip. The constable tapped his staff in warning. After a significant pause, Ned removed his hand from her. "I would prefer not to talk here, Miss Blythe. If you could take me to your friend's house where I might wash away this filth, I should be most grateful."

Her heartbeat doubled. "Yes, of course," she said.

And fervently prayed she wasn't making the most monumental misjudgment of her life.

Chapter Twenty

On arrival at Portia's house, the Earl of Stranraer eschewed supper with cold courtesy, and went upstairs to bathe. Cassie could only hope that once he'd washed away the smell of stale beer, he'd drop the show of chilling politeness and return to them in more friendly mood.

"I must say," said Portia as soon as he was out of hearing, "I'm a bit disappointed with your friend's manners. He's very distant."

"Ned blows hot or cold. There's no middle ground with him. And I'd hesitate to call him my friend. He does nothing but chide me."

"Maybe they behave differently in Scotland," Portia suggested.

"Stranraer is as English as you or I, despite his claim to hate the South." Cassie had been reading about his pedigree on the journey to Aston, just as a way of passing the time. It was certainly impressive.

"There was a lot about him in the papers after he went missing," Portia said, producing a battered canteen of cutlery from a drawer. "He has land in Yorkshire as well as Scotland. Gant's Ridge, I think the Yorkshire estate is called."

Cassie blinked and slapped her hand to her forehead with blinding comprehension. "I am such a fool! Gant's Ridge, Ganstridge—I should have realized."

"Ah, his alias." Portia nodded, then carefully queried, "Does Mr. Carnforth know of your connection with the Earl of Stranraer?"

"Of course not." She hadn't known it herself until a couple of days ago.

"Why not? Wouldn't it make him jealous? If he were, it could do no harm to your cause."

Cassie indeed looked forward to telling Julian she was acquainted with the Earl of Stranraer. *Well* acquainted. Just as soon as that vengeful, ungrateful rogue upstairs stopped playing at spy and resumed his rightful place in Society.

"I shall try it, of course," she said, somewhat disheartened. "But I need to get Julian thinking of me as something more than a sisterly friend before I have the slightest hope of making him jealous."

"More of those scandalous lessons you told me about in your letter? You really are too shocking! What if you'd been discovered?"

"I'm starting to see how foolish I was. I suppose I just needed to realize that for myself, rather than have an overbearing, controlling, exasperating man like Ned point it out to me."

"Ned?" her friend said with arched brows.

Cassie rolled her eyes. "I knew him as a servant. Don't read anything into it."

"Why not? I think he likes you. And he's very handsome."

"Even when covered in stale beer?"

"I quite like the bedraggled look. He has stunning brown eyes with delightfully long lashes and impressive eyebrows.

And his mouth! Although grim at the moment, it is beautifully sculpted. He'd be lovely to kiss, I'm sure."

Cassie's cheeks flamed, remembering just *how* lovely…

"Has he good teeth?" Portia continued. "I've not yet seen him smile."

"I really couldn't say." Still feeling hopelessly self-conscious, Cassie raised her eyes to the ceiling at a peculiar noise. "Whatever it is that?"

A dark stain was spreading slowly across the pitted plaster.

Portia exclaimed in horror, "Bless my soul, it must be water from his bath! You must go up immediately," she commanded, "and tell him to stop splashing about at once."

Cassie balked. "That would be most improper. You go."

Portia made a face. "I've only just met the earl. Send Ella if you don't want to do it."

"But she's just about to serve supper," Cassie pointed out.

"Oh, very well, I'll bang loudly on the door. But I shan't go in and mop up the mess. He'll have to do that himself."

"Tell him to stem the flood before the whole ceiling falls on our heads!"

Cassie hurried up the narrow stairs and stood before the door, heart pounding furiously. She knocked.

No reply, just a good deal of splashing.

She knocked again, as hard as her knuckles could bear.

Still no reply. Gritting her teeth, she opened the door and stood in the doorway, eyes firmly shut and averted.

"My Lord? Ned!"

The splashing ceased, as did the strange humming sound coming from the direction of the tub.

"Cassie? What on earth?" he demanded, clearly astonished at the intrusion.

Her eyes still shut, she pointed at the floor. "Cease your splashing at once, my lord. You're ruining the ceiling below."

There was a watery pause. Then he said, "Terribly sorry. I hadn't realized. But good God, woman. What on earth are you thinking, coming into a room where you know a naked man is to be found? Has Wycherley ruined your sensibilities completely?"

Irritation flashed through her. "Must you bring him into every conversation? You just can't let it lie, can you? You're obsessed with the man."

He said, more quietly, "Perhaps you've come in hoping for another of your indecent lessons? From me, this time."

She put her hand over her eyes in case she was tempted to peep, and snapped, "I wouldn't have needed to come in if you'd answered my knock."

"I didn't hear you. I must have been dousing my head."

"Or singing. Was that singing I heard?"

"It may have been…" he replied, sounding puzzled. "I always sing in the bath. Now, about this flood…"

There was a swilling sound, followed by a watery sucking noise. He must be standing up.

She mustn't look.

She truly mustn't.

She would *not* look!

"I'll get dressed," he said, "and you can send up a servant."

Thankfully, the man was insufferable. "Which servant would that be?" she demanded in irritation. "Ella's doing the supper. Portia's no servant, nor am I."

There was a wet thud, followed by another.

"You can open your eyes now," he said. "I'm decent."

Reluctantly, she removed her hand.

And did her very best not to stare.

Without success.

Define decent, she asked herself.

Great Juno! The Earl of Stranraer really did have the body of a young Hercules. His form proclaimed a masculinity and strength she had never expected to see embodied in a flesh and blood man. Julian would certainly not look like this out of his clothes, though she had done quite a bit of creative imagining of that.

An almost naked Ned was, in a word, magnificent.

The towel he'd wrapped around his lean hips was totally inadequate to hide…well, anything at all.

Thank God.

No! This was…wrong.

She struggled to avert her eyes and train them on his face instead of examining every bulge of muscle in fascinated admiration. And was gifted with a glimpse of his naked buttocks in the mirror, revealed by the delightfully scant towel.

Sweet Venus. She felt a peculiar lurch at her core, a welling up of something hot and exciting that traveled quickly to every part of her body. It was getting harder to breathe, and her face burned as she tore her gaze from the tantalizing reflection and forced herself to focus on his face.

Was that a smirk? Did he know how he was affecting her? And was he *enjoying* it?

Mortification sifted through her.

"I suggest you clean up the water yourself," she said testily. "You spilled it." When he opened his mouth to protest, she lifted a finger. "Remember you are a guest in this house."

He took a step toward her. "And may I remind you that *I* am not a servant, either, and that it's not my fault you left me in that stinking cell to be insulted and humiliated by the cursed locals with flagons of stale beer."

She moved closer, clenching her fists. "I much preferred you when you *were* a servant. You're lucky we troubled ourselves at all to rescue such an ingrate. The reason you were in the cell in the first place was because of your own ill-controlled temper."

His jaw stiffened, and he took another step toward her, his dark eyes glinting with a savage light. "I've had enough of your chiding, Miss Blythe. I don't like it one bit."

She tipped her head up. They were standing almost breast to chest now, and she could feel the spilled water soaking into her shoes, but she was too cross with him to retreat. "In that case, I'll get my friend to rescind your invitation, and I won't help you any more with your quest!"

"I never asked for your help," he said, but the anger was slipping from his expression. "Let's both calm down, Cassie, and not overreact." He regarded her for a long moment. "Though, I have to say, you look stunningly beautiful when you're angry."

She opened her mouth, then closed it again. He had taken all the wind out her sails with that compliment, curse the man!

And how could she stay cross when he was so close she could easily reach out and run a hand down his slick, wet flesh? If her lessons with Wycherley were a scandal, being here with Ned in his nearly naked state was a complete disgrace.

She didn't care.

"Cassie." His damp fingers reached out and caressed her face, his thumbs stroking the corners of her mouth. She didn't look into his eyes. She couldn't focus on anything other than his full, firm lips, hot and inviting.

Just a whisper away…

Through the blur of her lustful thoughts she registered the brush of a dropped towel. Then he pulled her against his body and kissed her.

For a moment, she froze. Then melted against him.

Yes, oh yes. She *wanted* this. To touch him, to be touched. To explore his tall, muscular body with eager fingers. She'd never reacted so powerfully to a man before, never wanted a man this desperately. Not even Julian.

Nothing mattered except experiencing the intense

sensations rushing through her body.

Ned's lips plundered hers, and with his hands holding her head still, she couldn't have escaped if she'd wanted to.

She didn't want to. Not in a million years.

Snaking her hands up into his dripping black hair, she caressed his head, pulling his mouth more firmly against her own, parting her lips so her tongue could taste him.

The whole hot, hard mass of his body pressed against hers, and she knew her gown would be soaked, but with the amount of heat passing between them, she felt only pleasure.

He wrapped his arms around her, pressing her breasts against the solid muscle of his chest, but he didn't release her from his kiss. Instead, without warning, his tongue delved between her lips, penetrating her slack defenses in one masterful movement. It teased and danced with hers.

"Damn, you woman," he growled, releasing her mouth for a moment. "You are making a lovesick fool of me."

She blinked, but her body was completely attuned to his, captured by the special magic that was filling her with such delightful, unfamiliar sensations.

"Don't talk," she commanded, pulling his lips back to hers. "Kiss me."

He deepened the kiss, his tongue probing her mouth in a relentless rhythm of advance and retreat. She ran her hands across the muscles of his broad shoulders, down the mounded upper arms, and along the sinewy forearms with their dark smattering of hair.

His hands had found their way to her waist, then moved slowly up her rib cage, dangerously close to where her breasts pressed against him. His thumbs began to circle the soft flesh of her curves, and she quivered at his touch, unconsciously stepping back to allow him better access.

Suddenly, a noise came from the doorway, along with a short, feminine scream.

Chapter Twenty-One

Cassie spun around to see Portia standing there armed with mop and bucket, staring at her, dumbstruck.

Ned slid his hands around her waist from behind and held her firmly. "Don't move," he whispered in her ear. "We don't want to shock your friend any more than need be."

His voice was so low, so enticing, a thrill of awareness sliced through her entire body. She wanted to lean back and feel his lips on hers again…and perhaps in other places, as well.

She gulped. "I'm so sorry, Portia," she managed. "I got a bit…distracted."

"I can see that!" exclaimed her friend, dumping the mop and bucket just inside the door. "I'll be downstairs setting the table for supper. If anybody still cares about eating."

"We've shocked her," said Cassie as her friend slammed the door shut. "What will she think of me?"

"She's been married," he said, and she loved the way his voice reverberated through his chest where he was pressed tightly against her. "She knows what a naked man looks like."

"But she's never seen *me* in the clutches of one before. How am I going to explain…this? What if she demands we marry?"

"She won't," he said easily, his breath stirring her hair. "We're in the country, not high Society. She'll understand. There was hardly time for more than a kiss."

"Wretched beast." Now that the sensual spell had been broken, Cassie couldn't find the courage to turn around and face the man who had just taken complete control of her body and her will. The temptation remained, but the madness had gone. "I'd better go to her. Salvage the situation, if I can."

"Very well," he agreed, releasing her. "I'll mop up the water before I come down. But I suggest you change your gown before supper. I would hate for you to catch cold."

She could hear the smile in his voice. Was he feeling smug, thinking he'd just won some kind of victory over her? She would have to put him right on *that* score. But for now, she must mollify Portia.

Not daring to look behind her, she hurried off to change her gown, then made her way quickly down the stairs.

Expecting to find her friend appalled and in total shock, it came as a huge surprise to see her sitting bolt upright at the table in the parlor, an unsliced ham in front of her, wreathed in smiles.

"Cassandra Blythe, who would have thought you had it in you!" Portia declared.

"I behaved abominably. I'm so sorry."

"Don't be. It was worth a damp ceiling to witness what I did. What superlative muscles the earl has—what I could see of them."

Cassie blinked in confusion. She'd expected rebukes and recriminations, if not an outright demand that she and Ned marry immediately. "But…you rushed away in horror!"

Portia's smile widened. "That was glee. I didn't want to

spoil the moment for you."

Cassie took a deep breath and let it out slowly. "I think you probably saved me from ruin," she said.

"Now, that would be a great shame," Portia said decidedly.

Cassie shook her head. "You must know I'm not interested in Lord Stranraer in that way."

Portia looked singularly doubtful. "Why ever not? I think his good qualities—particularly his physical attributes— outweigh the bad. His temper can be improved with a little work. I don't think his body can. It's practically perfect."

"Shame on you, Portia! I never knew you had such wanton thoughts about men."

"It happens when you've been without one for too long. But really, why do you say you're not interested? Your actions suggest the opposite."

A good question, indeed. One Cassie had started asking herself.

"I've loved Julian since I was thirteen years old. There is no other man for me." The words came out as if she was repeating them from a primer, having said—and thought— them so often over the years.

Her friend gave her a knowing look. "Are you quite certain? Don't you need to spend more time in the company of other gentlemen, like Lord Stranraer, so you can make comparisons?"

There was a creak on the stair, and Cassie's body trembled in anticipation at the approach of the man himself. This was ridiculous. He shouldn't have this much power over her person. She forced her shoulders down and tried to appear poised.

He ducked his head as he came into the room. He didn't look at her, but she knew instinctively he felt her presence, as she felt his. She could not take her eyes off him, drinking in the splendid sight, examining his face for a hint as to what he was thinking. Because what he thought of her, and her behavior, suddenly mattered very much indeed.

"Please take a seat, my lord. Shall I re-kindle the fire?" Portia asked.

"Only if you yourself wish to, Mrs. Fiennes," he said, with a courtesy Cassie hadn't thought him capable of. "I must apologize for the spillage. I hope your ceiling is not irretrievably ruined?"

How was it he'd never been this gallant to *her?*

"Don't trouble yourself. I can always have it painted over," Portia said, waving her hand dismissively. "Shall I carve you some ham? It's not at all the kind of quality you're used to, I'm afraid."

He sat down in the chair indicated. "Believe me, I've forgotten what quality tastes like, having lately dined only on the kind of food meted out to servants. And criminals," he added wryly.

If only he would look at her! She needed to see that flame in his eyes, she craved reassurance that she hadn't disgusted him with her wantonness. She was totally shocked by her own response to him and hardly knew what to do with herself. The ham was dry as cinders in her mouth.

"I believe you are familiar with my quest to find my sister, Mrs. Fiennes," he said. "I hope I can rely on your discretion."

"Of course, my lord. Please, help yourself to a piece of game pie."

"Ned, please. Let's not stand on ceremony. I've been just plain Ganstridge for months. The pie looks delicious, thank you."

Cassie couldn't tear her eyes away from him. It was in some ways a relief to see him safely dressed and respectable—his saddle bags containing spare clothing had been brought across from the inn—but also a disappointment. His hair was toweled dry and combed back from his face, revealing more of the chiseled bone structure which had always made her think him striking.

No. More than striking. In a masculine way, he was quite… beautiful.

Her knees trembled again. What *had* he done to her with those searing kisses?

He said, "Before that unfortunate misunderstanding at the inn, I was going to inquire if a young lady has moved to this area recently. My sister looks not at all like me, but is light of hair and medium height."

His gaze met Cassie's as he spoke, his eyes looking almost black in the dim evening light. She stirred uncomfortably in her seat, then, as he continued to subject her to his intense scrutiny, her discomfort turned to heat, collecting in the lower part of her abdomen, making her body feel heavy and languorous. She shifted again and looked away.

"I regret, no," said Portia. "The only new arrival came four or five months ago. An elderly lady now living by herself in a tiny cottage on the lane leading to the next village."

"You're sure of her age?"

"Well… She has white hair."

"Might it be a wig?" suggested Cassie. "Maybe your sister wishes to conceal her identity."

"Possibly. Has anyone actually seen her close up? Her face?"

"On the rare occasions she comes to Aston, she always wears a veil and a very broad-brimmed hat. I wondered if she had weak eyes and was trying to protect them."

"Has no one managed to get a good look at her, then?"

"Achilles, the constable, was walking past when she was in the garden with the veil pushed up so she could attend to her roses. He only saw the side of her face before she pulled the veil down, but he said her skin was most definitely wrinkled and creased, not that of a young woman."

"Hmm. It doesn't sound like a disguise," Ned mused. "But maybe I should call on her anyway, just to make sure."

"Achilles could take you there," Portia offered.

Ned grimaced. "Thank you, but I'm quite happy to avoid that gentleman's company. Just give me the direction, and I will make my way thither tomorrow."

"I'm terrible with directions," Portia said with a frown. "Cassie knows where the place is, though, don't you, dear? We walked that way the last time you came to visit. The little lane on our way back from the manor."

"Yes, I suppose—"

"I have to wait in tomorrow morning for the butcher's boy, so you must show his lordship the way," said Portia, beaming at her.

"Ned," he reminded her friend.

It was a conspiracy. Cassie conceded defeat. "Of course."

But she would certainly take Ella as a chaperone. Even walking out in broad daylight along a country lane seemed a dangerous business, given her inexplicable weakness for the handsome Earl of Stranraer's kisses.

She was going to have to be very careful from now on.

Chapter Twenty-Two

Ned had been much too long without a woman.

It was not due to lack of opportunity—he could have offered his services as a lover to any number of his female acquaintances, and would doubtless have been accepted. Even in his guise as a servant he knew he'd turned a few heads. He'd caught even proper ladies running their eyes over his physique, calculating his proportions and his looks, and finding a sum which apparently pleased them.

Nevertheless, the fire, the loss of Georgiana, and the awful rumors of her fate had eaten away at him, taken away his interest in the pursuit of pleasure.

But Cassandra Blythe had reawakened his passion. She was not the sort he was usually attracted to—indeed, was the complete opposite. No quiet, gentle, compassionate and sensible miss was Cassandra. She was proud, headstrong, misguided, at times idiotic… And she'd reignited a fire within him he'd thought quenched forever.

It was the next morning, and he looked at his reflection in the mirror, wondering what the day would bring. Boundless joy...maddening frustration...or deep sorrow?

He scraped a razor over the stubble on his cheek. It was fortunate he'd become so good at shaving himself. There was no one here who could do it, and Cassie would probably rather cut his throat than shave him, after the liberty he'd taken with her last night.

Though his mind had yelled at him that he was behaving like the worst kind of man, his body had been completely taken in. Cassie was beautiful, with that porcelain skin and those hazel eyes, and the shining bronze-colored curls she pinned up and hid away from admiring eyes. Her lips, her feminine curves, were everything he could wish for in a lover.

What would she be like as his lover? He didn't know what Wycherley had taught her—hell, he didn't *want* to know. But it was such a shame for a diamond of the first water to be learning the lessons of love through bland theory—or worse, calculated seduction—rather than from genuine affection and ardor.

Ned could certainly teach her a thing or two—if she'd let him.

Which she wouldn't. He'd already played that card.

Not a good idea, anyway. They might not suit in the long term, and he certainly did not want to be forced into matrimony with a woman so far below his own status. That would only complicate his life. Probably.

"So, hands off," he concluded, testing his chin to make sure it was smooth, then swilling the razor about in the basin to get rid of the shaving soap.

On the other hand, what did it matter that she was stubborn, misguided, and opinionated, when she was capable of such sublime passion? When the very thought of her made his heart pound and fired his blood?

Julian Carnforth was a very lucky man.

He shook his head at his reflection and backed away. No,

Mr. Carnforth had set his cap at Lady Lucy.

Cassie had been on a fool's errand asking Wycherley to show her how to seduce the oblivious man. Ned ought to tell her that Carnforth was a lost cause, that he had already been seduced by someone far more experienced than herself. But was she prepared to listen? Would she think he was just speaking from self-interest because it was obvious he desired her? After last night's episode, he wouldn't blame her for thinking exactly that.

After flicking water off his razor, he dried it carefully and examined himself in the mirror. Yes, he'd pass muster. He threw on his clothes and went downstairs to join Mrs. Fiennes and the ravishing Miss Blythe for breakfast.

Half an hour later, he and Cassie stepped out into the bright sunshine of early June.

Alone.

He smiled to himself in satisfaction.

Ella had been sneezing all morning, so loudly it had woken everyone. She claimed to have caught a cold while traveling on the box of the coach, and seemed most unwilling to get out of bed. Portia still needed to remain at home for the meat delivery and to tend to Ella, so Cassie was now accompanying him unchaperoned.

Which was rather a blow to his carefully honed gentlemanly indifference.

And a huge boon to that demon inside which was urging him to taste her again.

But first, he needed an answer about his sister.

And that thought was enough to cool his ardor. For now, at least.

Swallows swept over their heads as they set out, then darted low to feed on the dancing midges which swarmed like black smoke above the hedgerows. The road, broad and well-maintained, led Ned and Cassie temptingly onward, away from the village and into the wild unknown.

"Someone has started mowing already," he remarked, smelling the air, desperate to distract himself from the weightier subjects of beloved sister and desired kisses. "If they are lucky with the weather, they may even get a second mowing before autumn."

"You're interested in the land?" she asked.

"Very much so. My family's fortunes have from earliest times been dependent on our manorial holdings."

"And have things changed since then?"

"Not materially. But we've always kept up with the newest inventions, the latest ideas for how to manage the pasturing of animals and produce a good crop of hay. We've invested in the woolen mills and have subscribed to various turnpike, canal, and other transport schemes, and receive a tidy income from these, too."

"I approve of turnpikes," she said. "I cannot abide a bumpy road. I felt quite green the entire journey here."

"The going was better for me. On horseback, one can avoid the ruts. Do you ride, Miss Blythe?"

"Very little. I had a pony when I was small, and we do have a horse, Hannibal, at home, but as he was the one who threw Papa, no one has felt like riding him since."

"You didn't have the animal destroyed?" he asked hopefully.

"Oh no, we would never do that. It was Papa's mistake, not Hannibal's."

"Good. I can't abide to see a horse punished," he said with feeling.

"Nor can I."

They walked a few paces farther in comfortable silence. The hay fields had given way to green wheat, its stems long and sturdy, the ears nodding and billowing gently as the breeze whispered through them.

He smiled over at her. "But someone must ride Hannibal soon," he said. "Or he will be spoiled."

"Papa says he'll do it himself when his legs are stronger."

Ned nodded approvingly. "He sounds a brave man."

"Stubborn and determined, rather."

Just like his daughter.

"Perhaps I should come by and ride him for you a few times," Ned suggested. "Just to remind him of the feel of a man on his back."

Cassie paused and looked him up and down, gauging his size.

He felt a stirring at her close perusal.

"I think he is probably high enough to take you. But he has a soft mouth."

"I can cope quite nicely with a soft mouth," he replied and couldn't help but allow his gaze to stray to hers.

A delicate pink color blossomed in her cheeks before she turned her head aside. Damn that bonnet she was wearing! Every time she turned away from him, it hid her face. He wanted to see her.

"Aren't you too hot in that bonnet?"

"A broad straw hat might be better, but not quite the fashion," she said, chuckling.

Suddenly, she came to a halt, glancing around. "This part of the road has not been very well maintained. I wonder why."

"Different landowner?" Ned suggested, coming to a stop beside her.

A sizeable puddle lay before them, glinting in the summer light and attracting the interest of a large dragonfly, along with several flying things which looked as if they might bite. He didn't care for biting things. Particularly not since his hours in the cell.

As he stepped forward to wade through the water, her hand on his arm brought him up short. "I can't possibly walk through that. Let me run back and get my boots."

"Don't be silly," he said automatically. "I'll carry you over."

She backed away. "Oh no, I couldn't."

He turned and regarded her, his lip curving. "Miss Blythe," he said, "I would never have taken you for a coward."

Her chin lifted. "No, I meant I can just squeeze around the edge."

He looked over to where the verge met an overgrown hedgerow. "And pull your gown to pieces on the brambles there? No, I insist."

He gave her no time to evade him. She was in his arms, surprised and utterly delectable, in a matter of moments.

This was better. He could see her face now. The urge to strip the bonnet from her head and nuzzle against the silk of her hair was almost overpowering.

On the far side of the puddle he set her on her feet, but found he didn't want to relinquish his hold on her. He took her hand and placed it on his arm. She tried to pull away, but he laid his other hand over hers to prevent it.

"Ned," she said softly. "You forget yourself. You're still supposed to be playing the part of a servant, are you not?"

"Can a servant not support his mistress if she's tired? Anyway, there's no one here to see us but the skylarks and gadflies."

"And possibly your sister," she reminded him. "The old woman's cottage should be coming up soon."

The mention of his sister instantly doused his selfish desires. "I can't decide if I want it to be Georgiana or not. If it is her, living in abject poverty and ruin, I may have to break my promise to you and call out Wycherley," he said grimly. "Or kill him outright."

A tut of disapproval emerged from the bonnet. "I don't understand why you are so convinced Captain Wycherley is a villain," she said. "The only real evidence you have against him is Georgiana's name in a book."

"I think her use of the term 'dearest' in her inscription is good evidence of a relationship between them. As Wycherley has not quit the country, I have to assume Georgiana is alive but in hiding. Presumably in the place named in the inscription. Although there may be any number of places called Aston, which means we are very likely on a fool's errand."

"But think rationally about it for a moment," Cassie urged him. "If she fell in love with him, and somehow escaped the terrible fire, then moved to Aston for whatever reason—"

"Because he'd ruined her."

"But then she sent him a book of *love* poems in which she called him *dearest*? No. She cannot possibly be at odds with the man!" she finished exasperatedly. "If he had used her ill, either before or after the fire, would she be employing such affectionate language?"

Ned stopped in midstride. *Good God*. That had simply not occurred to him. Georgiana had been sundered from friends and family—presumably by Wycherley—yet she still wrote to him in terms of endearment.

"She may well love, or *have* loved the captain," he said with a frown. "But his conduct since her disappearance— No, I'll not sully your ears with tales of his libertine behavior."

"You're like a terrier with a bone," she muttered.

He put her hand back through his arm and started walking again. "It is a beautiful day, Cassie. Let us not spoil it by being at odds. Clearly, you like Wycherley and are determined to defend him against all aspersions."

"No, I merely believe he *can* have genuine feelings for a woman. He was decidedly jealous when Julian was flirting with Lady Lucy."

"I'm afraid a man being jealous does not necessarily signify any great love for the lady. It is more a case of needing to conquer a rival."

As he'd been jealous of Wycherley mauling Miss Blythe. He could admit that to himself now.

"There's no need to scowl. You said you didn't wish to fight with me, but you are arguing nonetheless."

She was looking up at him, one eyebrow arched questioningly, a slight hitch to the corner of her mouth. Curse that tempting mouth! He wanted to press his lips to it, explore its shape again, in a far more leisurely fashion this time.

Yes, definitely jealous.

He clamped his jaw. "I need to know more about your Mr. Carnforth. What is it about him that makes your heart skip a beat and inspires undying love?"

There was a long pause, during which nothing could be heard but the crunch of their feet on the lane and the repetitive call of a chaffinch from a hawthorn bush.

"It's hard to say," she said at length. "I've known him from childhood. We played. He let me ride on his rocking-horse, and when he had his first full-grown steed, he sat me on the saddle in front of him so I could admire his riding skills."

"Very romantic, I'm sure," Ned replied, unable to keep the sarcasm from his tone. He couldn't forget that Carnforth cared nothing for Cassie, and the knowledge that she was wasting her affection on such an undeserving recipient gnawed at his heart.

"When he went off to school, I missed him terribly, and when he came back he looked so grown up. I was so full of admiration for all he was learning, I felt I would burst. As he grew older, he became such a dandy."

Ned bit back a contemptuous snort. The man sounded a complete prig. Having met him, though, Ned knew him to be a personable one, at least.

Cassie chuckled, and he smiled down at her, but she was hidden in her bonnet, staring straight ahead, her mind locked on the past. He regretted having opened the subject. But soldiered on.

"And you have continued to admire him," he said.

But not love him. He had heard nothing yet that sounded remotely like love.

"He won all kinds of prizes at Oxford. He dances well, sings divinely, plays the pianoforte — "

"A man of many talents," Ned interrupted impatiently. "But there are plenty of other men who display similar qualities."

"So Portia keeps telling me," Cassie said wryly.

Ned's heart sped up. So, there was hope? Time to point out the obvious. "Has Carnforth ever given you reason to believe he felt the same way about you?"

She shrugged. "You gentlemen can be very hard to read. You play your games, have your rivalries, lay wagers on who will be the first to steal a kiss from a particular woman… Heaven forbid a man be straightforward."

Ah, but he *had* been, with Ned. Now would be the moment to tell her the truth.

That Julian Carnforth had eyes only for Lady Lucy and would never look on Cassandra as anything other than a sister.

"Has Julian ever kissed you?" he asked bluntly.

This time *she* halted in mid-step. She withdrew her hand from his arm and turned to face him. "That is an impertinent question."

"As one who has also kissed you, I have a right to know. Well, has he?"

She nibbled her lip. He wanted to nibble it, too.

Her gaze fell, and her mouth curved downward. "Not yet. That's why I came to Wycherley, to find out how to make Julian see me differently, to see me as a woman."

"And I've told you how foolish that is. Any man with eyes

in his head would see you as a woman. You already know how you affect me."

Tilting her head, she gave him a coquettish look. "Well, that's something, I suppose."

He stared at her. She was *flirting* with him?

"Stand still," he commanded. "There is something I need to do."

"What's that?"

"Trust me."

"But—"

The ribbons of her bonnet came undone without difficulty. He removed it and watched the sun turn her hair into threads of spun gold. It was a crime to hide such splendor from the light. He put the bonnet in her hands, then bent and placed a kiss on the top of her head, relishing the feel of the fine hair against his lips.

There was no movement, no response. He might as well be kissing the hair on a doll.

It was obvious she needed further instruction.

He lifted her into his arms.

"What are you doing?" she squeaked.

"I'm going to finish the lessons Wycherley began."

Chapter Twenty-Three

Cassie went absolutely still. The feel of Ned's powerful body moving as he carried her into the neighboring field was a compelling distraction from the chaos running rampant in her mind.

Her side was pressed against his firm, flat stomach, her feet floated just above the young stalks of wheat, and her head nestled against the muscle of his chest. Somehow, her hands were twined about his neck, her bonnet dangling from her fingers by its strings.

The urge to pull herself up so she could kiss the edge of his jaw was almost irresistible. But that would only encourage him.

Just how far was he prepared to take her "lesson?" She was terrified to find out.

More terrified *not* to find out.

He strode on until a stand of tall hawthorns hid them from the road. Then he set her down in the green wheat and, finally, bent his head to kiss her.

Her lips parted on a sigh, and she let her head sink back

to give full access to his firm, demanding mouth.

Visions of the previous evening's encounter swam through her head—his impressive body, slick with water, glistening in the candlelight, the darkness of his eyes, his expression suffused with desire. He had wanted her.

And she'd wanted him, too. Wanted him to sweep her up into his arms and kiss her and touch her, and… Lord, she didn't know what else.

His kiss became deeper, hungrier. Her bonnet fell to the ground, and she reached around his body, digging her nails into his back. He groaned and shifted, and pushed his hips against her in a shockingly suggestive way. She couldn't help herself. Her body just seemed to take over, and she pressed her hips against his in return.

This was not how she'd imagined things would be when she'd pictured Julian making love to her. There had been none of this deep, animal instinct, this fundamental lust to explore him intimately as a man. *All of him.*

Ned had awakened something in her she did not understand…but was eager to experience. She was the pupil, he was the master, and where he led she had no choice but to follow. Her whole being ached for…Ned.

Even as she felt her body begin to soften, to meld to his shape while blending her mouth with his, he unerringly undid the buttons of her pelisse and pushed it from her shoulders. His hands tugged at the lacing of her gown.

Sweet Venus, he was undressing her…

And all the time his skilled hands were about their work, his kisses grew deeper, more insistent, drugging and overwhelming in their intensity.

She felt her gown loosen, the breath of the early summer breeze on her shoulders, the fall of her hair caressing her neck. When had he freed it? She had no idea, but was glad. He'd told her he wanted to see it flowing free.

Her inner voice of reason was shouting at her to stop—
now!—before she fell completely under his spell…but he had
already stolen her will, and all she managed to do was shift
slightly and murmur a halfhearted complaint that they might
be seen.

His voice was soft and low as he replied, "There's no one
to see but the swallows and the skylarks, and they won't care,
as their minds are on exactly the same thing."

He shrugged out of his coat and placed her hands on the
buttons of his waistcoat.

"You want me to undo them?" She was surprised she
could still speak, with her lips so bruised, her tongue so slack
from the heated tangle with his.

"It seems only fair," he said, smiling down at her. "If you
want to, that is."

She did.

Knowing the glory that lay beneath his clothes, she felt
as if she was unwrapping the best gift she had ever been
given. It gave her the opportunity to run her hands over his
chest, feeling the ripple of muscles, the innate strength they
represented. Very quickly the waistcoat joined their other
discarded garments, down amongst the quivering crop.

He pulled her against him again, seeking her mouth, and
found her breasts beneath the loosened corset, and caressed
the soft flesh with his fingers.

How shamefully sinful! How deliciously wicked!

She arched her back, pressing her breasts more firmly
into his hands, reveling in his sensual touch.

He moaned at the invitation, and his fingers found her
beaded nipples and caught the aching buds between thumb
and forefinger, squeezing gently. She let out a breathy sigh in
response, and so did he.

He seemed to enjoy touching them as much as she
relished having them touched. His lips increased their

pressure as his tongue demanded full access to her mouth, and she welcomed it with her own, exulting in his desire and his need, and in the fact that every splendid masculine inch of him was concentrated on this one moment.

On *her*.

She splayed her hands over the crisp linen of his shirt and remembered what he looked like without it on. She felt a desperate urge to see his naked torso again. Touching was good, but seeing *and* touching would be even better.

She ran her hands down his flanks until she found the waistband of his breeches and started tugging his shirt free.

He released her from the kiss and held her away from him, looking at her in a daze. "Cassie, this is madness. Your enthusiasm is making me forget myself. To take this any further would make me as bad as Captain Wycherley."

Her entire being cried *no*! They couldn't stop now. What was she to do with this desperate, throbbing desire that had penetrated every part of her body, if not…this? She needed… something. His words and his confident touch implied he knew exactly what it was, even if she didn't.

She tried to think of the lessons Wycherley had taught her. But couldn't remember a cursed thing. So, she just reached forward, pulled at his shirt, and demanded, "Take it off. I want to see you again."

His face was still, with no expression but the blazing inferno in his eyes. For a moment she was afraid of him—of his size, his power, the obvious intensity of his feelings, and his ready ability to utterly ruin her.

His hand came over hers in the tangle of his shirt. "Be careful, little one," he warned. "You're playing with fire."

"What kind of gentleman is not prepared to oblige a lady her wishes?"

"A gentleman of honor," he replied.

Frustration surged through her. "Have we not already

gone well beyond the bounds of decency and honor? You were naked last night when you kissed me. We've already broken nearly every rule of Society."

He regarded her and said, "It's fair to say I started this, not you. But I *am* a man of honor, despite…everything…and I have every intention of doing the right thing by you."

"Good," she said. "Then take off your shirt."

Watching her closely, he caught at the edges of the linen, brought the garment over his head, and flung it aside. "There. Now what?"

Breaking away from the intensity of his gaze, she let her eyes rove over his superbly muscled chest with its fine smattering of dark hair. Yes, she had seen it before, but it hadn't been *hers* then. Now it seemed it might be—and if she didn't miss his meaning, hers alone.

She laid a hand appreciatively over his hard, male breast and let her fingers glide over the cool, smooth flesh, exploring carefully every mound, every dip of his torso. A primitive, pulse-pounding curiosity prompted her fingers to delve lower, over the softer flesh of his stomach, and even lower still, to see what the skin felt like there.

He groaned and whispered, "*Enough*. You are making me mad for you."

"Did you not say this was to be a lesson? Would you not teach me?"

The look in his eyes was dark and dangerous. "Damn your lessons! I'm flesh and blood, not an automaton. You don't understand what your teasing does to a man."

She rather thought she did. If it was anything like how he had made *her* feel, she wanted to do more of it.

Balancing up on tiptoe for another kiss, she reached around and started to explore his naked back. She pressed tightly against him and could feel his male member swelling as she'd once seen a stallion's do when covering a mare, and pushing against her abdomen.

His breathing was coming faster now—as was hers—and when he bent his head for another kiss, the meeting of their mouths became nothing less than frenzied. His hands cupped her head then burrowed deep in her hair, massaged her shoulders and rode swiftly up and down her arms as if trying to touch all of her at once.

"No!" he rasped, and pulled out of her grasp. "You're pushing me to a point beyond which I can no longer trust myself. I want to make love to you more than you can possibly imagine. But Cassie, you are young and innocent, and you're not yet mine. To take you now would be greed of the most selfish sort. I cannot do it."

"Oh, but—it all feels so good."

He gave her a shaky smile. "Hussy."

She studied his naked chest again, slowly, trying to tame the wild and wanton impulses that had taken over her body. "Yes. I suppose I am. Is that so very wrong?"

"In the marriage bed, not at all. But in a wheat field? Where anyone could come upon us?"

"It was you who carried me here," she said peevishly, frustration rolling through her like thunder. "What were you planning to do, if not this?"

"I wasn't planning to tumble you, if that's what you're thinking. I just wanted…something more than a kiss."

"Then take it," she urged quietly. "I offer it freely."

Her words were greeted with a low moan. "What manner of wanton have I unleashed in you?"

Very deliberately, she slipped the shoulders of her gown lower, then allowed it to slide to the ground, and stood before him in nothing but her loosened corset and chemise. Then she stepped out of the dress and wound her arms around his neck, pressing her aching nipples against him. Needing…

Relief.

His hands clenched on either side of her waist as if to ease her away, but then gentled. "If this is the way you want it, Cassie, then you must become either my mistress or my wife."

"As you wish."

"Ours won't be an easy relationship, I fear."

"I daresay we will learn each other's ways in time," she said, running her hands over his heated flanks. "I will try to be good, if you will."

He chuckled. "As long as you are only good with me."

She kissed his smile, planting brief, soft kisses along the seam of his lips and in the tilted-up corners of his mouth. As her hands moved over his body, continuing their delicious exploration, he made a small humming noise of appreciation and took his lips on a leisurely journey over her neck and her ear.

Shivers of fire coursed across her skin and her whole body quivered. She wanted to feel more of him, to gain mastery over his responses as he commanded hers. She ran her hands experimentally over the lower part of his back, and then farther down, over the back of his breeches. His flesh tensed beneath her touch, and she felt an overwhelming urge to squeeze, remembering how tempting his behind had looked in the mirror at Portia's.

How she longed to feel his nakedness again! His body called to her from every pore, awakening in her an overwhelming desire to own him—body, heart, and soul.

But at this specific moment, his body would do.

He found and untied the drawstring of her chemise and commenced distracting her with tiny sucking kisses along her throat, and across her collarbone, then over her bare shoulder.

Before she could think about how skillfully he was rendering her naked, he removed her hands from his body and placed them at her sides, then eased her loosened chemise down to her waist.

Feeling suddenly exposed, she grabbed for the garment before it descended any farther.

"You may hold it there if you wish. I don't mind," he told her with a wicked smile. "Because you'll have no hand free with which to restrain my actions."

Why would she want to restrain him? She was enjoying every touch, every new sensation, and her body had moved to a whole different level of awareness, drunk on the heated pleasures of the physical realm.

His hands cupped her breasts. Her naked breasts. His eyes held hers with a smoldering, triumphant look.

She swallowed as his warm fingers moved over the tender skin, found the erect, demanding nipples and caressed them, squeezed and rubbed across the peaks. A bright arc of sensation burned a path from the aching buds right to her womb and the heated place below, making her press her legs together in pure, sizzling delight.

A steady pressure on her shoulders urged her to her knees amongst the springing wheat, then he knelt before her. With quiet determination, he removed her hands from where they clutched the chemise, and placed them on his shoulders. She felt the linen slowly slide down, taking the corset with it, giving him unhindered access to her naked torso.

Bending his head, he touched a nipple with his lips. His tongue slid across it, and when his teeth nipped it gently, the feelings of need in her lower body cried out. His lips parted, and she felt the moist warmth of his mouth and tongue as he suckled her.

Sweet, heavenly Venus.

She shuddered with delicious shock, her head fell back, and her body arched, greedily requesting more of the same. His mouth moved over one breast while his fingers toyed with the nipple of the other.

She was trembling uncontrollably. She felt intensely

naked and exposed, here on the fecund earth beneath the blue sky, one with Nature and the pulse of the world. Heat pooled in her belly, between her legs, and then her lover found that place, too, and was stroking it with strong, clever fingers, causing waves of incredible pleasure to wash over her.

In one last, faint glimmer of sensible thought, she realized he was doing everything. She was doing nothing for him in return.

She reached for his head, delving deep into the thick waving hair, caressing his ears and the sturdy column of his neck. She worked down his shoulders, across his chest, stroking the fine curling hair, circling the small, hard male nipples, fascinated to find they responded in the same way as hers. His sharp little intakes of breath told her he liked her touching them.

His head came up, and he pressed his cheek against hers. "Are you all right, sweet Cassandra? You would tell me if you were not?"

"Too much talking, Lord Stranraer. Continue your lesson. I need to find out what happens next."

"Very well," he growled. "Just remember you asked."

Chapter Twenty-Four

There was no going back.

So Cassie decided there was no point in being coy. She wanted to know what was going on beneath Ned's breeches.

She pressed her hand against him. He sucked in a breath between clenched teeth.

"Am I not to touch?" she asked, halting to look up at him.

"It is…very forward of you." There was an unmistakable tension in his voice.

"Do you mind?"

"Not at all," he said with a voice that sounded a bit like he was choking. "I'm just surprised. You really are a very extraordinary woman."

She ran her hand over his swelling manhood. The tip of it now projected above the waist of his breeches. It felt… squashed in there. Which must be uncomfortable. She reached for his buttons.

His powerful hand came over hers. "Are you sure?"

She knew it was pure folly. Worse, these few moments of boundless pleasure would almost certainly change her life completely…and not necessarily for the better.

And yet…

"I've never been more sure of anything in my life," she whispered.

"I've never wanted any woman more than I want you," he murmured. Still kneeling, he leaned forward and kissed her deeply, his tongue thrusting in and out, setting up a rhythm which she copied with her hand on the formidable bulge in his breeches.

He sucked in a breath as if she'd hurt him, but kissed her with even more fervor, so she knew it was not pain but pleasure.

A little more effort with the buttons and his breeches went down over his hips. Oh, but his buttocks were so delightful to squeeze, so much taut, masculine flesh in her hands. His hips pushed against her stomach, and she felt his long, hard shaft, skin to skin against her. She'd never before seen a man like this—except in some sketches of statues recovered from Pompeii—but she knew instinctively she was experiencing one of life's fundamental miracles, the change in a male animal that allowed him to couple with a female. In humans, it was said to be a change brought about by love, by skill, by desire. She prayed fervently that Ned felt all three.

She reached for him and felt the ripple of sensation that flowed through his body, changing him from coherence to incoherence, making him moan and rock and buck and gasp her name against her cheek.

It felt so amazing!

But he was large. *Really* large.

He removed her hand and pressed his member down through the curling hair between her legs. She didn't quite understand what happened next…but it was too late to voice her fears.

He placed his arm behind her waist so he could lower her

to the ground, holding her in his strong embrace as though not wanting to break the contact between them any more than she did.

The green stems of wheat bent and crackled, tickling and scratching her skin as her naked body pressed into them. He suspended himself above her, supported on his arms, and she reached out to touch him again.

So hot, so hard, so silky, with the softest skin.

She ran her hand up and down his shaft, increasing the pressure, and he groaned and rocked above her. Leaning down on one elbow, he used his free hand to burrow in amongst her feminine folds. The hand moved easily—through a slick of moisture that had gathered there.

"Don't frown," he whispered, as though sensing her questions. "This is exactly how it's meant to be."

With a shock, she realized his finger had entered her— perhaps more than one finger? She couldn't tell. Then it was removed, and she felt the broad tip of his manhood following the path of his finger.

She tensed as it dawned on her what he was about to do.

His free hand caressed her face, and he tenderly kissed her eyelids, then her forehead. "Don't worry, little one. You must relax. There will be a pinch of pain to begin with, but it will quickly pass. I'll be careful, I promise."

And he was very careful, very patient with her, though she could tell from the look on his face that it cost him dear to go slowly. As he pushed in deeper and deeper, her body seemed to expand to accommodate his width, and, after a short stab of pain, she knew at last what it was to be truly a woman.

Truly *his* woman.

Her heart raced and her legs parted as she felt every glorious inch of him press slowly into her. They entered a different world—a world of taking and giving, of sensation and yearning, a world in which she was drunk with pleasure and no longer had any control over the demands of her body.

He began to move inside her.

She inhaled in surprise. But each movement, each teasing withdrawal and triumphant return pushed her higher and higher, until she felt completed, at one with another being, in total understanding and communion.

Her breathing became labored.

So did his.

His strokes moved faster. She squeezed with muscles she hadn't known she possessed. When she tensed, she could feel the friction, the slide of his member back and forth inside her, with every nerve she had.

He moaned.

So did she.

His head hung over her, dark hair flopping over his brow, concealing his face, and she reached for him, clutching at his back, reveling in the feel of the powerful muscles working as he moved harder and faster, harder and faster.

Then came a moment of absolute stillness. He arched his back and shivered inside her, and she pushed down, hard, and suddenly felt herself open like a flower to the sun. Her flesh blossomed, and she rose above herself to ecstasy, and the waves of pleasure washed over her again and again and again.

He gave a soft, strangled cry, and leaned down, his hair softly grazing her face, and kissed her so tenderly, so delicately, she thought she might weep with joy.

He was still inside her. There was no discomfort, only a blissful feeling of satiation, fulfillment, completeness. She wanted to lie like this, with him filling her, holding her as if he loved her, forever.

When he moved to pull out, she mewed in disappointment, but he caressed and soothed her, rolling onto his back and cradling her against his side where she fitted perfectly, her head on the pillowed muscle of his shoulder. He gazed up at the sky and the wheat stalks, and she drank in the beauty of him—the noble profile, the firm, sensuous mouth which had given her such pleasure, the long lashes that rested against the high cheekbones.

He was beyond comparison. She could not have asked for more. She could not have given more. It was perfect. *They* were perfect.

"Ned?"

He turned his head and kissed her on the forehead. "Yes, my darling?"

"Was that good?"

"Unsurpassable. For me, at least." He laughed. "But I shall do my utmost to increase your pleasure, next time."

There was going to be a next time? The thought warmed her. She said, "I like it when you laugh. I like it when you smile."

"You have given me a good deal to smile about, Miss Cassandra Blythe."

He reached across and pulled her on top of his naked body, his half-erect manhood pressing against her bare abdomen. It was the most erotic feeling— she could so easily be aroused all over again.

The sound of a goat bleating brought her suddenly back down to earth. Here she was, lying naked in the middle of a field with her lover—who just happened to be an earl—and it wasn't even lunchtime yet. Could the day get any stranger?

And what, if anything, was going to be the outcome of this extraordinary lapse of self-control?

Chapter Twenty-Five

Ned hated to leave this idyllic place with this wonderful woman, but alas, it was time. Cassie was fully dressed and looking breathtakingly lovely, her eyes shining, her lips bruised from his kisses, and her cheeks stained pink from their lovemaking.

He rescued her bonnet and rolled it between his hands, pressing it back into shape. "I'm sorry," he said, returning it to its accustomed place on her head. "We seem to have crushed it at some point."

He tied the ribbons, smiling down at her, struggling to control his still-rampant lust and remember the kind of behavior expected of a gentleman.

"There. Back to normal," he said, giving her bonnet a final adjustment. He smiled again because it seemed the right thing to do, and looked around him. "I'm quite certain no one has seen us, except that goat peering through the hedge."

She followed the direction of his gaze, laughed softly, and looked up at him, waiting.

Taking her hand in his, he placed it on his arm. They must

carry on with their errand as intended, but slowly, giving their aroused bodies time to calm down before meeting the old woman. And allowing his tormented mind time to find the right words to ensure that Cassie would marry him.

For, of course, they *must* marry after this. There was no question of anything else. He assumed she knew this, but he couldn't quite bring himself to raise the subject.

What was he afraid of, rejection? Because of Carnforth? How could she reject Ned after what they had just done? It would be madness. She was his now, whether she liked it or not. Though, he sincerely hoped she liked it.

But he couldn't find the right words to say to her. To banish forever her stubborn clinging to the childhood *tendre* she had so clearly outgrown. But how to convince her of that? Or would she even need convincing? His thoughts were in such turmoil, all he could manage were banal pleasantries as they strolled along the path.

"Are you satisfied now that any man with eyes in his head *must* see you as a woman?" he asked.

"Hmm? Oh yes."

"I trust you no longer feel the need for Wycherley's lessons?"

She gave a light laugh. "Are you fishing for compliments, Ned? Do you wish me to award you a golden apple so you can be sure you are the better tutor?"

He frowned. Not the response he'd hoped for. She didn't seem the least bit worried that he'd essentially ruined her. "Perhaps I *am* that vain. I don't know. I just hope you realize now that Carnforth is not the only man who can make you happy."

She gave him a mischievous look. "Well, I can't make a proper comparison until I've persuaded Julian to make love to me as you have just done."

He stiffened in outrage. "I would much prefer you did

not."

Her smile widened.

She was joking. She had to be joking.

"I think this may be the place," Cassie said, stopping to indicate a timber-framed cottage with a thatched roof.

"Ah." They had come upon it too soon. Much too soon. He wanted to talk about their lovemaking. About their marriage.

But they could still do that on the walk home, after he'd learned the identity of the woman who lived in this cottage—and if she was his beloved sister.

The moment of truth had arrived.

The sun reflected brightly off the glossy leaves of the roses which trailed and spread all about the wooden fence enclosing the cottage's garden. Great hollyhocks strove to reach the eaves of the ancient-looking thatch, but had not yet opened their rounded buds in flower. Lavender bloomed along the edge of the path, creating a refreshing scent.

A woman wearing a broad-brimmed straw hat with a veil was in the front garden, a trug on the ground in front of her and a pair of snips in her hand. A pair of gloves lay beside the basket. She was so engrossed in removing some bindweed which was threatening to choke a rose stem, she did not notice their arrival.

As Ned gave the woman a cautiously cheerful, "Good morning," he saw with a shock that the skin on her hands was fresh and unblemished, not those of an old woman.

His breathing became shallow, and he pressed Cassie's hand tightly against his side.

The woman straightened, her large straw hat throwing her face into shadow. She cocked her head and peered up at them. Then she sucked in a horrified breath.

And fainted clean away.

Ned darted forward, sprang over the fence, and collected the limp form in his arms.

"Cassie, see if the door is open, please."

She responded to the urgency in his voice and raced forward to open the door, allowing him to carry the woman into the house. He passed through a tiny kitchen and into an equally tiny parlor, where a shabby sofa from the previous century proved just long enough to lay his burden gently down upon.

"Cassie." His voice held a tremor he was unable to hide. "Help me."

His fingers shook as he struggled with the veil and the hat. Cassie knelt by his side and loosened the ties under the lady's chin.

His heart was hammering, and he was starting to feel sick. He looked at Cassie, and she understood. Together, they carefully removed the veil.

A peculiar strangled sound came from deep within him, and he pressed his knuckles against his teeth in an attempt to contain his emotions. He was dimly aware of Cassie sliding an arm about his shoulders and squeezing him with all her strength.

"Georgiana," he said on a strangled breath.

It *was* his sister.

But she was so changed, he barely recognized her.

For a moment he felt only anguish, a pain that struck through him right to his heart, cutting him so deeply he knew not how he could bear it.

The woman on the sofa looked like some strange creature concocted by Blake or Fuseli. Half her face was pale, smooth-skinned, and would have looked youthful were it not for the white eyebrows and the white hair which swept in thin wisps across her forehead. The other half of her face was wizened and discolored. In places, the skin looked like parchment, stretched so tight it seemed ready to tear. The eyelid on that side was reddened and drooped in grotesque fashion. She was half monster, half angel.

Ned's heart shattered for his dear sister. For her ruined face, and the lost beauty of his adored Georgiana.

Slowly, the anguish gave way to anger, and the anger gave way to fury. He shot Cassie a glare as she gazed up at him, white-faced.

"*Wycherley did this*," he erupted. "He tried to run away with her and must have set the fire to deter pursuit. But something went wrong, and Georgiana ended up like *this*. I am going to hunt that man down and slaughter him like the vermin he is!"

"No!" Cassie burst out. "You can't do it. That would be murder. Take a moment, I beg you, and think!"

But he was already on his feet, striding toward the door.

"Ned! Wait," she pleaded with him, rushing to place herself in the doorway of the little room. "Your sister is more important now! Georgiana *needs* you. I'll fetch her some water. You support her head, make sure she can breathe easily."

He hesitated, never before so torn.

"And when she is recovered, she'll be able to tell us the whole truth."

That did it!

"Truth? *Truth*? If she was so blinded by love as to hide her affair with Wycherley, how can I expect her ever to tell me the truth? No! Out of my way, Cassandra."

She retreated before him through the kitchen, then pressed her back against the door, looking up at him beseechingly. "I can't let you go when you are in such a towering rage," she said. "You already know how easily your temper gets you into difficulties. Besides, you *promised*. Will you so quickly discard your promises to me, my lord?"

The double implication of her words brought Ned to a halt, and he stared down at her, jaw clenched. To have, such a short while before, experienced such ecstasy with her, only to be now thrown into abject despair, was enough to crush a man's soul.

"You must do nothing about Wycherley until you've heard Georgiana's side of the story," she urged.

His sister was ruined, her beauty gone forever. He wanted to weep.

But at least she was alive.

And there was neither sight nor sound of an infant. *Thank God for that.*

He took in a shuddering breath and tried to concentrate on Cassie's sympathetic face. "Very well," he said. "We tend to my sister first."

"And you won't harm Wycherley?"

"I must confront him. But I'll just talk with him."

"It is your sister you need to talk to now, Ned. How will she feel if she comes round and discovers you have charged off in a fury in search of her lover? Hasn't she suffered enough?"

His shoulders eased a little, and he took another deep breath. "Maybe you're right."

"Do you not think, perhaps, that is exactly why she has been in hiding? For fear of just such a reaction?"

"Cassie, I—"

Before he could frame the words he needed to say, a horrified scream rent the air. He rushed into the parlor, where Georgiana was now sitting up and staring wildly about her in obvious shock.

"Georgiana!" He was on his knees before her in an instant, taking her in his arms and cradling her against him.

"Ned? Is it truly you?"

Suddenly, the door flew open behind them, and Ned felt a strong hand on his collar, trying to pull him roughly away from his sister.

He shot up, grabbed his assailant about the neck, lifted

him off his feet, and slammed him, none too gently, against the wall.

He recognized the man instantly.

"Matthews?"

Good God, what was Wycherley's footman doing here?

As Matthews started to go red in the face and splutter, Georgiana rose and tugged earnestly at Ned's coat.

"Let him go, Ned. He's done nothing wrong!"

Of all people, *Matthews* had known of Georgiana's whereabouts all along?

Ned felt fury building up again, but before he had a chance to lower the man and take a few calming breaths and recover his self-control, someone cannoned into him, making him release Matthews, stumble over a small footstool, and fall helplessly onto his back on the hearthrug.

Cassie, of course.

Her spirited leap had thrown her off-balance, too, and she collapsed on top of him, her limbs flailing. Matthews slid down the wall into a breathless heap, and Georgiana collapsed back onto the sofa, fanning herself rapidly.

Ned lay there, staring up at Cassie, and beyond her to the plaster ceiling above, where a shadowy cobweb billowed in a faint draft.

All at once, the tension exploded in his chest, and he laid his head back on the rug and laughed until the tears ran from his eyes.

Chapter Twenty-Six

Some people might have chuckled at seeing a young woman topple the Earl of Stranraer. But the last person Cassie would have expected to laugh at that particular moment was the earl himself.

He rolled sideways, tipping her off, then sat cross-legged and hid his face in his hands, his shoulders quaking with amusement.

Matthews glanced at Cassie, and recognition dawned in his eyes. Then he looked at Ned, and his face darkened.

Alarm sprang through her.

Thankfully, Georgiana said quickly, "It's quite safe, Matthews. This is my brother, Edmund."

Cassie laid a hand on Ned's shoulder. She hoped no one else had noticed what she had—that there were sobs racking that stalwart frame, interspersed with the laughter. He was quite literally crying and laughing at the same time, so overcome was he with emotion.

"Your brother?" exclaimed Matthews. "How can that be? Your brother is an earl. This man is a servant in Captain

Wycherley's employ."

"In *Francis's* house?" Georgiana's face went almost as pale as her hair when she glanced at Ned. Cassie noticed she kept the damaged side turned away from them.

Poor girl. What pain she must have suffered. What distress!

Ned wiped his palms across his eyes, then turned to Matthews. "What my sister says is true. I've been searching for her ever since the fire at my aunt's house. I suspected a connection between her and Wycherley, so I decided to spy on the captain in the guise of a servant. It was this young lady, Miss Blythe, who finally found the clue that led me here."

Using Ned's shoulder for support, Cassie got to her feet, hands outstretched toward Georgiana. "Forgive me," she said. "I had no idea you'd suffered burns, or that you might be deliberately hiding from the world."

"Of course I forgive you." Georgiana took both her hands and squeezed them warmly. "You have merely brought about something that was bound to happen sooner or later. Francis kept telling me I should contact my family, let them know I am alive and well. I just… I was just struggling to find the confidence."

Ned came to Cassie's side. "Georgiana, meet Miss Cassandra Blythe. I must warn you, she is a regular firebrand, and has no fear of me, the dictates of Society, or what is considered proper conduct for a young, unmarried lady. But I'm hoping to change that soon. Matthews, fetch some water for my sister, if you please."

Cassie blinked. Change what part? The firebrand, the fear, or…

Matthews didn't respond immediately. Ned just raised an aristocratic eyebrow, and said, "Well, man, what are you waiting for?"

There was no mistaking the lofty tone in his voice. It was enough to convince Matthews. "At once, my lord," he said, and disappeared into the kitchen.

Cassie, however, was awash in a sea of uncertainty.

Not the least of which was not wanting to interfere in the reunion between brother and sister. They had a lot to talk about, not all of it pleasant. But when she turned to go, the brief touch of Ned's fingers on her arm prevented her.

"Stay," he commanded softly.

She stayed.

The water was brought, Matthews was dismissed to the garden, and Georgiana moved to sit in a chair. It must have been her favorite—it was placed so only the back of her head could be viewed from outside, while to anybody in the room, her face was thrown into shadow by the light from the window.

Ned took the sofa, and after a moment's indecision, Cassie joined him there so Georgiana could address them both. The earl's fingers trembled where they rested on his thigh. Feeling as much overwhelmed by the man and his emotions as by the moment, Cassie reached across and squeezed them. When she made to break the contact, he curled his hand around hers and prevented her.

"I expect," he said to his sister, "you have quite a tale to tell me."

"I think, brother," said the disfigured young lady, "that is rather an understatement."

Chapter Twenty-Seven

Despite the dramatic discovery of his sister and his horribly mixed feelings about her circumstances, Ned was still blindingly aware of the young woman sitting next to him, who had helped bring about this reunion. The woman he had just compromised in a wheat field. Despite her youth and lack of worldliness, she was currently a tower of strength. He had seized her hand, offered in comfort, as a drowning man clings to a rock or a spar. This was a journey into the unknown, and he was quite happy not to make it alone.

"I've loved Captain Wycherley since the very first, and he has loved me," Georgiana said. "No, Ned, it is the very purest kind of love. You don't need to worry about my honor."

Her honor? He would be a fine one to question it, after what he'd just done with Cassie…

"We met secretly—"

"But why could you not have been open about it? Told me of your feelings?" he interrupted, half flummoxed, half hurt by that.

"You would not have approved."

"How could you know that without asking?" he asked, even though he knew she was right. "Am I that intractable that you couldn't hope to persuade me?"

Was he that intractable?

Maybe.

He could feel her keen gaze on him, even though her eyes were in shadow.

"You are so much older than I," she said. "I have always been rather in awe of you."

He ran a hand through his hair. Did he really frighten the very people he cared about? He'd only ever meant to protect them.

Just as he'd wanted to protect Cassie from a rake, his conscience prodded. And look how *that* had turned out.

"I'm sorry," he said sincerely. "I wish you and Wycherley had just asked my permission. Tried to persuade me. If I'd given in, none of us would be where we are now."

Georgiana bowed her head. "We are both very sorry for all the trouble we've caused. Especially Francis. He is racked with guilt over this."

Ned stared at her in disbelief. He'd seen no evidence of anything resembling guilt during his time with that rogue. But he would not wound his sister by pointing it out.

"You still love him?" Ned asked instead. He couldn't believe the answer would be yes.

"I do. And he loves me."

At that, he let out a contemptuous snort. "I do not —"

Cassie gripped his hand in warning, but Georgiana cut him off, a smile in her voice. "You needn't say it. I know all about Lady Lucy Dyer. And the others. Yes, he tells me everything." Ned could swear she gave a sidelong glance at Cassie. "We have an understanding. I am his secret, and we both firmly intend it will remain that way."

"You can forgive him his philandering?" Ned asked,

stunned at his sister's generosity.

She flushed. "He has needs. He wouldn't be doing it if I would agree to marry him."

Stunned turned to shocked. "Wycherley has asked you to marry him?" Ned demanded, incredulous. This new view of Wycherley as a lovelorn martyr was one he found difficult to swallow.

She nodded wistfully. "Regularly. Each time he visits. But I don't want him leg-shackled to a monster who can't go out in society."

At that, there was a soft gasp from Cassie. "Why can't you go out in society?" she asked, askance.

Georgiana just shook her head, her lips turning sadly downward.

"Well, that's just nonsense," Cassie said, straightening in her seat with authority. "Much can be done with cosmetics. And wigs. Moleskin can replace eyebrows, broad-brimmed hats can be worn at just the right angle. Veils can conceal—"

Ned pressed Cassie's fingers. She was trying to help and he appreciated it, but he could see his sister was not persuaded.

"Dear Miss Blythe, you are quite right, of course," Georgiana said. "But I don't have the confidence. People will still *know* I look like a freak. If we marry, Wycherley will be pitied for his choice of wife. I wouldn't want that for him."

Her pronouncement sounded so brave, and yet so forlorn, Ned's heart broke into even smaller pieces.

"We can decide the best course of action later," he said. He was still too dangerously angry at Wycherley to discuss any potential marriage rationally. "Right now, I want to hear what happened on the night of the fire. I shall endeavor not to judge you."

Georgiana nodded and then thought back for a quiet moment, looking pained.

"Francis and I met for the first time at the library," she

murmured. "We were both leafing through books of Byron's poetry. There was an instant attraction which neither of us could deny, and as the days passed, we liked nothing better than inventing schemes so we could be alone together. I know it was very wrong of us, but love makes people do foolish things."

It did, indeed, thought Ned. And just look at the consequences.

He would have some consequences of his own to deal with shortly. Hopefully, much happier ones, though—the only fire he intended setting was one in Cassie's heart. Lifting her hand, he kissed her knuckles, then turned back to Georgiana.

"On the night of the fire," Georgiana continued, "I'd arranged a tryst with Francis. He had, in his eagerness, arrived well before the appointed hour, which probably saved my life. I had washed my hair and was trying to dry it quickly by the fire up in my room. Suddenly, my hair sizzled and spat, and I feared I'd set it alight."

Surprise froze Ned to the spot. "The fire was an accident? Not deliberately set?"

Georgiana looked confused. "Deliberate? Goodness, no. In my panic to beat the fire out with my hands, I knocked over an old oil lamp, which set the hearthrug ablaze. I screamed to raise the alarm, but only Francis, waiting in the shadows below my open window, heard me."

"Thank heaven he was there!" Cassie exclaimed.

Ned didn't dare look at her. Damnation, she'd been right all along. Wycherley *hadn't* set the fire.

Georgiana smiled shakily. "Francis scaled the vine outside and was in my room in seconds. But by now, my clothing was alight, and I was screaming and coughing in the smoke, stumbling blindly about, trying to escape the excruciating pain. I must have pulled on the burning bed curtains because the next thing I knew the canopy had fallen down, hitting my head. After that, I knew nothing at all. Until I awoke in a strange room, in agony, with my head swathed in bandages. You cannot imagine the fear I felt until I heard Francis's voice, telling me to be calm."

God have mercy. Ned shuddered, horror sluicing through him. How awful for his beloved sister to go through that terrible experience! And he'd been nowhere nearby to help. He'd been wining and dining with Paxton that night, with no idea of what had occurred until several hours later.

He felt once more the grim hopelessness of sorting through the ashes, trying to discover any trace of what had happened to his sister.

Anger rose up in him anew. "And what was Wycherley doing while you lay insensible?"

"He first carried me down the stairs out of harm's way, then roused the house with the gong, banged on our neighbor's doors, and alerted a night watchman. Then he rushed me to the nearest physician, who happened to be a friend of his from the Peninsular wars, a man familiar with burns. A bed was made up for me there, and Wycherley barely left my side for days, terrified I might worsen."

Remembering the destruction Ned had seen when he arrived at what was left of his aunt's house, he could taste again the awful nausea which had roiled up from his stomach. The terrifying loneliness which had confronted him for his sister, the ghastly fear of her loss he had endured.

"Why were we not told you'd been hurt?" he asked bitterly. "Surely, that should have been his first thought after he'd made you safe?"

She looked contrite. "He wanted to, but I begged him not to. I was so sick, so frightened. The fire was my fault, and I could not face poor Aunt Claudette, who had lost everything. Is she well, Ned? I owe her so much, and I behaved so poorly."

"I moved her to Gant's Ridge. She has been grieving over

you, Georgiana, even though I urged her not to despair since I had found no evidence you'd died in the fire. Could you not at least have written me a note?"

Cassie murmured, "Ned, this is no time for recriminations. Your sister has been through enough misery. Besides, you went missing for a while yourself, remember? To all manner of speculation."

"Yes, I heard. And I tried not to worry," Georgiana said. "I knew the ugly rumor that you'd done away with yourself in a fit of guilt couldn't be true. You are too strong-minded to contemplate self-destruction."

It had crossed his mind, to be sure, but he had been too resolute to find her to give it serious consideration. And too determined to wreak his revenge when he found the responsible party.

He said, "I was desperate to find you, and Wycherley was the only clue I had. I thought it very suspicious he'd raised the alarm about the fire but not stayed to help fight it. So I decided to investigate him."

Understanding lit Georgiana's eyes. "Which was why Matthews took you for a servant."

"Aye. I became Mr. Ganstridge, and with a bit of help from friends in high places, I infiltrated Wycherley's household."

"I'm trying to imagine the proud Earl of Stranraer as a servant," Georgiana said with a chuckle, the weight of her confession easing in her smile.

"I've learned considerable respect for the serving class, now I know what we put them through," Ned confessed with a grimace.

"You didn't show much respect to Matthews," Cassie chided. "You nearly strangled the unfortunate man."

"I refute that," he said contritely. "I knew exactly how much force to use. Pray, don't tease me." Not when his emotions were scraped so raw.

She returned his gaze sympathetically. Which only made him feel worse.

"Matthews must have been so confused when he came in and saw you just now," Georgiana said with an amused shake of her head.

"What happened to you after convalescing at the doctor's house?" Ned asked.

She grew serious again. "I was taken to the home of another friend of Francis, a very nice gentleman called Babcock, whose wife looked after me. No one recognized me — I had lost most of my hair and my eyebrows in the fire — and when my hair grew back, it was white. By the time I was permitted to look in a mirror, the worst of the damage to my face was beginning to scar over. You can imagine my feelings when I first saw my reflection." She sucked in a breath and dabbed at her tears of memory.

Instantly, Ned was kneeling at her feet, her hand clasped between his. "It must have been terrible for you, my darling. But you will always be beautiful to me, to the rest of the family. You mustn't believe we would ever think even a fraction less of you."

"I am but a shadow of my former self," she said despondently. "When I saw that awful reflection, I knew I needed to become someone new and forget all about the past. I persuaded Francis to find me somewhere quiet where I could live out my days in solitude, tending to my garden, reading my books, and writing my terrible poetry. He argued against my decision — he still wanted to marry me. But I said it was bad enough that one of us must lose all hope of ever going out in the world again. I didn't want him to be tied to a wife who would only bring him down in society."

This generosity of spirit was too much. Bitter gall rose in Ned's throat, and he got to his feet. "You were prepared to set him free, not hold him accountable, even after everything he did to you?"

"It wasn't his fault," she insisted.

"It was!" Wycherley may not have deliberately set the fire, but he was still ultimately to blame.

"Ned." Cassie's hand was on his arm, but he shook her off.

"You sent your maid away early because you had a tryst with him," he accused. "That is why you were doing your own hair, and why the accident happened. Wycherley has made you pay a terrible price for loving him."

He clenched his fists as his anger grew and threatened to spill over. Wycherley was still his enemy.

There was only one way to deal with an enemy.

Destroy him.

He strode toward the door.

"Ned, where are you going? We have so much to talk about!" Georgiana's voice was full of alarm.

"I'm going to find that man and make him pay for what he has done to you. For what he has done to *us*."

"Ned, don't. You're too angry to think clearly." Cassie stepped in front of him, trying to block his way. He shook his head, lifted her up, and placed her behind him.

"Cassie, I need to do this."

She pushed past him again, placed herself squarely against the kitchen door, and faced him down, her elfin chin tilted and determined. Before he could stop her, she had locked the door and dropped the key down the bodice of her gown.

He blinked. And gaped.

And his thoughts instantly galloped off in another direction entirely.

Her cheeks pinked as she watched his face, and her lip trembled slightly. He remembered the feel of those lips against his, the soft silk of her breast beneath his hand, and the emotion in his heart when he'd made her his own.

His anger ebbed away somewhat.

"Do you think that an effective deterrent, Miss Blythe?" he inquired gruffly. "What's to stop me reaching in and retrieving that key?"

Her eyes widened, and Georgiana coughed.

"But no, that would distract me too much from my purpose, as I'm sure you know. So in the interest of haste, if you don't give it to me, I'll just tip you upside down and shake you until it falls out."

"Ned! For shame!" Georgiana was behind him now, her voice an exact imitation of their old nanny.

He rolled his eyes to the ceiling and took a deep, shaky breath. "God in heaven, I have been unmanned and out-gunned by two naive chits who actually think I have a conscience. Well, let me tell you, I don't care nearly as much about propriety as I used to. So, Miss Blythe, that key is most definitely not as safe as you might imagine."

"As it's my key," Georgiana said archly, "I think I may be the best judge of when to use it, so perhaps Miss Blythe would be prepared to relinquish it into my keeping?"

He lifted a brow at Cassie. After a moment, she dipped her hand into the cleft between her breasts and fished for the key.

Ye gods, how much he wanted to help her with that! But with his beloved, long-lost, and suffering sister standing right behind him, he knew he must summon up all his strength and curb his improper lusts.

Cassie knew exactly what she was doing, the little tease. Her eyes never left his as she felt about in her bodice, and the half-smile that sneaked onto her face informed him that she had learned her lessons in seduction well. She was quickly mastering how to gain the upper hand in the game of love.

He stifled a groan as she brought the key out and leaned past his shoulder to present it to Georgiana.

"If you promise not to upset your sister, I'll go back to

Portia's now, so you two can discuss your family matters in private," Cassie said. "Matthews can escort me, then return with your things, Ned, if you wish to stay here with Lady Georgiana."

He hesitated, and became lost in the warm depths of those hazel eyes. He desperately wanted her to stay. But she was right. He hadn't seen his sister in six months, and there was so much that needed to be said and planned for.

He shook off his need for Cassie, along with his craving for immediate revenge. "Very well, Wycherley escapes retribution. *For now*. However, I can't say the same for you, Miss Blythe. We *will* talk later."

Her smile told him she thought she'd won. Well, she would have to think again. Summoning up his very best manners, he raised her hand to his lips, swept her an elegant bow, then ushered her outside and into the care of Matthews.

He hurried back inside, and as soon as the door was closed, he enfolded Georgiana in his arms and held her there for a long time in silence, lost in the heady mix of love and relief swirling in his heart, and offering up silent prayers of thanks.

"Words can't say how happy I am to have found you again," he whispered.

"As am I, my darling brother."

She glanced up, and he saw her eyes were moist. He couldn't stand to see her cry. He never had been able to. He pulled her back and gave her another long embrace.

Eventually, she pulled back and gave him a warm smile. "You like Miss Blythe," she said after a brief hesitation.

"The girl's a menace," he responded, not wanting to talk about Cassie at the moment.

"On the contrary," Georgiana said knowingly. "I think she has a good heart. She's thoughtful and kind."

"And infuriating, and misguided, and headstrong."

Georgiana laughed as they made their way back into the parlor. "Is she the one Francis told me about? With the lessons?"

Ned grimaced. "You see my point, then."

"Francis saw no harm in them, just a little innocent tutoring in flirtation. With the prospect that, at the end of it, Miss Blythe would get the husband she wanted."

Ned's skin went cold. "She won't get Mr. Carnforth," he informed her. "He's infatuated with the same Lady Lucy with whom your Captain Wycherley has been having an affair. Carnforth thinks of Cassie as a sister. I'm sorry to be blunt, but there it is."

Georgiana stoked up the fire in the range and filled a kettle from the kitchen pump. "Poor Miss Blythe. But that is good for you, isn't it?"

"Why would you say such a thing?" he asked. How did they get on this topic, anyway? He'd stayed to discuss Georgiana, not his love life.

"Because I've never seen you look at a woman like that before."

"I don't want to have this conversation," he stated, crossing to the window and drumming his fingers on the sill.

Outside, a robin flitted from branch to branch of a plum tree, making the young green fruits quiver as it passed.

"She would make you an excellent wife," Georgiana said, laying out tea things on the table. "You wouldn't want someone who can't stand up to you. Someone sweet but dull. You'd never be bored with Miss Blythe."

She didn't know the half of it, he thought as he gazed out at the lane which Cassie and Matthews had taken back to Aston.

"Is she of good family?" she asked softly, when he remained silent.

He turned from the window, and his sister looked so

earnest, he gave in and said, "Quite. Not titled, but her family traces itself back to the Conqueror. Georgiana, why are you grinning at me like that?" he demanded irritably.

"Ladies don't grin. They smile secretively."

He rolled his eyes. "You haven't changed." He smiled, his heart filling with warmth. "Not that I'm complaining."

"You have clearly had her investigated, so you must be interested in her."

He shook his head. "She was associated with Wycherley. I wanted to find you, so I made it my business to find out about everyone he was acquainted with."

"Tell me about Lady Lucy's pedigree, then."

"Touché." This conversation was definitely not going the way he'd planned. "Let's just say Miss Blythe intrigued me."

"Past tense? We've only been reunited half an hour, and already you are obfuscating."

"My feelings don't matter. I fear her heart still belongs to another."

"And yet you're hoping she'll reappear outside with Matthews when he brings back your luggage, and that she'll stop and take tea with us so you can look your fill on her exceedingly pretty face."

Ah. So that was what his sister was preparing for.

"I was, in fact, hoping he would bring *Maxim* along, not Miss Blythe," he demurred. "I'm not keen on the idea of going back to that pox-ridden inn to fetch my horse."

"Besides, you said she will never win that other man," Georgiana persisted.

He gave her a quelling look. "I have no intention of discussing young ladies with you."

Georgiana's face was all innocence. "Is there any reason for you *not* to attempt to get to know Miss Blythe a little better?"

He certainly knew Cassie a lot better now than he had at

breakfast, but he wasn't going to tell his sister that. He would marry Cassie, of course.

Take Cassandra Blythe as a wife?

Despite what they had shared, the reasons for an earl not to get more deeply involved with her were glaringly obvious. She was impulsive, headstrong, with no regard for Society's rules. What if she continued to behave with thoughtless impropriety, as she had with Wycherley, as she had with Ned himself, and dragged him and his family into disrepute?

The hypocrisy didn't escape him. He, the very man who had despoiled her, was thinking her possibly unworthy to be his wife because she'd let him do it.

Why had she let him do it?

Not that it mattered. She *had*, and if he possessed even an ounce of the honor he was so concerned about, they must marry. And that was that.

Which meant he must somehow disabuse her of her annoyingly persistent obsession with Mr. Julian Carnforth.

Chapter Twenty-Eight

"You've been gone an age!" cried Portia the moment Cassie stepped through the front door. "Have you found the earl's missing sister? What's happened to him? Who was that servant who collected his things?"

Cassie smiled and removed her bonnet, feeling like she'd lived two lifetimes since seeing her good friend that morning.

"Yes, we've found her. Could we have some tea? Telling you all about it is going to be a thirsty business, and I'm exhausted."

"Oh, I'm so happy! What's she like? But you don't look as pleased as you should. Has something upset you?"

Bother it. Portia was far too perceptive. As was Ned.

Cassie was suddenly struck with the uncomfortable realization that she must be far less subtle and poised than she'd thought.

Only Julian was still unable to divine her feelings. How obtuse *was* the man?

Or perhaps it was she who was being obtuse…?

She had spent the better part of the morning with another

man, lying naked in a wheat field, surrendering her innocence to him. And liking it. Immensely. The entire time, she hadn't once thought about Julian. Nor could she ever imagine doing with Julian anything like what she'd done with Ned.

And with *that* thought came a second, far more uncomfortable realization. Could it really be that she had fallen slightly in love with the Earl of Stranraer?

Maybe even more than slightly?

"Well?" Portia asked as she poured hot tea into cups Cassie hadn't even noticed had been prepared and set. "What happened?"

She forced herself back to the present and related the whole story of finding Ned's sister, Lady Georgiana.

Portia beamed with pleasure. "This is quite the most exciting thing that has ever happened in this quiet little village. But you seem pensive. Are you worried for her? Or sad your adventure is over?"

"Not at all," Cassie reassured her. "I'm just a bit overset by all the drama, I suppose. We've been in the throes of deeply felt emotion all day. I've never seen a man so moved as Lord Stranraer was at finding his sister."

Except, perhaps, when he'd been making love to Cassie…

She cleared her throat. "I think the earl's heart is in proportion to the rest of him, though generally, he prefers not to show it. He's a most impressive man."

By Jove. She hadn't meant to voice that thought aloud.

Portia was looking at her with increased interest. "Am I to understand that you've finally found another gentleman to admire? Is the fickle Mr. Carnforth now forgot?"

"How can you say that?" Cassie chided. "You haven't met Julian above half a dozen times and can have no reason to condemn him as flighty."

"He has no regard for your feelings." When Cassie made to protest, Portia waved a hand and said, "Yes, he struck me as affable, with a good degree of drawing room wit, acceptable manners, and pleasant conversation. But there was no spark to him. Not like Lord Stranraer."

"Do you call Julian dull?" Cassie could hardly believe her ears. "Surely, you cannot think that? Julian rides, reads widely, dances most elegantly, and has opinions on a great variety of subjects."

"And does he share any of those things with you?"

"I… He—"

"I didn't think so. Beneath his veneer of civilized interests, he is scrutinizing the year's crop of young ladies in search of a potential bride."

Cassie winced, and thought of the way he looked at Lady Lucy. "No, I'm sure you're quite wrong."

Except she knew instinctively her friend wasn't wrong. That he'd, indeed, already made his choice.

And it wasn't Cassie.

"Let him go. There's a spirit, a passion in you, Cassie Blythe, which Julian Carnforth can neither match nor satisfy. From what I've seen of the Earl of Stranraer, there's more than enough of him to satisfy any woman—in every way possible."

Cassie's teacup clattered onto its saucer, splashing tea over the side. *Sweet Venus.* Her friend had no idea. "Portia! You shock me!" she cried, to conceal the vivid memories that statement evoked in her mind…and her body.

"*Hmph.* As I recall, it wasn't *me* in the embrace of a naked man last night. So, truly, who is more shocking?"

Cassie wriggled in her chair and turned her heated face toward the window. Portia really had *no* idea.

Thank God.

Her friend pushed out a sharp breath. "You are in thrall to Lord Stranraer, but too stubborn to let go of your idealized view of Mr. Carnforth, a man who couldn't hold a candle to the earl."

Cassie turned back to her friend. "If you have such admiration for him, why don't you make a play for him yourself?" she said, not knowing where her sudden pique came from.

This brought a gale of laughter from Portia. "Because Lord Stranraer has eyes only for *you*, my dear. I would be wasting my time."

Cassie stared at her friend for a long, confused moment, then gathered herself and said, "I've splashed tea in my saucer. Have you a cloth?"

Portia sighed. "So you don't want to talk about Stranraer. Very well. I wouldn't want you to be in a pet with me for the rest of your visit. I'll fetch you a cloth."

No, she didn't want to talk to Portia about Ned. Her feelings about him were too chaotic to attempt sorting them out right now. Besides, there were other things to worry about. Wycherley, for one. How could she rest easy when the earl still seemed bent on ruining him? She was concerned for Lady Georgiana, too. Cassie had taken a genuine liking to Ned's sister and wanted to see her restored to her rightful place in Society.

What an unselfish character that young woman had! Despite still being madly in love with Wycherley, she'd had the courage and selflessness to refuse his suit, putting concern for him before her own feelings.

It made Cassie's love for Julian look terribly selfish. All these years, she'd only thought about *her* feelings for him and what *she* wanted, not about his feelings and what might be best for *him*. If Julian only wanted to be her friend, it was very wrong of her to plot to seduce him, potentially trapping him into marriage.

Good heavens. Ned had been right when he'd said she was on a fool's errand with those lessons.

Portia was still smiling when she reentered the room. "He is quite a handsome man, though."

Cassie wanted to groan. The woman was relentless. And quite right. "I suppose he is."

"Extremely eligible, too," Portia went on, unabashed by Cassie's warning look. "I've been reading about him in an old copy of the Courier. Did you know he has—"

"Stop, I beg you. I don't wish to speak of him."

Portia pouted. "You would deprive me of any entertainment in my loneliness."

"If you're lonely, you must go and befriend Lady Georgiana, for she, too, has been very lonely. I'm sure you would take to her."

"If she's anything like her brother, then I assuredly will." When Cassie gave her another pleading look, she narrowed her eyes and said, "Clearly, something has happened between you two. You must tell me at once."

"No, there's nothing more to tell than I've told you already," Cassie insisted, but found it impossible to look her friend in the eye.

Portia tipped her head and then looked toward the window. "Hmm. Perhaps I should confront the man himself. He might be more forthcoming."

Following the direction of her friend's gaze, Cassie was aghast to see Ned giving them a cheery wave as he strode toward the cottage.

No! She couldn't see him now. During their visit to Lady Georgiana, Cassie had managed to block her thoughts and feelings about what she had done with him, what she had lost to him, what she had felt for him. And still felt. But on the walk home, all those thoughts and feelings had resurfaced in force and taken her over completely.

She needed to sort them out.

Decide her best course of action, if the worst happened.

Decide what, in fact, *would* be the worst thing that could happen...

"Tell him to go away. That I have the headache," she instructed and went upstairs as fast as her legs would carry her.

There was a confident rap on the door. It opened and was followed by the sound of voices. Portia surely wasn't going to invite him in?

She pressed her ear against the bedchamber door.

The conversation continued for a moment or two, then the front door closed.

Anxiously, Cassie approached the window and peered out.

And looked straight down into Ned's eyes. Her stomach flipped over and she clutched the window sill for support. How could one man have the power to affect her so, even at such a distance?

Ned smiled broadly at her and waved. Then he was striding away across the village green. She saw him pause in front of the Blind House, shake his head, and move on until he had vanished from sight.

Where was he going? What was he going to do?

When she went downstairs again, Portia was hopping from one foot to the other with excitement, holding a folded piece of paper.

"What is it?" Cassie asked.

"The earl left a message for you. He wishes to meet with you, to talk."

Cassie's heart sped up. She unfolded and read the note, hoping Portia would fail to notice how it quivered in her hands.

She looked up. "Lord Stranraer wishes to meet me in the churchyard at eleven o'clock tomorrow morning."

Chapter Twenty-Nine

The following day was just as beautiful as the last had been, although Cassie greeted it somewhat bleary-eyed after a restless night. Yesterday's events had played through her mind in a never-ending merry-go-round of emotions she was powerless to stop.

She knew she had to hear what Ned had to say to her—and she imagined he'd have plenty—but that didn't make confronting her own wanton behavior with him any easier.

Or, indeed, her new-found feelings for him.

Had he replaced her safe and familiar desire to wed Julian Carnforth with the dangerous and uncertain fantasy of being the wife of a tempestuous earl?

Would he even want her in that way?

Or perhaps he was only interested in acquiring a mistress. Yesterday, he had mentioned both possibilities equally, and she hadn't demurred from either. Why had she not protested at the less honorable suggestion?

Perhaps he was meeting her simply to explain—in a chivalrous manner, of course—that it had all been a terrible mistake?

After a fretful morning, she set out for the churchyard and arrived, her mind still in a whirl, exactly on the stroke of eleven.

"Cassandra!" Ned came toward her with every indication of pleasure written across his handsome features. She had to admit, seeing him cheerful and in the full light of day, that he *was* extremely handsome. He could easily compete in that regard with Julian or Wycherley and win. Physically, he outshone them both. It had just taken a little while for her to get used to him being well-built and so...so overwhelmingly male.

"Ned?"

He grinned, showing a set of very even white teeth. And a dimple in each cheek she'd somehow not noticed before. Not only handsome, but dashing, too. Butterflies began fluttering in her stomach.

"Isn't it a splendid day?" he said. "This dreadful village looks almost jolly with the sunlight upon it."

"You're turning into a poet," she said wryly.

"Ah, you have stumbled upon one of my secrets. I *do* write poetry, but only for the entertainment of friends and family."

Really? How intriguing. She'd written a few verses herself, but they were mostly about Julian and most decidedly *not* for the entertainment of family and friends.

"You're in an ebullient mood today," she said, wondering when he was going to dispense with the pleasantries and come to the point. She was anxious to learn her fate.

"Indeed, I am. Georgiana has agreed to return home to Yorkshire with me. It is such a joy to have her back again, to know the good news I shall be bringing to Aunt Claudette and the rest of the family. I want to thank you for your help. I don't know if it was your luck or mine that made you pick up that book in Wycherley's house, but I will be eternally grateful you did so."

"You're quite welcome." Impatience made her blurt out, "But that can't be what you wished to speak to me about. I've been wondering what you can have to say that is fit for a graveyard but not for Portia's ears."

"Blunt, as always," he said with a sigh, then regarded her for a moment. "About yesterday…"

Her mouth felt suddenly bone dry. "Your sister?"

He gave her a telling look. "No. Us."

Suddenly, she wasn't ready to hear it. She swallowed heavily and opened her mouth to say something to stall him, but he held up a hand to stop her.

"I could apologize for what happened yesterday between us," he said, "only, I don't feel sorry at all. And I believe you enjoyed our…intimacy as much as I did."

His dark eyes glittered at her, sending a skitter of awareness along her spine. That was an understatement.

"Well," she said, "possibly. But perhaps you took your 'lesson' a bit too far. I never intended—"

His lips curved, and he moved a little closer as he interrupted her. "I won't be put off, you know. But before we descend into an argument, you must let me tell you that you're looking very lovely today, Cassandra."

He never gave such gallant compliments. She was instantly wary. Was this a prelude to a kiss…or her dismissal?

"Goodness," she responded, hoping he wouldn't notice the way her voice kept hitching in her throat. "You *are* in a good mood."

"Indeed. I feel as if all my ships have come in at once. Only one more thing needs to happen to complete my happiness."

"Oh?" She was truly terrified to ask.

Was it her imagination, or had he edged still closer? She felt like a rabbit mesmerized by a stoat. But if she stepped away, he would think it cowardice.

Perhaps she *was* a coward.

Definitely, she was a coward, because instead of all the questions raging through her head, she said, "So, Lady Georgiana will be leaving soon. That's a pity. I'd hoped to get to know her better. Has Wycherley been informed?"

Ned's advance halted. "Why should he be informed?" he queried with a frown.

"Because he's taken care of her every need for the past six months. You can't just whisk her away without so much as a by-your-leave."

"Can I not? I think you'll find I can, and will." There was steel in his tone now.

"Just as he took her from you? Do you not remember how terrible that felt, to have her simply disappear?"

He scowled. "That's different. I'm her brother. He has no right—"

"Doesn't it matter to you that she loves him? That he loves her?"

Ned waved a dismissive hand. "He has other women. And she has refused to wed him. She will get over him soon enough, as he will her."

"The other women were because he couldn't have the one he wanted most. She encouraged him to take lovers, so don't try and make him out to be a villain," Cassie countered.

Ned took another step toward her, and she had to crane her neck to hold his gaze. He was dangerously close. And yet, not nearly close enough…

"Why do you care so damned much about that scapegrace?" he asked, visibly frustrated.

"I consider him my friend, so I care what happens to him." She had to stand her ground on this. She *must* stand her ground, to prevent broken hearts, and a possible disaster.

"Well, he isn't *my* friend. Had he been honest and open about his feelings for Georgiana and done the right thing, she would not now be hiding in a cottage at the back of the North Wind with only half a face and no self-confidence!"

"It was an *accident*, Ned." Would he never understand? Of all the stubborn—

"Stop defending him!" Ned's voice had become a low growl, and the heat of his annoyance radiated out from his body. A muscle worked in his cheek.

Maybe arguing with him at such close quarters was not the best idea. He was more deeply angry than she had ever seen him, but she couldn't fathom the reason.

"Someone needs to," she said, trying to keep her tone even. "You have not yet heard his side of the story."

"Anyone would think you had a *tendre* for that gentleman," he shot back.

"Don't be ridiculous," she snapped, her own temper rising. "You know exactly why I started seeing Wycherley."

"Feelings can change. Make up your mind, Cassie. Who's it to be in your bed? Carnforth? Wycherley? Or me?"

What?

She straightened her spine. "That, sir, is a gross insult. I am not… I am not *that* sort of woman." *By Juno, that hurt!* How could he possibly think…? She was almost too angry to speak but managed to spit out, "I don't wish to be in your odious presence any longer." She turned to go, but he caught her arm and spun her around to face him.

"I'm not finished with you yet," he said, his voice deceptively soft.

How *dare* he manhandle her in public? "Let go of me," she demanded, lifting her hand to beat him off, but he caught her by the wrist and pulled her roughly against his body.

Then he bent his head and kissed her.

With a hunger which was astonishing.

She struggled against him. "No."

"Yes."

He kissed her again.

She didn't struggle quite so hard. Especially when his grip softened and his lips turned seductive rather than angry.

He didn't break the kiss.

She stopped struggling and melted into him.

Desire fizzed between them—a desire only heightened by their battle of wills, their profound attraction making a mockery of their harsh words.

Sometimes, Cassie thought as she surrendered to him, the demanding touch of an aroused man was a powerful aphrodisiac, not a punishment.

If it was the right man.

When he released her hands, she fastened them about his waist. She opened her mouth to the bruising pressure of his, tilting her head so he could deepen the kiss, and lost every ounce of decorum she possessed.

Then, just as brutally, he tore his lips away, and when she opened her eyes, she was momentarily blinded by the sunlight reflecting off a white marble monument in the churchyard.

Ned was no longer standing in front of her.

Where on earth had he gone?

Chapter Thirty

Another face swam into view as Cassie stood blinking in confusion.

It took a moment.

"Julian?"

"Cassie." Julian's usually cheerful face was dark as a summer storm, his eyes pallid with anger. "Are you all right?"

Why, what did he think had happened to her? Good lord, had he witnessed that tumultuous kiss? Embarrassment shot through her from her ears to her toes.

Not waiting for her answer, he turned around and hissed, "You insolent mongrel! If I had it with me, I'd use my horsewhip on you until your back was a sea of red!"

It took a horrified moment for Cassie to realize he was no longer addressing her. The kiss had unsettled her so much she still felt as if she were in a dream, or at the bottom of the sea, with everything swirling around her in a miasma of sensual, emotional strangeness.

"What the devil? Good God, Carnforth! Take your hands off me at once, sirrah!" Ned's voice.

As Cassie's world steadied, she realized the two men were standing just beside her, almost breast to breast, bristling with anger.

Julian said, "Wait, I know you! We met just the other day in Oxford, during that downpour."

Ned scowled down at him. "We did. Now what the deuce is the meaning of this outrage against my person?"

Julian's eyes narrowed dangerously. "I came to find Cassandra. And not a moment too soon. I should call you out! In fact—" He started to remove his riding glove.

Still in shock at Julian's sudden appearance, Cassie quickly stepped between the two men. "Julian, his lordship meant no harm. It's not what you think."

He turned to her in astonishment, glove half off, his fists clenching. "You mean you *welcome* the attentions of a man in full view of anybody walking past? I cannot believe it. He has importuned you, taken advantage of your innocence! I *will* call him out."

She shot back angrily, "Don't be a fool, Julian. You'll be arrested. He is the Earl of Stranraer."

"I know damn well who he is. A title doesn't make him any less of a churl."

"Julian, please. I didn't mind him kissing me!" she cried in frustration.

"No, no, no." Julian shook his head and squeezed his eyes tight shut as if in pain. "This is all wrong. You can't love someone else. You're supposed to be in love with *me*."

"I beg your pardon?" A frisson of shocked fear shot up Cassie's spine. What was going on here? How could he know that?

Ned started toward Julian but Cassie put out an arm to bar his progress. He obliged, but she could tell from his stiffness he was mind-numbingly angry.

"Explain yourself, Carnforth," Ned said icily. "Or I may

decide to call *you* out for that insult."

Julian straightened his shoulders and puffed out his chest in a manner most unlike him. "I have come," he said imperiously, "to ask Miss Blythe to marry me."

"*What?*" Cassie and Ned spoke in chorus as her heart squeezed in confusion.

"It's quite simple. Cassie is to be my wife. Both our fathers wish it, and have done for some years. She is old enough now to know her own mind—"

"I *beg* your pardon?" she exclaimed, outrage eclipsing her shock at his unexpected words. She'd been old enough to know her own mind since coming out of leading strings. And she'd always wanted Julian. But not after—

"You mean," Ned interrupted her fury with his own, "that you have just discovered the stocks which make up her dowry have recently shot up considerably in value."

Cassie spun to look up at him. How did *he* know about her dowry? He'd delved more deeply into her business than he'd admitted. Of all the cheek!

"Not at all," Julian answered in affront. "I am very fond of Miss Blythe, and I think we will have an extremely comfortable marriage. I happen to know she loves me, and I hold her in the highest esteem."

Cassie's heart shrank even more painfully. No mention of love.

If Julian didn't love her by now, he never would. It was a dismal discovery. Ned had been right all along.

Surprisingly, the idea no longer filled her with despair. Was it relief she felt? Or total confusion because her dearest wish for the past six years had finally come true…and all she felt was indifference. How could this be happening to her?

"Julian—" she began cautiously.

"Cassie, let me deal with this," Ned commanded, stepping past her. "Carnforth, you told me you were betrothed to Lady

Lucy Dyer."

Betrothed? Cassie felt suddenly sick. When? How long had they been engaged?

And why in heaven had Ned not told her? He knew how she felt about Julian! Or had felt…

Sweet Venus, she was so muddled she didn't know *what* she felt anymore.

"I am no longer engaged to that lady," Julian replied, reddening. "It turns out she is far too…mercurial."

Cassie's stomach roiled with humiliation. So, he'd only come after her because Lucy had thrown him over. And to think, a month ago she would have welcomed him with open arms.

"That is regrettable," Ned said. "But you are too hasty, sir. Cassie is no longer interested in you."

"Excuse me?" she demanded. "I can speak quite well for myself." Not that he was wrong, but…

"Keep out of this, Cassie," Ned warned her. "Carnforth and I will settle this between ourselves."

Furious, she pushed at the unyielding muscle of Ned's chest and stopped just short of giving him the pummeling he so deserved. "You will not! This is *my* life you are commandeering. *I* am the one who decides who I am to marry!"

He caught her by the shoulders and tried to pull her against him, saying, "Cassandra, please. Carnforth doesn't love you. Your obsession with him is making you do foolish things—"

"Take your hands off her!" Julian roared.

Cassie spun round in alarm, just as he lunged forward. Ned stepped smartly out of the way, hauling her with him.

Julian's momentum carried him forward, and he caught his foot on the curbstone of a tomb. He toppled over. There was a ghastly *crr-ack* as his head struck the edge of a neighboring grave marker. He crumpled, limp as a puppet.

Cassie flung herself to the ground and cradled his head between her hands. "Julian! Speak to me!"

Oh Lord, he was bleeding. Copiously. Her head swam, and her stomach clenched with nausea and fear. She looked up at Ned for help.

He grimaced. "Damnation! He should never have come at me like that. I'll carry him back to Mrs. Fiennes's house and send for a physician."

"You'll have to be careful, his head is— Oh!"

Astonished, she saw Ned's eyes roll up, showing the whites, and the next second he, too, had collapsed onto the ground, unconscious.

For a moment she didn't recognize the man who stood directly behind him, a hefty stick in his raised hand.

The man's eyes widened. "*Cassie*? What on earth are you doing here?"

It was Wycherley.

"I'd ask the same," she said with a gasp, trying to will her galloping heart back to its normal rhythm. "But I wager I already know."

He gave her an uncomprehending look, then glanced down at Ned. "Clearly, I was not mistaken. It really *is* Ganstridge. I'd know the brute anywhere." He moved his gaze to Julian's limp form. "And, if I'm not mistaken, that's your Mr. Carnforth. I remember him from Paxton's ball."

"Yes, yes. But—" She tried to cut him off.

"What is the meaning of this carnage?" Wycherley ignored her and raised the stick again, as if expecting more trouble.

"Captain Wycherley, do stand down!" she cried up at him. She tore off her pelisse and folded it to pillow Julian's head, then twisted round so she could examine Ned. "There is no need for violence."

He kept the stick poised, but thankfully, didn't strike. "It seemed called for, under the circumstances."

"You know nothing of the circumstances." She carefully lifted Ned's head and cradled it in her lap, feeling gingerly for bumps or breaks. When she examined the back of his skull, she could feel the burgeoning swelling beneath his hair. "Do you not care that you have just knocked your sweetheart's brother senseless? And for no reason. Julian's fall was a pure accident."

Wycherley froze. "My sweetheart's *brother*? But how—"

"I know all about Lady Georgiana," said Cassie impatiently. "And this is the Earl of Stranraer."

"*Ganstridge?*"

"Yes! Oh, don't just stand there gawping, fetch a doctor. There are two injured men here. Explanations will have to wait."

"No." Ned's head shifted in her lap as he came round and eased himself into a sitting position. "I'd like one now," he said hoarsely. "Did that damned lothario just hit me?"

"A simple misunderstanding," Cassie quickly assured him, supporting him as he attempted to stand up. "He thought you'd attacked Julian."

"And *still* you defend him," Ned growled. He set her away from him and loomed over Wycherley. "Bludgeon a man from behind, would you, you cowardly cur? I'll give you a taste of your own medicine!" He seized Wycherley by the lapels and dragged him forward.

"No!" she cried. "Stop!" All her nightmares were coming true at once.

But she was never to find out what Ned had in mind. Achilles Marsh, the constable, arrived at a run. "Halt!" Without waiting, he dealt Ned a sharp blow on the side of the head with his weighty staff.

The earl staggered against the pedestal of a marble angel

and clung there, dazed.

"I knew it!" proclaimed Marsh with smug satisfaction. "I *knew* that villain was trouble. It don't matter how highborn he be, it's a sin and against the law to brawl on the Lord's Acre. Back to the Blind House, he goes. Sorry, Miss, if you and Mrs. Fiennes don't like it, but he needs to learn proper respect. I'm going to fetch some help and lock up these two felons until they have cooled down a bit."

"Two?" Cassie demanded. She took hold of Ned's arm, holding him up. His face was as white as Julian's, and his eyes unseeing. Such blows to the head could not be healthy for any man.

The constable indicated Ned and the still prostrate Julian.

"No, Mr. Marsh. You don't understand. It was all accidental. These men need a physician, not a night in a dank cell." There was a stream of red bubbling down the side of Julian's face and stealing in a wave over his collar. She'd never seen anything like it.

Fortunately, Ned's two wounds seemed less serious. Already there was an angry, knotted bruise coming up where the constable's staff had struck him on the temple, but the skin wasn't broken.

"The law's the law," the constable told her. "I'm sorry, Miss. Once they're secured, you and Mrs. Fiennes are welcome to go in and bandage their pates. Stay right here. I won't be long." He strode off.

Wycherley stood watching the scene, his previous anger turning to wry amusement.

"Captain, do something!" she said in frustration. "Tell the constable it was all a horrible mistake, I beg you."

His blue eyes narrowed as he looked at Ned, whom she was still struggling to support. "But that wouldn't be the truth, would it? I swear I saw murder in his mien."

"Facial expressions are not illegal," Cassie said. "He didn't lay a finger on Julian, and all he's done to you is crumple your coat."

"The intention was there," Wycherley said coldly, giving Ned an inscrutable look. "Not to mention him lurking in my household, spying on me. I'm sure there's a law against *that*."

"But he's Georgiana's brother! How will she feel if you bring charges against him? She'll be mortified."

"I'll take that chance," was Wycherley's response.

Ned shook off Cassie's support and stood up, swaying slightly. "Damn you, Wycherley," he said hoarsely, "You have dishonored my sister and ruined her life. You don't deserve to live."

"That sort of talk could land you on the gallows," proclaimed Achilles Marsh, coming up behind them, a group of doughty-looking laborers in his wake.

No. This was ridiculous.

"Captain Wycherley," she snapped, "if you do not stop this nonsense now, I will go straight to Lady Georgiana and tell her she's in love with a heartless rogue who'd rather see her brother thrown in prison than tell the truth."

He folded his arms. "Miss Blythe, you are in no position to dictate to me. What I know about you would curl the pages of the Gazette—"

"How dare you insult Miss Blythe like that!" Ned stormed, lurching unsteadily forward.

The mass of men brought by the constable halted just inside the lych-gate, apparently unwilling to intervene in the drama before it had played out.

"Ned, don't make things worse," she begged, clinging onto him.

"I may as well be hanged for a sheep as for a lamb," he growled. "First he insults my sister, and now he insults the woman I intend to make my own."

She had no time to react to that unexpected declaration

because at the very same moment, the constable signaled the villagers forward. In seconds, both Ned and the barely conscious Julian were in irons.

"Mr. Marsh!" she said, taking the constable by the arm and drawing him aside, thinking furiously.

"What is it, miss?"

"I really don't think putting the two gentlemen in the Blind House is a good idea," she said in a tempered tone. "When the earl is freed, which we both know he will be, he can make life very uncomfortable for you."

"The law is the law," the man said, tapping his baton against his thigh. "I can't change it, even if I wanted to. Which I don't."

"Stranraer is very well connected," she said conspiratorially. "He probably rubs shoulders with the local magistrate. I have it on good authority that he dines with the king, and numbers the Duke of Paxton among his best friends."

The constable shot a sideways look at the gaggle of men waiting to haul his captives away. It would not do to make him lose face in front of them.

"I have a solution," she said, "which might serve. Put the two gentlemen under lock and key at the Rose and Crown. And if the doors there cannot be locked, then station yourself or one of your assistants outside. The prisoners can remain manacled, but they will at least get to lie in decent beds and can be tended to while they recover from their injuries. *Accidental* injuries," she added meaningfully, "to which Captain Wycherley will attest." When she got him to see sense.

"The third gentleman, you mean? The one with the splendid cudgel?"

"Yes."

Marsh pressed his plump lips together and pondered a moment. Cassie held her breath.

"Very well. But I'm not paying for their keep. Landlord

will want his fee."

"The earl will pay for everything."

"He doesn't seem that obliging—"

"I'll talk him round, I promise. One way or another, I'll make sure you're not out of pocket."

The constable rocked back and forth on his heels a couple of times. Finally, he said, "Very well. I'll do what you say."

Relief flooded through her. One problem averted, at least. "Thank you."

"You'll tell Mrs. Fiennes I've done what I can to assist you?"

"I'll tell her."

The constable marched off to command his troop, and Cassie finally felt able to breathe again. But she had only eased the situation in the short term and had come nowhere near resolving it.

The potential outcome was too awful to contemplate. Wycherley was unrepentant and would doubtless provoke Ned at the first opportunity. For his part, Ned was out for blood and likely to get himself hanged if he let his need for revenge win over reason.

Most shocking of all, Julian had, after all her years of heartfelt yearning, finally decided to propose to her. And what had her reaction been to this much longed-for declaration? Not joy. Not delight. Not eagerness to marry the object of her heart's desire. But rather, a smug satisfaction that he'd finally come to his senses, and the irrefutable knowledge that she no longer wanted him.

Could the situation be any more insane?

Possibly not.

Ned never had the chance to explain what he meant by "making her his." Did he mean to do the honorable thing and ask her to wed? Or had he planned to propose to her a much less honorable position in his life?

What if the man she no longer loved offered her marriage, and the man she loved with all her heart only offered her infamy?

What on earth should she do?

Chapter Thirty-One

Well, at least the Rose and Crown had softer beds to lie on. Though, Ned couldn't convince himself they were any cleaner than those in the cell. At least no one would be able to sling the dregs from their tankards upon him. He hoped.

Still, his trials had not yet ended. Not only did his head ache like the very devil, but he was forced to endure the intermittent moaning of Julian Carnforth from the other side of the room.

"Be a man, Carnforth," Ned commanded. "It can't be as bad as that."

"What reason have you to taunt me?" his fellow inmate complained. "If you were in the amount of pain that I am, you would moan, too. I'm blinded by blood and am like to cast up my accounts at any moment. I hope you're pleased with your handiwork."

Ned shook his head, then wished he hadn't. The pain was excruciating. "I did not do this. You charged at me, tripped, and hit your head on a tombstone. Miss Blythe will attest to all that."

Carnforth gave a fruitless tug on the manacles binding

his hands. "She'll say whatever you want her to say. You're an earl, aren't you? Don't earls get whatever they want?"

Ned sighed heavily and glanced around their new prison. The thickly plastered walls were dark with tobacco smoke and soot marks, and the smell of stale beer was drifting up through the floorboards, bringing unpleasant memories with it.

"Very rarely," he stated. "The mores of Society dictate what one may and may not have. As a peer, I have less freedom than the lowest laborer. But I wouldn't expect you to understand."

Nor did he expect sympathy for his situation—or want it. He just wanted people to realize how important his family was to him, and the lengths to which he would go to defend them, or avenge the wrongs done to them.

"I wouldn't have thought mauling a young lady in a public place would go down too well with Society," Carnforth pointed out irritably.

"True," Ned conceded. Cassie made him do things he could never have imagined. His behavior had become unconscionable. Little better than that of the accursed Captain Wycherley. "We all make mistakes," he said shortly.

"You regret kissing her?" the other man inquired.

"Not at all. Nor do I regret a minute of the time she's spent in my arms."

"You may be an earl, but you're the very worst sort of rake," Carnforth said heatedly, his eyes flashing. Then he winced. "Oh Lord, but my head aches! I believe I am about to vomit. Is there a pot in here?"

"There'll be a chamber pot under the bed."

"How can I grasp it with my hands constrained?"

"Good God, man, *I'll* get it for you if you're so helpless!"

Ned eased himself carefully off the bed, mindful of his head, and placed the pot on the floor in front of his rival.

He lay down on his bed again, turned his back on the

scene, and tried to ignore the nasty noises coming from the other half of the cell. Of all the damned luck, to be locked in a flea-ridden bedchamber with a retching milksop who thought himself a paragon of virtue. The man who possessed the one part of Cassie Blythe that Ned had not touched.

Her heart.

After a moment, the sounds subsided, and a weak voice said, "Don't think she'll ever take you. She loves me. Always has. You told me that yourself."

Ned rolled onto his back and groaned. Yes, he'd certainly implied it, and now he regretted it enormously. "You don't know that she *still* loves you," he insisted. "By her actions, if not her words, she has given me every reason to believe she does not."

"You have dishonored her!" Carnforth was outraged.

He refused to dignify the accusation. "I have every intention of making her my wife. If she'll have me."

Of course he was going to marry her. How could he even consider a future without Cassandra Blythe in it?

"I still say she won't have you," countered Carnforth. "You are not at all well suited. Cassie needs a quiet existence, with no drama or crises. I am more than happy to rusticate in the country with her if she's tired of Oxford."

"Then you don't know her at all," Ned asserted. "Cassie is young, energetic, and resourceful. She needs stimulation, adventure, and likes to experience new things. She would tire of *you* in no time."

As true as the words were, he realized how ungracious they sounded. And petulant. But there was no point scrapping with Carnforth for her, like two dogs over a bone. Cassie had already stated she would make her own choice. Which was only right. The decision to marry Ned *should* come from her.

And if her choice didn't fall his way, well, he would just have to find a way to make her change her mind.

Chapter Thirty-Two

An hour later, having consumed a tankard of weak ale, a hard-crusted mutton pie, and a sliver of cheese, Ned sat on the edge of his bed, glaring balefully at the man who was threatening to take Cassie away from him. Well, he could make his own threats. He said, "Does Cassie know you always intended to marry Lady Lucy? I'm sure she'd find that most interesting."

Carnforth, who hadn't touched his food, cradled his head in his hands. "Don't plague me, sir, I beg you," he said. "I still feel most unwell."

"To prefer Lady Lucy over Cassandra…" Ned made a deprecating noise. "You are a complete fool."

There was a scraping sound as a key was turned in the chamber door, and a new voice said, "Who's a complete fool? Pray tell."

Ned groaned aloud. There were two things in the world he *really* didn't need right now. One was having to listen to the righteous prating of Cassie's would-be husband, the other was to have Francis Wycherley come and gloat over him. Not when he was in no position to rearrange that gentleman's face.

"How good of you to visit," Ned said sourly.

"I need to speak with you, Stranraer," said Wycherley. "Sooner rather than later, I think."

"Have you, perhaps, come to apologize for turning my life upside down? For stealing my sister away and letting us think she was dead? For cheating on her with other women and breaking her heart? For allowing her home to burn to the ground and disfiguring her beautiful face? Destroying all her hopes of future happiness? All roads lead back to you, Captain."

There was a long silence, then Wycherley said, "All true enough. But you must believe me, I was, and still am, very much in love with your sister. Perhaps even more so now that I've seen how stalwart of spirit she is, and how brave."

Ned thought about that for a moment, his mind still clouded with the pain and fug of his injuries. The immediate temptation was to correct Wycherley and say the word "misguided" might have been better. However, he now understood only too well that people didn't always behave intelligently when it came to matters of the heart.

"You cannot understand how the family has suffered, not knowing what had become of her, fearing her dead, or worse," he admonished.

"You knew she was alive," Wycherley countered, "or you would not have entered my employ as a servant, snooping about in the hope of finding clues."

"I thought you had run away together and had started the fire to delay pursuit."

Wycherley looked genuinely horrified. "Great heavens, no! How could you have so poor an opinion of me? Of your own sister?"

Ned ran a hand through his hair, and his manacles clinked and chafed. "When confronted by the worst, one's imagination takes flight. Yes, I assumed she must still be alive, but was being hidden away until a babe was born. I was determined to find evidence and force you to marry her."

Wycherley made a deprecating noise. "You considered an arsonist and despoiler of innocents a suitable husband for your sister? If I were truly as bad as you imagined, you would have been damning her to a life of misery."

"I concur," said a weak voice from the opposite corner.

"Stay out of this, Carnforth," Ned said ominously. "This matter is private, and I'll have your balls for a bellpull if you speak of it to anyone."

"I say, you don't have to threaten. Just asking can be equally effective."

Ned sank his head into his hands. Had he ever been in a more insufferable situation than this one? Trapped with not just one enemy, but two? And utterly unable to extract himself.

Trying to temper his tone, he told Wycherley, "I feel somewhat differently now I know the truth. But I shall still demand an apology from you, since it was your rash behavior, your cowardly unwillingness to ask my permission to court her in the accepted manner, that has brought about this whole sorry business."

Wycherley suddenly glanced up and strode to the chamber door. "Well, sir," he said, "you're going to have to decide damn fast. I can hear Georgiana outside, chatting to the constable."

Ned looked up, eager to see his sister.

"This should be interesting," averred Carnforth from his side of the room.

"A *bellpull*, Carnforth," Ned reminded him.

As soon as Georgiana was admitted, Wycherley caught her in his embrace and kissed her soundly. "My darling!" he exclaimed. "How I've missed you!"

"Hush, love, not in front of my brother, please," she said,

pushing him gently away. "Goodness, how pale you look, Ned!"

She hovered uncertainly between him and the captain, then knelt by Ned's side and took his hand between hers.

He attempted a smile. "It's very kind of you to come. I know you have no desire to go out in public."

"I've taken Miss Blythe's advice and styled my hair to cover the worst of the burns, and have donned a deep bonnet. I may take up hat design to amuse myself while I complete my recovery."

"You look wonderful, Georgiana," he said. "And it's good to see you in such good spirits."

"I wish I could say the same of you," she responded with a grimace. "But I understand the other gentleman, Mr. Carnforth, is in an even worse state. I assume that's him on the other side, apparently asleep?"

"I never touched him," Ned responded, running a hand lightly over the side of his head. "Even so, your gallant Captain Wycherley struck me down."

"Forgive me," said Wycherley. "I misunderstood the situation."

"Evidently."

Georgiana squeezed Ned's hand. "I'm sorry it happened, but you'll mend, darling. You always do."

"How on earth did you hear of the altercation?" Ned suddenly wondered.

"Cassie ran out to the cottage to tell me. She said you were struck twice on the head. I'm very pleased to see you're still rational."

Was he? He was starting to doubt it. None of this was making any sense.

"Miss Blythe went all that way to fetch you?" he asked.

"She knew I'd be worried when you didn't return. And of course, I was dying to see Francis, whom she told me was here.

Is there anything I can do for you, anything you want?"

"The constable's head on a platter?" Ned suggested with menace. "Preferably with lots of sharp things sticking into it." At her gasp of reproach, he waved a hand and said, "Thank you, no. I'll endeavor to survive the night."

She smiled bleakly and started to rise. "Very well. Then I'll see — "

He gently grasped her arm. "But what am I going to do about you and the miscreant standing behind you?"

"Oh, please don't be angry with Francis," Georgiana pleaded. "Everything was as much my fault as his."

"It *is* his fault," Ned said with a scowl. "He is a man of the world, and you were an innocent. He should have courted you properly."

"About that…" She sat back on her haunches and regarded Ned steadily. "I've been thinking a lot lately. And I have now started to consider my future in a more positive light. If Francis still wishes to marry me, I would like to accept him."

Wycherley rushed forward. "Georgiana! I can't believe my ears!"

"It's true, my darling."

There was a great rustle of silk as Wycherley swept her up and pressed her to his chest.

Ned wanted to shout at them to stop. *Please, not here, not now.* How could he bear to look on the happiness of others when his own felt so threatened?

His sister eased out of her lover's embrace and gazed hopefully at Ned. "We would value your blessing, brother."

"Now is not a propitious time. But I promise I'll think about it," was all he could manage for the moment. Of course he would consent. But let the man stew a little.

"Miss Blythe warned me you'd be like this," Georgiana declared. "She said while you're making up your mind, I must exact your solemn promise not to harm Francis. You're not to call him out, do him violence, or attempt to ruin his prospects."

"I am not accustomed to caving in to ultimatums," he retorted. "What if I won't promise?"

Georgiana bit her lip. "Then you will never see us again," she said sadly. "We will disappear, go to the Colonies or India, where fortunes are to be made. Isn't that right, Francis?"

"It's an exciting idea," offered Wycherley, but to his credit, his cautious gaze was directed at Ned, as if imploring him to reconsider.

"But not a wise one. I could easily stop you," Ned replied, though his heart wasn't in it. He'd lost his sister once, and he may have lost Cassie to his rival. He wanted his sister back, at least.

She seemed to sense the spreading cracks in his determination. "Yes, but you won't." Smiling, she tenderly patted his hand. "Seeing you again has been such a tonic, Ned. But I'm feeling weary now. Francis, can you take me home? We'll all feel better after a night's rest. We can make our plans in the morning." She took the captain's arm and held him close in an intimate gesture.

Irritation sluiced through Ned. "You seem very sure I'm eventually going to let you marry Wycherley."

"I know you will." She tipped her head and gave him a sly look. "Because you've been learning about love yourself lately, and know you cannot stand in its way."

He stilled. "Where would you have come by such a ridiculous notion?"

"Why, you and Miss Blythe, of course."

He felt an invisible knife to the heart. "Love?" he scoffed. "You are quite mistaken."

"I think not. Anyone would be blind not to see you have feelings for one another."

Try telling *her* that. Or *him*, he thought, and cast an

unfriendly eye on the sleeping form of Mr. Carnforth.

"You are imagining things," he said.

"Perhaps. Perhaps not," she mused with a knowing smile. "You should give this one a chance, at least."

He ground his teeth. "Leave it, Georgiana. My romantic life, or lack of one, is none of your concern."

Her smile only widened. "Francis and I will be dropping in on Miss Blythe. Shall I tell her to come to you?"

"You'll do no such thing!"

Georgiana tilted her head. "All right. You don't want Miss Blythe to see you in this sorry state. I understand."

Another twist of that knife. "I know you mean well," he retorted, "but I'm weary and would like to sleep now. Be sure Matthews accompanies you home." He cast Wycherley a curt, meaningful look. "You still have a reputation to maintain, Georgiana, and I have a scandal to hush up."

Wycherley coughed and shuffled his feet, but Ned ignored him. If he wanted to court Georgiana, it was time he played by the rules.

"I am *so* glad you came to find me," she told Ned. "This week has been a turning point for us all. Farewell for now, darling. Let me kiss you."

"I'm very glad, as well," he said with heartfelt sincerity.

"Dear Edmund, I do love you!" She pecked him on the cheek. After calling out to thank the constable, she and the captain finally left Ned alone with Carnforth, and his own tempestuous thoughts.

Chapter Thirty-Three

Cassie paused uncertainly outside the door to the chamber that served as jail cell. Locked in that room together were two men about whom she'd had overwhelmingly powerful feelings. She knew, though, deep within her soul, which man she wanted.

Ned.

But did he want her? The insult he'd given her just before their kiss in the churchyard, it still stung. Badly. The kiss had been glorious, but had started in hurt and anger. How could she know how he truly felt about her, deep down? Whether he intended to make her his wife, or only his mistress?

Should she follow her heart...or take the safe path offered by Julian, the path she'd followed for most of her life? Counting on Ned's feelings would be an enormous risk to take...

"Miss Blythe!" announced Constable Marsh. "Have you come to mend these ruffians' pates?"

She would hardly call either of them "ruffians," but let the man savor his small victory while it lasted. Which she hoped would not be long.

She lifted the basket on her arm to show him its contents. Bandages, a flask of clean water with a little witch hazel in it, some arnica salve.

"Mrs. Fiennes does not come with you?" the constable asked, visibly disappointed.

"No. We weren't sure if we'd both be allowed in."

"Oh, the more the merrier," he said, rocking back on his heels. She thought she heard the clink of coin in his pocket, and hoped she'd brought enough for her own bribe.

"There's already been two visitors," Marsh informed her as he stealthily relieved her of her shilling.

Who could be visiting Julian and Ned? Lady Lucy? Cassie sincerely hoped not.

"Captain Wycherley and the new lady who lives out on the Kenville road have been here already."

Wycherley? With Georgiana? Good Lord. How would Ned have dealt with that scenario? Especially after his cutting question about whether Cassie would prefer Ned's bed or Wycherley's?

"Everything was amicable, was it?" she cautiously queried as the constable put the key in the lock. "No arguments, raised voices?"

"None at all. I wouldn't have allowed any altercations, you know."

"Of course not."

So, Wycherley was still in one piece. Good news, indeed. Her heart lifted a little as she stepped into the room where her lover—and her former love—were both incarcerated.

"Cassie!" Ned leaped up and reached for her hands, and she winced at the touch of cold iron from his manacles.

"Ned, how are you? What's happened to Julian?"

She didn't quite know how to act with him. She still felt wounded by his thoughtless comment. But then, he'd kissed her so passionately. Perhaps the best approach would be to keep things polite and businesslike until they had a chance to talk.

He nodded toward the other side of the room and grimaced. "I must stop moving my head so suddenly," he said, then added, "I think he's asleep."

"I'll attend to him in a moment, then. Sit down, Ned, please. Let me see your injuries."

He sat, and she set her basket down and ran her hands gingerly over the back of his head.

Oh, it felt so good to be close to him again! Recalling what they had shared, and all he had made her feel, she prayed he felt the same about her as she felt for him.

She heard his sharp intake of breath as she probed, and resisted the urge to tease him, knowing he could do very little to protest with both hands shackled together. Then she saw the ugly bruise on his temple, and her wicked thoughts evaporated in a cloud of concern.

"That looks painful. Portia recommends arnica ointment, if the skin isn't broken."

"Portia has turned out to be a very useful friend," Ned said wryly, as Cassie dipped her fingers in the salve and started gingerly anointing both the bruise and the bump.

When she'd finished with the ointment, she wiped her hands on a handkerchief, then looked over her shoulder.

Julian still lay with his back to them, apparently asleep. Now might be a good time to ask Ned what he'd meant by saying he was planning to "make her his own" when they were in the churchyard. Whatever his offer, she'd like to have time to prepare her answer.

"Ned—"

"Cassie, is that you?"

Blast.

She turned to see Julian sitting on the edge of his bed,

supporting his head in his hands and looking decidedly unwell.

"Julian, you're so pale! Excuse me," she said to Ned, grabbing up her basket and hurrying across to examine her childhood friend.

Julian wasn't just pale, he was positively green. There was a nasty gash where his head had struck the tombstone, and his shirt collar was dyed dark with blood.

"I've felt better," he declared weakly.

Ned gave a derisive snort. "I'd say we both have."

Could he be jealous because of Julian's proposal at the churchyard, worried she might prefer Julian to him? She smiled. Perhaps it would do him good. He was always so cocksure of himself. And of her.

She dabbed a cloth in the water and set about gently dabbing around Julian's wound. It felt so odd to be this close to him, closer than she'd been since they were children, closer even than when they'd last danced together. She could appreciate the high cheekbones, the light, waving hair, the aristocratic nose and brow. Despite the pallor of his skin, he was no less handsome than she'd ever thought him.

What an ironic twist of fate that he would suddenly wish to marry her, and she would no longer want him as more than a friend.

Julian seemed a stranger to her now. She had known another man's touch—Ned's touch—and the thought of Ned sitting just a few feet behind her affected her infinitely more deeply than Julian's nearness.

"Are you going to take all day about that?"

Ned again. Yes, he was definitely jealous. And absolutely no good at hiding the fact. Did that bode well for his feelings for her? He *had* been ready to call Julian out, before all hell broke loose at the churchyard…

She smiled again. "I'll just put a bandage over this to keep the wound clean," she said, "and then I'm done."

She thought she *was* done, and was about to turn back to Ned again, when Julian suddenly slid from the bed onto one knee and seized her hand between his.

"I know this isn't a propitious moment, with me being accounted a felon, and us having an unwelcome audience, but… Please, Miss Cassandra Blythe, would you do me the honor of becoming my wife?"

Oh no. Not again!

There was a deep choking gasp from the other side of the room, and she could feel Ned's eyes boring into her back. Curse Julian Carnforth! What an insult to offer an earl! And to herself.

This was absolutely not the place and most certainly *not* the time to be proposing marriage.

"Julian, you are concussed," she told him sternly. "You don't know what you're saying." She tried to pull her hand away, but he refused to release it.

"I know exactly what I'm saying." His words sounded a little slurred. He was definitely not in his right mind, but continued regardless. "Your father wishes it, my father wishes it, and I know you love me."

It was hardly a shock that he'd somehow discerned her feelings for him. She'd made them clear enough over the years. She just wondered why he'd chosen this exact day to declare for her. It was maddening of him, really, to wait until the precise moment she'd changed her mind.

But had she? Changed her mind?

The uncertainty of Ned's feelings returned to plague her.

She said stiffly, "I will not deny that I once had…strong feelings for you, Julian. But I was very young when they began, with no idea what love truly is. I do love you as a friend, though—"

"Do not think of rejecting me, Cassie—"

"I didn't say I was—"

"She *is*, though," pronounced Ned, infuriatingly.

Hands on hips, she spun to face him. "Please, Ned. Let me deal with this."

"You'd do well to accept me," Julian warned. "Stranraer is far too high in the instep for you. I, however, can be forgiving. I don't mind marrying you, even though Stranraer has obviously severely compromised your reputation. It doesn't matter to me one iota if you have let him—"

"*What?*"

Cassie couldn't believe she was hearing this. Her heart seemed to shrivel up inside her, while her mind blazed with fury. She turned on Ned.

"You *told* him?"

"I most certainly did not! He obviously witnessed you in my arms, and our kiss, but I never said there was anything more than that between us."

She clamped her jaw, grinding her teeth. *Lord*. If Julian hadn't known before that she and Ned had been intimate, he surely knew now, after she'd blurted out her accusation.

She was heartsick. Those precious, stolen moments in the wheat field, that wonderful feeling of being one with a man, being one with Nature, had all been intensely private…and should have stayed so.

And now Julian knew. Who else would he tell, should she refuse his proposal? This was as dainty a morsel of gossip as the *ton* had enjoyed in many a day. It was all too humiliating.

She drew herself up, using anger to stop her from collapsing in a heap of abject misery. "You are despicable. *Both* of you. I don't want to see *either* of you, ever again."

"I say!"

"Cassandra!"

Ignoring their protests, she grabbed up her basket, avoided Ned as he surged to his feet to stop her, and thundered with her fist on the dusty wooden panels of the door.

It was opened with alacrity by a surprised Achilles Marsh, who stepped in and placed a warning hand against the earl's chest.

She turned round, glaring at Ned and Julian in utter fury, and snapped, "I wouldn't marry either of you, not if you *begged* me. In fact, I don't think I want to marry *anyone*. *Ever*."

Chapter Thirty-Four

Nothing on God's earth was going to take Cassie away from him. Having—after a lengthy and heated discussion—bribed the constable for his freedom, Ned ran straight to Mrs. Fiennes cottage, only to discover that Cassie had boarded the last coach of the day and left Aston.

He threw himself onto Maxim's back and rode harder than he ever had in his life, fortunately catching up with the mail coach just as it reached Devizes.

Was Cassie inside? She *had* to be. It would be ill-luck, indeed, if he'd chased halfway across Wiltshire after the wrong equipage.

Yes, there! He'd know her figure anywhere, the bronze curls that caressed her neck beneath the shade of her bonnet, that purposeful but sensuous way she walked…

Thankfully, she wasn't going into the Pelican Inn for refreshments. She was walking away from it, in the direction of Caen Hill. Good. He didn't want their conversation to be in public.

He leaped down from Maxim's back, threw the reins to

a stable boy, and ran down the hill in pursuit. Cassie had just settled herself on a quaint wooden bench beneath a willow tree a few feet away from the canal when he caught up with her.

Slowing to a halt, he gave himself a moment to drink in the sight of her. *Thank God* he'd found her. He couldn't let her walk out of his life. Especially over a complete misunderstanding. He cared too much. More, perhaps, than he was prepared to admit to himself. But whatever this feeling was that had held his heart in a grip of ice ever since she'd left the inn at Aston, it was too painful to be allowed to continue.

"Cassie," he said softly, every nerve on edge.

"Ned!" She dropped her reticule in astonishment, but he was there in an instant, handing it back and settling himself on the bench beside her.

Was she pleased to see him? Was the sparkle in her eyes, the pink in her cheeks, due to anger or pleasure?

He hoped the latter.

"Whatever are you doing here?" she asked, somewhat breathlessly.

"When Mrs. Fiennes told me you'd taken the next stage back to Oxford, I knew I couldn't let you go. There was too much that remained unsaid."

How he longed to touch her, to peel the glove off that tender hand, press his fingers between hers, and tell her he loved her, that he couldn't contemplate a future without her. But her last words before leaving had not been encouraging.

"How is it you're no longer under house arrest?" she asked warily. "Surely, you haven't earned a reprieve? Where's Julian? Is he not with you?"

Naturally, she *would* ask about the meddlesome rogue.

"I came alone, thanks to giving that wretch of a constable a hefty bribe. Added to those he'd been given already."

"Julian is also free?"

Ned held onto his patience. "Despite everything, I'd have felt a churl if I'd bought my own freedom and left him behind." He regarded her closely. "You're quite certain you're not going to marry him, aren't you?"

"I believe I made myself quite clear the last time we spoke," she said stiffly. "I don't wish to marry *either* of you."

"But definitely not Carnforth."

"I don't know. I've wanted him for so long..." She turned away so he couldn't see her expression.

His heart felt like lead, and panic erupted in his chest. She was just teasing him, surely?

"I would far rather you marry me," he said, reaching for her hand.

She didn't pull away. A good sign? His fingers tightened, as did his chest. Right now, she could destroy him with a single word.

"Is that a command, Lord Stranraer, or an offer?" she asked tartly, turning back to face him again.

"Both," he replied with a smile because she hadn't rejected him outright.

She was silent for a long moment. "All I can say is I'll think about it. You and Julian have given me a lot to mull over."

"I'd be most grateful if you forgot about him," he said, attempting not to sound petulant. "I want you to think only of me."

Her lips curved downward. "Such vanity!"

"Hardly," he said, looking down at his travel-stained clothes and dusty Hessian boots. He hadn't even stopped to put on a coat. "If I were vain, I wouldn't dream of courting you in anything less than my best Parisian silk suit."

She chuckled. It was the sweetest sound on earth. "I can't imagine you in anything that fine, Ned. I've yet to see your full trappings of grandeur."

"Next time, I will put on the finery I wear for Court," he promised, "so I might impress you."

"Do you hope to win my heart by dressing up?"

"Oh no. I have a good deal more in my arsenal than that."

Things seemed to be taking a positive turn, and he should push home his advantage. Snaking an arm about her waist, he pulled her to him and pressed his lips to hers.

Oh, the honeyed-peach of her mouth! So sweetly innocent, yet generously giving. How could he ever have enough of this woman?

He slid his tongue over the crease between her lips, then bit down gently on the lower one. To his delight, she shifted against him, pushing closer, and tilted her head to deepen the kiss, opening her mouth and welcoming his questing tongue.

He rolled his head, his fingers caressing her cheek, anchoring themselves in her hair, and kissed her with the hard, heavy hunger which had been brewing in him ever since he'd made love to her in the wheat field. By God, if there were anywhere private nearby, he'd do it again, and again, until he was too exhausted to move.

But he was forgetting himself. He'd not ridden here pell-mell to throw Cassie on her back, however tempting that might be. He'd come here to win her hand.

And, if at all possible, her heart.

He withdrew and kissed her lightly on the forehead before easing himself away.

"Will you marry me, Cassie?"

Her face became serious. "I appreciate that you have ridden all this way to find me," she said. "But as you can probably guess, I cut short my visit to Portia so I wouldn't have to see you or Julian again. At least, not until I'd decided how I feel about you both."

His heart did cartwheels inside his chest. "And what do you feel?"

"Very confused."

"If you want an apology, let me give you one. I apologize, with all my heart, for kissing you in public. For discussing you with Mr. Carnforth. I should never have done either."

"And for that horrible remark in the churchyard?"

He frowned. "What remark?"

Her mouth drooped. "You don't remember? Your cruel question about whose bed I'd prefer to share…?"

He grimaced, mortified by his unforgivable insult, and took her hand again. "I'm so very sorry. I shouldn't have said that. I was angry and— No, it was inexcusable, and I shall regret it to my dying day."

She eased out a breath. "Yes. I've no doubt. But how am I to know it's not how you truly feel about me, deep down? From my first meeting with Captain Wycherley, you were convinced my behavior lacked propriety. And I've done nothing but prove you right."

"Not true! I was worried for you because you were an innocent, and I knew Wycherley was less than honorable."

She looked up at him. "And yet, your sister loves him, and he wants to do right by her, and do the honorable thing."

"Evidently." He scowled. He didn't want to talk about that now. He still hadn't secured Cassie's promise.

But before he could turn the subject back to their own betrothal, she asked, "Are you going to permit her to marry Wycherley?"

"I haven't decided," he said shortly. "I haven't forgiven him for what he did to her."

"Oh, but you must. For her sake. She loves him!"

Damn it, they were arguing again. How did this always happen?

"I'll bear it in mind," he said. "Now, can we get back to—" But his words were cut off by the loud blast of the coachman's horn.

Cassie seized her reticule and leaped to her feet. "The coach. I must go."

He caught her by the shoulders and pulled her against him. "No. Stay. We are not yet finished talking."

"I need time to think, Ned," she said, pulling away from him. "About your offer, and Julian's. Grant me that."

The next instant, she was running back up the street toward the coaching inn.

He should run after her, catch her, and kiss her senseless. Kiss her until all doubts and all thoughts of Julian Carnforth were banished from her mind. By which time the coach would have departed and she would be his to look after, his to convey back to her papa, his to cherish and to love and to marry…

But his feet refused to move.

He didn't know if his heart could take any more uncertainty. Was she truly considering accepting Carnforth over him? Even after she'd so willingly and lovingly gifted him her innocence? His pride rebelled at the idea of pursuing her any further until he knew he'd succeed.

But he had no choice.

He could *not* lose her.

She would marry that fickle, venal Mr. Carnforth over his dead body!

"I *will* find a way to win her hand," he vowed aloud.

He would think of a grand gesture that would amaze and impress her.

And win her heart forever.

Chapter Thirty-Five

Cassie had been back in Oxford for a full two weeks when one morning her papa shuffled his paper and exclaimed, "What remarkable news! The elusive Earl of Stranraer has been found."

Her spoon crashed onto the edge of her porridge bowl, and when she tried to rescue it, she was all fingers and thumbs, which became an immediate point of interest for her family.

"This news has clearly overset you," her cousin Becca stated. "But I cannot imagine why."

Her reaction had been so patent, there was no demurring. "It's all a bit complicated to explain, but I am acquainted with Lord Stranraer, you see."

"Good Gad!" exclaimed her papa. "How did you fail to mention you've been rubbing shoulders with an earl?"

Rather more than shoulders, she thought, feeling the all-too-familiar stab of pain. A whole fortnight, and she'd heard nothing from him. Somehow, she hadn't expected him to give in so easily.

"I met him in Aston while he was incognito," she

managed. "He was looking for his missing sister but didn't want to cause a scandal. I promised not to reveal his identity or his whereabouts."

Becca gave her a penetrating look. "You certainly became his confidant in a very short time. You were only at Aston a couple of days."

"I hope you didn't make a nuisance of yourself," Papa admonished lightheartedly.

Becca continued to gaze intently at her, increasing her discomfiture. "Uncle, pray do not tease poor Cassie. We must assume that her encounter with the earl upset her in some way, which is why she is looking so self-conscious."

The earl had, indeed, upset her. But not in the way they imagined. He had turned her world on its head, undermined all the truths that had been sacred to her, and opened up places in her body and her heart that now felt like chasms of aching emptiness.

Chasms not even a marriage proposal from Julian Carnforth could fill.

The former love of her life was now but the pale ghost of a memory compared to the powerful, energetic, infuriating, passionate Earl of Stranraer.

Had he not proposed marriage to her, as well? Had she but imagined that short conversation at the coaching inn? A dream? Wishful thinking?

Just hearing Ned's name at the breakfast table was exquisite torture. How she wished it were possible to rewind the clock, to undo the demand for time she had made at their last meeting. Why had she stubbornly insisted on being allowed to think things over, when her mind had already been made up long before?

Then again, if Ned genuinely wanted to pursue a relationship with her, would he not have made every effort by now to convince her?

Maybe, now that he was returned to his proper sphere in life, he'd realized he was far too lofty and important to consider a liaison with plain and lowly Miss Cassandra Blythe.

She was about to push her bowl away, having lost all appetite, when Papa asked suddenly, "So, will you both be fit and well enough to go to this ball, d'ye think?"

Cassie blinked, rearranging her thoughts. "What ball?"

"A masked ball at Highmore House. The invitation arrived with the post."

"But we don't have anything to wear for a masked ball," said Becca, her expression disappointed.

"Don't worry," Papa said cheerfully. "There's a note on the back saying costumes will be sent to us."

"How very singular," Becca mused. "I suppose we should consider ourselves privileged. The Duke of Paxton can't possibly be sending costumes to all his guests. How would he know their sizes, for a start?"

"A ball sounds…diverting," Cassie said. It was during a ball at Highmore that she'd first met Ned. It seemed more like years than mere months ago.

"Is Julian coming?" she asked conversationally.

"I believe he's received an invitation, as well."

"We need to know if he'll be coming with us, Papa. He's very accomplished at getting you in and out of your chair." Although, her next meeting with Julian would doubtless be highly embarrassing, for many reasons.

Not the least of which was his unanswered marriage proposal, which she had no idea how to respond to. Everyone would be shocked if she turned him down, after years of pursuing him. They would demand an explanation which, of course, she couldn't give without compromising herself. And how could she accept his proposal when she knew she would only ever truly love one man?

A man who had forgotten all about her.

She stifled a growl. How could she ever have fallen in love with such an infuriating man?

She became aware of a tension in the room and looked from her cousin's anxious face to her father's frown.

"Papa, what are you not saying?"

Becca reached for her hand with a solemn look.

"Now you're frightening me!" Cassie exclaimed. "Stop it, both of you, and tell me what's the matter." What had they been talking about before her dive into self-pity?

Her papa said, "I don't like to be the bearer of bad tidings, my dear, but…"

Julian. She'd been asking whether he would be at the ball.

"What?" she demanded. "Is it something to do with Julian? Is he ill?"

His head injury had been unpleasant but, surely, he would have been over that by now? Unless infection had set in.

"Not exactly," her father replied. "But I doubt you'll be pleased to learn he intends to accompany Lady Lucy to the ball."

What? Cassie's mind whirled, but she managed to say, "Oh. I see."

So, his offer of marriage to Cassie had not been in earnest.

Brilliant. Now *both* of her suitors had abandoned her.

"There's more," her father said, shifting uncomfortably in his seat. "He hasn't made it public yet, but I received a note from him this morning. He wanted us to be the first to know."

She took a deep breath. "I think I know what you're going to say," she ventured. "Has Julian asked her to marry him?"

"He has, and has been accepted. I confess, I am much disappointed by his choice. I'd always hoped…but no, it is no matter." Her father sighed.

"I think he's making a massive error of judgment," Becca protested. "She must be a good ten years older than he, and her reputation is appalling!"

"He appears devoted to her," Papa said. "I don't understand it myself, not when he has the whole world to choose from. I suppose marriage to Carnforth will bring Lady Lucy respectability again."

Well, that would save Cassie the awkwardness of having to refuse him, had he persisted in courting her. She couldn't help but pity him, though. How long would it be before the fickle Lady Lucy made a cuckold of him?

The family's ruminations on Julian Carnforth's fate were interrupted by the squeak of the garden gate. Cassie experienced a painful constriction of her stomach at the possibility that the caller might bring a letter from Ned, or even better, be Ned himself.

However, it turned out to be the arrival of their costumes, individually addressed, for the Duke and Duchess of Paxton's ball.

The first thing Cassie pulled out of her box was a wig. It was made of pale horsehair and formed into a tall mound with several different layers and a delightful frill of ringlets all around the edge. Next came a pair of white silk shoes, with slender heels and large rosettes to decorate them. These were followed by a mask—half face only—with slanted eyeholes and winged edges.

And then came the dress.

"By Juno!" She held it up in front of her, admiring the watered-silk petticoat with its pattern of yellow roses exposed by an open-fronted gown, and the bronze-colored silk damask skirts. Such a pity she must wear the white wig, for the gown matched her hair perfectly. The stomacher was also patterned with golden flowers, and the neckline, rather lower than she was used to wearing, had a delicate edging of lace. The sleeves frothed with lace, as well—gorgeous handmade Belgian lace in the style of the previous century.

It was truly lavish, far more splendid than anything she'd

ever worn. It must have cost a fortune!

The only items she would need to provide were the underthings, particularly the boned corsetry required to correctly fill the tightly tapered shape of the upper part of the gown, and the structures necessary to fan out the skirts so one wasn't constantly trampling on them. Still, with two weeks to go until the ball, there was ample time to make these.

Cassie smiled to herself. For the first time since her return from Aston, she felt almost cheerful. Behind the mask, beneath the sumptuous clothing, she could pretend to be whomever she wanted, just like Cinderella in the fairy tale.

But for her, there would be no Prince Charming at the ball.

She would just have to close the door forever on her love for the Earl of Stranraer and make the best of whatever Fate chose to throw at her.

Chapter Thirty-Six

"Doesn't the place look splendid?" exclaimed Becca. "It will look even more spectacular after dark."

It was the night of the ball, and they had just reached the front of the long line of carriages.

"The beauty fair lifts one's heart," agreed Cassie as she stepped down from their carriage under the imposing stone facade of Highmore House.

The flambeaux were all lit and glittering radiantly, just as she remembered from the previous ball. But how changed she was since that time!

She sighed, then realized she shouldn't, as it made her breasts rise rather too precariously within the confines of the tightly-laced corset. Her waist was cinched in so much she had to make a real effort to breathe, and she sincerely hoped the dances wouldn't be too lively, lest she faint clean away.

She wandered off to one side while the task of unloading her father's Bath chair from the roof of the carriage was undertaken, and gazed up at the bright windows of Highmore, remembering the way she had felt all those months ago, on the night she first met Wycherley and his intriguing manservant. A young girl, full of hope and excitement, consorting with dashing rakes, dreaming and scheming over Julian...

It was from one of these windows she'd first spied Ned and felt that shocking thrill of attraction, that immediate connection between them. Her eyes misted.

"Well, *I* think you should have put a chemise underneath it."

What? Cassie turned about sharply. That was Julian's voice, surely? Was he addressing her, or...?

"Don't be such a bore, Julian. You know you like to see what I have on display."

Cassie's hand flew to her mouth, and she stared in horror at the closed chaise which had just crunched to a halt behind their own equipage. Lady Lucy and Julian had arrived together in her chaise. And they were having an argument before the evening had even started.

"At least wear the fichu over it. You would not wish to take cold."

"It's a hot night! Oh, you're being so dull, Julikins. I thought we had come out to enjoy ourselves."

Julikins?

Ugh. Julian had always been hugely averse to the idea of pet names. If he now answered to Julikins, he must be truly smitten.

"I know what this is about. You wish to show yourself off in case Captain Wycherley is here. You want him to be jealous, to regret what he has missed out on by throwing you over for Lady Georgiana Talbot."

Cassie pricked up her ears. It was public knowledge that Wycherley was courting Georgiana? Did this mean Ned had given the couple his blessing? That he'd finally forgiven the errant captain?

He'd seen sense at last. Or...had he done it...for *Cassie*?

No. Now she was just being fanciful.

She wished she knew what had become of Ned. Why had he not sought her out? Had she destroyed any chance they might have had of finding happiness together?

It was all too depressing.

But one should not be miserable at a ball. So she rejoined Becca and Papa to help supervise two impressively-built footmen in lifting his Bath chair up the steps.

After greeting their host, resplendent in a Louis XIV Sun King costume, they entered the ballroom. It had been decked out splendidly with all manner of flora, trailing ivy and vines, and swathes of evergreen bay and laurel.

Would she really be able to enjoy herself, despite the absence of the only man she wished to see?

Perhaps she should seek solace with some of her former admirers—perfectly suitable gentlemen she'd ignored because she had eyes only for Julian. She could try to win them back. A lady must marry, after all, and it might as well be while she was still young enough to attract a good catch.

There was Harold Spencer who had red hair, so he would be easy to see if he wasn't in a costume wig. Perhaps Archie Carlisle was here, as well—the one who talked a great deal about angling. If she set her cap at him, she'd have to learn how to swim. And put worms on hooks. And wrap feathers round fearsomely sharp flies.

Carlisle was quickly crossed off her potential husband list. Neither he nor Harold Spencer had ever made her heart beat faster, as Julian had. No, there was only one other man who had ever done so, and he had made her heart pump so much harder.

She looked up from her bleak thoughts with a start. A tall man, very elegantly attired in a long black silk coat with embroidered waistcoat and black pantaloons, was bowing before her. His face was mostly obscured by the mask he wore, his hair hidden by a wig which was the masculine version of her own. He cut a very fine figure. A figure which—surely?—she recognized.

Scarcely daring to hope that it was really *him*, that it could truly be the Earl of Stranraer, she answered his bow with the obligatory curtsey—quite a task in such voluminous skirts—and inclined her head. Then she held out the wrist from which her little ivory dance card and pencil were suspended, for her prospective partner to claim his dance.

He took the liberty of supporting her wrist as he wrote his name.

That heated touch, those strong but knowing hands! Her heart thundered so loudly, all other sound was blotted out.

Ned.

She was sure of it, even as he released her and moved off into the crowd.

But why didn't he say anything?

Chapter Thirty-Seven

Cassie's hand was trembling so much as she brought the card up to her mask, she couldn't read the signature.

"Becca!" she called. "What does this say?"

Her cousin pored over it, the feathers in her elaborate headdress jiggling about as if they were alive.

"Good Lord!" Becca looked at her wide-eyed. "It says Stranraer. Well, he certainly didn't want to hang around and indulge in small talk, did he? Did he not recognize you from Aston, perhaps?"

"Maybe because of the costume," Cassie replied, hoping her cousin wouldn't notice how breathless she'd become.

Becca gave a *harrumph*. "If he's not too top-lofty to desire a dance with you, you'd think he would be happy to exchange pleasantries before moving off. Is he shy, perhaps?"

Shy? Well, it was possible. But he hadn't been in the least bit shy with her before, so what had made him so reticent all of a sudden?

"I don't think he cares much for the manners and modes of the *ton*," Cassie murmured.

"I'm beginning to think your earl must be very eccentric," Becca said as she wandered off into the crowd.

Not mine.

There was no doubt in Cassie's mind that Ned had recognized her. But how had he managed to pick her out from this heaving mass, disguised as she was? There must be three hundred people here at least, all bewigged and masked, in a vast array of colored silks and satins, damasks and velvets. Yet she had barely been in the ballroom a few minutes and he'd come straight to her.

Craning her neck, she tried to identify him in the crowd. With his height and size, it should not be difficult. However, many of the old-fashioned wigs the gentlemen were wearing gave them deceptive stature. She would just have to wait on tenterhooks for the third dance.

If her nerves—and corset—didn't cause her to faint in the interim.

After her papa was delivered to a comfortable corner of the card room, the musicians struck up, and she stepped out for the first measure with a gentleman she had never met before. His cold hands felt like dead fish, and he smelled evilly of tobacco. His dancing was only moderately good, but for some reason her own was little better. She was looking out for the gentleman in black, to see who, if anyone, he was dancing with.

"Oh, I'm so sorry." She had bumped a rather grand lady wearing scarlet.

"I beg your pardon." This time she'd jostled elbows with a fat man in a gold-colored waistcoat which looked likely to pop all its buttons at any moment.

"There is quite a crush in here tonight," said her partner kindly. "Avoiding collisions is very taxing."

When the music came to a halt, she felt exhausted, a bundle of nerves and anxieties. The next dance was booked to a gentleman who had simply drawn a cross on her card. She hastily dropped him a curtsey and stared beyond his shoulder to see if Ned might have been watching her deplorable performance, but there was no sign of him.

"Cassie, do you not know me?"

"Oh, Julian! I was distracted for a moment. I do beg your pardon. How are you?"

"How polite you are," he said, taking her hand and leading her into their set. "I don't normally get such a bland greeting from you. Are you trying to behave like a proper lady now, after that embarrassing episode in Aston?"

"No lectures, please, or I will be forced to remind you of your very ungallant, and—as it turned out—meaningless proposal to me. But how did you recognize me? I hadn't spotted you."

A few months ago, her eyes would have been glued to the door of any ballroom or assembly room, waiting for his entrance. She would have been dying for him to take her in his arms and whirl her about the floor. But now, she only wanted to feel Ned's hands upon her, even if he danced no better than a carthorse.

"I saw your father, of course," Julian said. "Not many beautiful young ladies make their entrance accompanied by a gentleman in a Bath chair."

"Oh yes. How silly of me." The orchestra struck up, and they parted, then joined hands with the rest of their set.

"Cassie, you're going the wrong way."

"Am I? So sorry. It's these huge skirts. I just can't work out where my legs are underneath, and I keep barging into people or losing my place."

"Might I suggest you concentrate more on the steps and less on staring at everybody else?"

"Was I? Forgive me." She tried to pay attention to her feet.

"I must say, your outfits are splendid. Did your family all go to the same costumier?" he asked.

"No, they were sent to us by the duke."

"Really?" His head went back in the way he had that meant he was perplexed. It suddenly reminded her of a tortoise stretching its neck.

"There was a note on the back of the invitation, so we assume they were from Paxton…"

"You are privileged, indeed. No one else has received such bounty that I am aware of."

He gazed down at her consideringly, and she looked up into his green eyes, shaded to a dark emerald by the mask. Yes, green was a very pleasing color for a gentleman's eyes. But brown eyes… Eyes the color of aged whiskey were something very special.

"Cassie?"

"Hmm?"

"You seem to have forgotten how to dance."

She came to with a start. "Sorry!"

What was wrong with her? These skirts, this tight-lacing, no doubt. They made movement a very different experience.

"Cassie."

"Yes, Julian?"

"Concentrate please."

She did her best. She was aware as the dance progressed that Julian's eyes were boring into hers, and his smile had vanished.

"Oh. And I'm to congratulate you, of course. Do you think Lady Lucy will make you happy?"

Clearly, this was the right thing to say. Cassie had to spend the next few measures, each time they came together, listening to Julian recite a list of Lady Lucy's charms, achievements, and pedigree.

How exceedingly dull. Had he always been this boring?

It was a mercy when their dance came to an end. She curtsied briefly then just stared past his shoulder, dismissing him with barely a thought.

The gentleman in black was striding toward her.

Lord Stranraer.

He bowed, took her in his arms, and almost lifted her off the ground as he swirled her around in time to the music. She didn't bang into anyone, get her skirts caught, trip, elbow, nor was she elbowed. He sliced his way through the throng with the precision of a diamond cutter, light and sure on his feet, and not in any way, shape, or form similar to a carthorse.

He took total control, and she barely had to think about the steps or the music. She and he were one. They moved and danced as one.

Why did he not speak? She waited, held captive by his eyes and his hands, floating along as if on a cloud. How was it that she, too, was tongue-tied? She had so many questions. So many things to tell him. All around them was a hubbub of gay chatter, dancing partners conversing and laughing. They were the only pair who remained silent.

The tension built to a point where she could stand it no longer.

"Ned," she said on a strangled breath. "Don't you know me?"

The brown eyes behind the mask twinkled at her. "Of course I do, foolish wench, just as you do me. I would know you anywhere."

She watched the slow smile below the mask, the appearance of those dimples which made him seem so much more human. "I know you by the way you hold yourself, the way you walk, the little movements of your head when you speak. I can tell you're in a good mood, which augurs well."

"Am I not always in a good mood?" Well, she hadn't been lately, but hopefully he would change all that tonight.

"Not with me, that's for certain," he replied. "But I hope to win you round eventually. I have a gift for you, too."

"Winning me round may require more than a gift," she teased, though in reality it would take merely a look from him.

He laughed wryly. "Don't I know it."

She smiled back. "Then why have you been silent?"

"I have much to say to you, but this isn't the time. Will you trust yourself to my company for a short while?"

"What, and disappoint all my would-be beaux?"

He feigned affront. "I sincerely hope so."

Soon after the set ended she found herself alone with Ned in a small room lined by glass-fronted cases filled with antique Chinese porcelain.

It didn't seem real, standing alone with him, both of them wearing the outlandish fashions of the past, both masked and mysterious, yet so achingly familiar.

She wasn't even quite sure how she'd arrived there. She didn't remember the end of the dance, nor the walk down the darkened corridor.

But she did recall the sound of a key in the lock.

Which meant that this time, *she* was the one imprisoned.

Chapter Thirty-Eight

Ned raised his mask and willed his heart back into a steady beat. Cassie had revealed nothing of her feelings beyond her usual attempts to tease him. Yet the fact that she seemed happy to be in his arms again had turned a flicker of hope into a blaze of optimism.

She wouldn't be alone with him like this if she were now betrothed to Carnforth.

Would she?

His throat was dry as he said, "Will you not lift your mask, Cassie? I want to see you."

She did so, and appreciation rippled through him. She was such a beauty! Even in the high wig and voluminous skirts, she could turn a man's head.

"I hope you're enjoying your evening," he said, at a loss as to how to proceed. He wanted to know her status with Carnforth but was terrified to ask and have his whole world crushed.

Should he just kiss her and be damned?

"How polite you are, Lord Stranraer," she said. "I hope

you're enjoying the evening, yourself. I must say, you look rather splendid in all that black silk, with the white lace at your collar and cuffs."

"How kind of you to say so," he said drily. "It's my Parisian silk suit—I'd hoped to impress you with it. My valet has added a few bits and pieces to make it more like the fashions of our forefathers. I must confess, I'm not much for flowered waistcoats in the normal run of things."

She chuckled, and he relished the sound. Her eyes sparkled as she said, "Ned. No one of your stature could ever look foppish."

Her appreciation made him bolder. He took her hands, and she didn't shy away.

"I wasn't certain if the costumes would serve," he said. "But it was you who gave me the idea."

Deuce take it, why were they making polite conversation when her peach-colored lips were mere inches from his own?

No.

Control yourself, Ned.

He must go slowly, as planned, or risk ruining everything.

She looked puzzled. He noticed there was a beauty spot glued to one cheek, and another tantalizingly placed on the curve of one breast.

"Did I? What idea was that?" Cassie asked.

She must have added the patches herself, to make her costume more authentic. He would never have thought of it. But they were perfect.

"Hmm?"

Especially the one on—

"You said I gave you an idea?"

He tore his eyes away from the steady rise and fall of that tempting patch. "You recommended Georgiana try the fashions of the last century. Powdered wig, slanting hat, and what have you. A masked ball was the ideal opportunity to bring her back into Society."

"She's here?" Cassie asked distractedly.

How he loved the way her eyes shone with wonder. Like a young girl, but still very much a woman.

A woman he wanted very badly.

His voice sounded a bit hoarse when he answered, "She is."

"How splendid. What is she wearing— Oh!" Her eyes widened. "It was *you* who asked Paxton to throw a masked ball, so she wouldn't have to reveal her scars. How clever of you."

He relished the note of admiration in her voice. "Her costume is the twin of yours, only in silver," he said. "I thought yours should match your hair."

Ah yes, *that* was an expression he liked to see—warmth, gratitude, a bosom heaving with emotion.

"*You* sent the costumes?"

It seemed he had played his hand well. So far.

"I did." But he hadn't come here to talk about ball gowns. "Forget the costumes. I want to—"

She stepped closer to him, an indefinable expression in her eyes. "Stop talking, please."

"But I have a good deal more to say."

"You always do. But first, let me thank you."

She went up on tiptoe, laid a hand on his chest, and brushed her lips lightly across his.

So, that was how it felt to be hit by a lightning bolt.

In a pleasurable way.

If only he could keep his unruly body under control until he had done what he needed to do and said what needed to be said.

He lifted both her hands and kissed them. He daren't allow himself to do more.

"Cassie, Georgiana has taken a great liking to you."

"And I to her."

Ned swallowed and took a deep breath. "*I* have taken a great liking to you, too. More than that, in fact…"

Pray God she wouldn't tease him now. He didn't know if he could bear it.

"Then I am doubly favored." Her face was alive with emotion…and she wasn't laughing.

"I know we've had our differences."

"A few."

"But I would like us to be friends. If you should ever have need of me, should you ever want a shoulder to cry on, I will be there for you. Always."

He wanted far more than friendship from her, but he was desperate for some sign that she cared for him, too.

"As a friend?" she asked, brows raised.

Was that a look of disappointment in those hazel eyes?

He summoned up every ounce of courage he possessed, and said, "No. As more than a friend. If you want me. But I understand I may be speaking out of turn. That this may not be the time, if your heart is still held captive by Mr. Carnforth."

One of her hands slid up the edge of his tight-fitting waistcoat. He wondered if she had any idea how erotic the gesture was. Her fingers caught on a button, and she rolled it between them. That gesture, too, was inflammatory. He caught her hand in his and refused to let it escape.

Gazing down, he waited for her reply, feeling like a tightrope walker balanced above a precipice. One false step and his world would come crashing down.

"Ned," she murmured, "Mr. Carnforth is a friend of long-standing, and I hope he will remain so. But I no longer think of him in any other way."

This was exactly what he had hoped to hear. But he'd never felt like this about a woman before and was riddled with doubts. He needed something more from her.

"You mean you have not accepted his offer?" He sent up a silent prayer as he waited, barely breathing, for her answer.

"Of course not. I said I would take neither of you, if you remember. Have you been worried about that?"

That would be an understatement.

"I have been breaking my heart over it," he said slowly. It was a confession he had never expected to make.

"Darling, foolish Ned," she said, stroking his cheek. "I've barely given Julian a thought since Aston."

Tears glistened in her eyes. He wanted to kiss them away. In fact, he wanted to kiss every single inch of her.

Happiness was within his grasp. He could feel it.

"No other gentleman interests me. How could they, after I've given myself to you? Or did you really think me a light-skirt, which you accused me of being when you first dragged me into Wycherley's closet?"

"God, no. I just didn't know if what happened in that wheat field meant anything to you, other than another lesson you would put to use for Carnforth's benefit." He was struggling to find the right words now. Everything sounded so selfish and insulting.

"Of course it did," she whispered. "It meant all the world to me."

Her hand had flattened out against his chest, and he wondered if she could feel the pulsing of his heart. To him, it sounded as loud and furious as a cavalry charge.

Her hand strayed appreciatively across his chest and down his ribs, where she discovered the small box he had tucked into a hidden pocket beneath his waistcoat.

She touched the bulge with a finger. "What's this?"

"I have a gift for you. In case my words are not enough to persuade you to hear me out."

"I'm listening to you now, am I not?" She tilted her head coquettishly.

He grinned. "I'm not sure you've earned it yet."

"What must I do to earn it?"

"Admit that you love me."

"Oh!" She pulled away in shock, but he caught her back into his embrace, pressing her hard against him, her face turned up to his.

He bent his head and gently tasted her lips. She reminded him of late summer honey. The feeling was so exquisite, he did it again.

The idea of any other man kissing those peach-tinted lips, ever, was unthinkable. Cassandra Blythe must be his alone.

Now and forever.

"Very well. I accept that you may not yet love me as I do you, but that's no obstacle to marriage. Many husbands and wives were less than friends when they married, but have made one another happy, nonetheless."

Her hands fluttered within his, like captured birds. Her eyes widened. "You love me?"

"I believe so." He gazed down at her tenderly. "It may, of course, be a mere infatuation, so if I were you, I would marry me quickly and secure your future before I come to my senses."

She blinked wordlessly up at him.

"Will you marry me, Cassandra Blythe?"

She pressed her lips together and frowned.

Did she not believe he was in earnest? Or perhaps…

"Do you want me to ask your father for your hand first? I don't know if I can wait for everything to be done properly. We've already spent nearly a month apart, and it was unbearable," he said.

Her eyes filled. "Then you must come now and meet Papa."

Ned wanted this precious moment to last forever. The door to his heart had been opened, and to close it again and appear to the outside world as if nothing had happened would be impossible. "I cannot let you go until I've given you your gift," he said to stall her.

"But was I not to have earned it first?" she asked uncertainly.

"You have special dispensation. Please turn round."

As she did so, he took out the little box and opened it to extract a brilliant ruby on a delicate silver chain. He laid it carefully round her neck, trying to avoid touching the tempting silk of her skin. For if he did, how would he find the self-control not to explore further—the sensitive pulse below her ear, the column of her neck, the delicious cleft between her breasts?

"There." Taking her by the shoulders, he turned her about to see how the family heirloom looked on the woman he dearly hoped would become the newest member of that family.

Her hand came up beneath the pendant, and she gazed at the ruby then sucked in a breath. When she looked up at him, he could not believe the change in her face. Hurt and betrayal had stolen the roses from her cheeks and lips, and her eyes were hot with unshed tears of pain, not love.

"How could you?" she cried. "Is this some horrible joke? Well, it's not funny, Ned. Not funny at all."

Numb with shock, he watched in disbelief as she yanked at the chain until it broke then threw the precious pendant into a corner. Before he could stop her, she surged across to the door in a flurry of bronze silk, unlocked and wrenched it open, and disappeared into the corridor beyond.

For a few moments, he just stood there, his heart racing in consternation. What had he done? How could he, with that simple but meaningful gift, have distressed her so?

Feeling sick at heart, Ned forced his limbs to move. He couldn't let Cassie go now, not like this, not when he felt he'd come so close to winning her. With no idea what he was going to do or say, he strode out of the room, not even stopping to pick up the precious ruby. He was damned if he'd let yet another silly misunderstanding tear them asunder. Whatever this new problem was, he would find a way to deal with it.

She cared for him. She definitely cared for him. Bolstering his courage with this certainty, he broke into a run, determined she would not evade him.

Chapter Thirty-Nine

Cassie ran blindly down the corridor, just needing to escape. There was a mill of people in one direction, so she took the other. She couldn't face light and noise — her distress needed a haven, somewhere dark and quiet where nobody would find her.

That awful pendant. Had Ned been listening and watching Wycherley's lesson on how to attract a man's attention? What did he mean by invoking it? Had his heartfelt proposal just been a sham? But to what end? She had already given herself to him.

She was so confused.

Hot tears trickled down her cheeks, and she swept them away with her palms. She felt betrayed, and the pain of it pressed on her lungs and tightened her throat, forcing her to drag the air down in great gulps. Her body felt like a yawning, aching chasm of pain.

"Cassie!" Ned was following her.

Spying an open door, she charged through it, down some steps, and out onto the broad lawns behind Highmore House, where she paused.

Which direction should she take? Where could she hide?

In a flash of inspiration, the answer came to her.

The maze.

But only if she could evade him long enough to reach it. She spun round to see if she was still being pursued.

Ned had stopped at the top of the terrace steps, his gaze fastened upon her.

The moonlight carved his face into stark highlights and shadows, rendering him as implacable as a granite statue. Then, to her complete astonishment, he very slowly started unbuttoning his waistcoat.

Surely, he wasn't planning to disrobe in front of everyone? Was he hoping to change her mind by reminding her of his delectable, muscular body and reviving memories of her glorious surrender to him in the field of wheat?

He cantered down the steps then started running swiftly across the grass, directly toward her.

She squeaked in terror, hitched up her skirts, and set off again, around the margin of the lake. Her heart pounded madly. She pushed through a line of laurel bushes, and suddenly her feet were crunching on gravel, and she looked about to see moonlight glinting off the roofs of glasshouses.

The knowledge that she had almost reached her goal spurred her on, despite the crushing pressure of her stays. As soon as the dark mouth of the maze appeared, she shot into it. She carried on running, angling back and forth through all the twists and turns until, finally, with hardly enough breath to remain conscious, she reached the platform in the middle.

Once her breathing had returned to normal, she should be able to listen for Ned, then use the maze's twists and turns to evade and escape him.

"Cassie."

Sweet Venus. How had he found her so quickly?

There was nothing she could do. She had exhausted every last ounce of strength. She was now entirely in Ned's power.

He stood before her for a moment, hands on hips, his chest rising and falling rapidly. Then, without a word, he pulled her to him and held her against his body, rocking her back and forth.

She felt like a rag doll in his arms, bereft of strength, bereft of will.

Nuzzling her hair, he said, "Tell me what I've done wrong, my love. I never meant to upset you. Did you think I was trying to buy you with a family heirloom? I swear, I wouldn't hurt you for the world. I love you. On your happiness depends my own."

She forced back a tear and hung her head, not daring to believe him. The ruby was simply too big a coincidence.

But there were bloodstains on his stockinged feet. Someone who was prepared to risk cutting his feet to ribbons on gravel, might, just possibly, be genuine in his feelings.

Following the direction of her gaze, he said, "I couldn't run in those damned shoes. I don't know how you managed in that get-up. I picked up your stomacher, by the way. Did you know it had fallen out?"

She looked down again. Her low-necked chemise was now revealed beneath the loosened lacing of the bronze gown. The stomacher would have to be put on again if she had any hope of returning to the ball without her reputation in tatters.

Of course, it was probably too late for that. Everyone on the terrace had witnessed their moonlit chase.

To give herself thinking time, she asked, "How did you navigate the maze so quickly?"

"Paxton and I have been friends for years, so I'm well acquainted. The labyrinth, however, is far easier to understand than you, my love. You must never doubt the strength of my feelings. I would run across the gravel again if it would prove them to you."

Her distress slowly started to crumble. "Truly?"

"Tell me," Ned demanded, holding her head up so she was forced to look at him. "What did I do wrong?"

The feeling of betrayal started ebbing into embarrassment.

"I'm sure you already know."

"I don't." He gave her a gentle shake. "You *must* tell me, Cassie. I'm not letting you out of my sight until you do."

She couldn't look him in the eyes. "The ruby pendant…"

He frowned. "A family heirloom. What about it?"

She took a deep breath, looking chagrined. "Wycherley advised me to wear one like it to entice a man."

Ned appeared genuinely confused. "A ruby?"

"Between my… To make him think about my…" Her face blazed, and she glanced away in mortification. "You must know what he said, as I'm sure you were spying on us through the keyhole."

Her fists clenched and unclenched at her sides. She wanted to throttle Ned for putting her through this horrible chaos of emotions. But a small part of her just wanted to run her hands over the mounded muscle of his upper arms and up into his tousled dark hair, to forgive him and pull him close for a kiss.

Her mind was telling her one thing, her body and her heart another. The agony of this conflict was close to unbearable.

"I did no such thing," Ned replied firmly. "I already liked you more than I should, and it would have been anathema to watch him touch you. What, exactly, did Wycherley teach you about rubies and the art of seduction?"

She had to clear her throat a couple of times, and knew she was blushing furiously, but she told him the story. His eyes grew rounder with every word. When she finished, he chuckled and gave her an affectionate squeeze.

"That sort of ploy might affect a more shallow, lecherous

man, I suppose. But the last time I saw that pendant around a woman's neck, it was Georgiana's, and before her, my mother's. So all the associations in my mind are most innocent. That damned Wycherley! I cannot believe I've agreed to take him as a brother-in-law."

She looked up in surprise and smiled. "Really? You agreed to their betrothal?"

"Given your defense of him, I assumed you wouldn't marry me otherwise." He grimaced. "I may yet come to regret my generosity of spirit."

Could it be true that Ned had completely abandoned his dire intent? Had he finally learned to forgive and put the happiness of his sister above his need for revenge? *Thank goodness.*

"He is forgiven?" she asked hopefully.

"Not entirely, but for Georgiana's sake, I have curbed my desire to ruin him and instead will allow him to attempt to win me over."

He was smiling, revealing the dimples that she so loved to see. As she gazed up into his dark eyes, she knew she was utterly smitten and could forgive him absolutely anything. She unclenched her fists and slid them around his waist.

It felt so good to be touching him again!

He responded with a sigh, held her closer, and brushed his lips across her temple.

"So," he said, his voice so soft she could barely hear him. "Are you going to marry me or not?"

Her whole body felt deliciously, gloriously alive. A wave of joy crashed over her, and she knew exactly what she wanted.

His love, *his* heart, *his* smile.

She pushed up on tiptoe, lifting her lips for a kiss.

His mouth was just a whisper away, but he said, "And can I be certain that you no longer have any tender feelings for Mr. Carnforth? I couldn't bear it if even just a fragment of your heart belonged to anybody else."

Cassie never knew what prompted her to tease her poor, long-suffering lover after this heartfelt confession. Because, after all, she'd told him she had happily refused Julian's offer of marriage. What more proof of her devotion did he need? But there must have been a little imp inside her that wanted to provoke him into an even stronger declaration of his own love.

She replied, "Well, I can't exactly say one hundred percent. But I daresay time will tell."

He suddenly let out a great roar of frustration. The next instant, she was hauled up and thrown over his shoulder, knocking all the breath from her body.

As soon as she recovered from the shock, she kicked out wildly and pummeled her fists against his broad back and buttocks.

To no avail.

Her wig fell off, and her head bumped up and down like a puppet's as he strode out of the maze with her and back along the gravel path toward the lawn. She let out a shriek, half defiance, half fear, and was immediately silenced by his threat of throwing her across his knee in front of everyone at Highmore and giving her the spanking she deserved.

Unbelievable!

The rogue carried her up the steps and in through the open French doors of the ballroom. Everyone gaped at them as he strode to the center of the dance floor. Without their masks, Ned and Cassie were easily recognizable, so there was no hope of hiding.

The ability to faint at will would have been helpful right now, but she was wound up like a clock, and even if he set her on her feet there was no way she could have swooned convincingly.

She was also—and it was terrible to admit it—singularly

aroused by Ned's indomitable strength and sense of purpose. But what that purpose was, she hadn't a clue.

He came to a halt. Her head still hung down toward the parquet floor, her face thankfully obscured by her cascading hair. Her heart thundered.

And she knew that nothing that ever happened to her for the rest of her life would ever be as humiliating as this very moment.

Chapter Forty

Ned stood in the middle of the ballroom with the woman he planned to marry draped over his shoulder, feeling like some ancient Scottish ancestor of his, carrying off a maiden from a rival clan.

Much as ripples spread out from a stone thrown into a pond, the dancers gradually stilled, then the conversations at the edges of the ballroom hushed, and when the ripple reached the orchestra, they, too, fell silent.

Feeling ludicrously self-conscious and already singularly regretting his impulsive act, Ned lowered Cassie gently to the ground, then knelt before her.

An astonished murmur ran through the crowd, and he became aware of disturbances as individuals began to push their way through. He'd better get this over with quickly before Paxton had him thrown out on his ear.

"Miss Cassandra Blythe," he said, in a voice loud enough to carry right up to the twinkling chandeliers, "for the third and final time, will you do me the honor of becoming my wife?"

There were a few shocked gasps and exclamations from the

onlookers. Then the room fell so quiet it was impossible to believe it held a good three hundred people. Heads were bobbing up at the back as everyone struggled to get a better view.

Ned looked up into Cassandra's face and waited, hardly daring to breathe. If she refused him now, he didn't know how he would bear it.

She pushed her tangled hair back from her face, smoothed down her skirts, and put her hands on either side of her slender waist. Then she took a deep breath, and he bent his head, fearing the storm of recriminations that was sure to erupt.

"Ned Talbot," she said, each word like a bullet to his heart. "You are the rudest, most infuriating, pig-headed man I have ever come across."

There was a movement in the crowd, and Ned looked up to see two familiar gentlemen step forward. Wycherley and Carnforth. One of them was pushing a Bath chair containing a very angry-looking elderly gentleman.

Damn it all to hell.

If he had to fight them over this, they would *all* be thrown out. Except the older gentleman, of course, who must be Cassie's father.

Cassie's hazel eyes softened, and the corner of her mouth quirked up then quivered. Was she laughing? No, she was crying. Both?

"Forgive me," he said, in a voice meant for her only to hear. Please God, she didn't mean to refuse him again?

His heart felt like lead in his chest, his limbs so heavy he could barely hold himself up. It was an agony to look at her, so he bent his head again, waiting for the ax to fall and destroy his hopes of happiness forever.

"But I don't think you're entirely beyond redemption," Cassie continued with a hint of laughter in her voice. "So, the answer is yes, Edmund Talbot, and yes, and yes again. Now kiss me, damn you, before I change my mind!"

He leaped to his feet. Oh thank *God*. He threw his arms about her, clasped her to his heart, and brushed his face against hers, eyes tight shut, wanting to see nothing that would distract him from the joy of having her in his arms once more.

For good, this time.

The people around them came back to life, shuffling their feet, the ladies fluttering their fans and the gentlemen whispering to one another. But the music did not start up again, and nobody moved forward, no doubt in case the scene had not yet played itself out.

It hadn't.

Ned released Cassie and looked into her upturned face. She reminded him of a flower, newly opened to receive the warmth of the sun, fresh and full of life. Her eyes were focused on his mouth, her lips slightly parted, and he knew exactly what she wanted. But that would only make the scandal complete.

As if it weren't already.

"There's something I want to hear from those beautiful lips of yours," he said. He drilled his gaze into hers, willing her to understand, begging her to say the words he so needed to hear.

Her face shone with joy as she said, "I love you, Ned. With all my heart."

The room erupted into hefty sighs and loud hurrahs from the men, giggles and tears from the ladies, and, louder than everything else, the thunder of riotous applause.

Oblivious to the commotion, Ned threw propriety out the window, bent his head, and kissed Cassie full on the lips, enfolding her tightly against his chest.

And as they clung to each other, he thanked heaven and the earth that had made her for giving him the most perfect gift of all.

Miss Cassandra Blythe, who had shown him the beautiful, awe-inspiring power of love.

Author's Note

Why name this Entangled Scandalous Series "Wayward in Wessex"? Wessex is actually another name for the South and South-west of England. I first came across it when studying Thomas Hardy's novel *The Mayor of Casterbridge* at school.

Hardy used the term "Wessex" to cover a geographical area stretching from Oxford in the north to Plymouth, Devon, in the west and Hampshire in the east. This reflected the extent of the Anglo-Saxon kingdom of Wessex, a name deriving from the term "West Saxons." The most famous king of this region was Alfred the Great (d.899 A.D.), credited with uniting English resistance to Viking attack.

Wessex is a stunningly beautiful region, encompassing the savage splendor of Cheddar Gorge in Somerset, the granite outcrops of Dartmoor, the chalk downs of Wiltshire and Berkshire with their ancient hill figures, and the genteel Georgian city of Bath. Each book in the "Wayward in Wessex" series has at least part of the action set in this remarkable and romantic part of England, where it is now my privilege to live. I will also be using this area as the backdrop for another series, written for the Entangled Select Imprint. So watch out for "Wedded in Wessex"!

Acknowledgments

I am extremely grateful to Nina Bruhns, my editor, who saw a glimmer of potential in my #PitMad competition entries, and has been my guiding hand in getting the first three books in the "Wayward in Wessex" series into shape. I look forward to working with her again on my two forthcoming historical romances for the Entangled Select Imprint. Thanks are also due to the Entangled team who, right from the start, have welcomed me and dealt kindly with my rookie mistakes.

My friends and fellow authors, Anna Albo and Shelley Inōn, have supported me every step of the way on my journey to publication. They have dispensed advice, made me laugh, and helped me recover from my melt-downs. I am so glad we found each other, ladies. You are both absolutely awesome writers!

I would also like to thank fellow romance authors Annie Burrows and Barbara Monajem for their support, and the amazing Tamara Gill for letting me come to her splendid Facebook parties.

Thank you to all those friends, both real and virtual, who

didn't fall about laughing when I said I wanted to be a writer. Thanks also to my Wattpad followers for reading, critiquing, and voting on my works. You've given me some much-needed confidence boosts and saved me from making some embarrassing mistakes!

About the Author

Elizabeth Keysian felt destined to write historical romance due to her Cornish descent, and an ancestral connection to the Norse god Odin. Being an only child gave her plenty of time to read, create imaginary worlds, produce her own comics, and write sketches and a deplorably bad musical for an amateur dramatics group.

Three decades spent working in museums and archaeology fired Elizabeth's urge to write, as did living on a Knights Templar estate, with a garage full of skeletons, a resident ghost, and a moat teeming with newts.

Elizabeth lives near Bath in England with her partner and cats.

More information can be found via her website or by signing up to her "Key to Romance" newsletter. Don't forget to visit the Entangled website for more ravishing romances!

Discover the **Wayward in Wessex** *series…*

DISTRACTING THE DUKE

Get Scandalous with these historical reads…

THE ROGUE OF ISLAY ISLE
a *Highland Isles* novel by Heather McCollum

Cullen Duffie is the new chief of Clan MacDonald. Determined to prove he's not his father, Cullen works to secure his clan against the English. When a woman washes onto Islay's shores, he protects her from his uncles' schemes. Waking up not knowing who she is or where she comes from, Madeleine is at the mercy of the man who found her. Through dreams and flashes of her past, she rebuilds her memories. But the more she recalls, the more she realizes the jeopardy she is bringing to Islay, Clan MacDonald, and the Highlander who has captured her heart.

HOW TO LOSE A HIGHLANDER
a *MacGregor Lairds* novel by Michelle McLean

In this Highlander *Taming of the Shrew* meets *How to Lose a Guy in 10 Days* tale, Sorcha Campbell and Laird Malcolm MacGregor are determined to break the bonds of their forced matrimony. To do so, they'll have to keep their hands, and hearts, to themselves, or risk being permanently wed. But there's a thin line between love and hate, and even their feuding clans might not be enough to keep their passion at bay.

Falling for the Pirate

a *Men of Fortune* novel by Amber Lin

Juliana Hargate is the daughter of Captain Nate Bowen's enemy. Nate vowed he would have his revenge, but he never expected to have the tool of his revenge to be so desirable. And at his complete mercy…

Captive. Juliana is imprisoned by a tall, imposing, and entirely unscrupulous pirate. A pirate whose eyes seem to look past her skirts and many petticoats, and whose touch sends delicious ripples of desire through her. With every passing day, she finds herself tempted to give him the very thing he's determined to take…

The Elusive Wife

a *Marriage Mart Mayhem* novel by Callie Hutton

Newly arrived from the country for the Season, Lady Olivia is appalled to discover that her own husband, Jason Cavendish, Lord Coventry, doesn't even recognize her. She's not about to tell the arrogant arse she's his wife. Instead, she flirts with him by night and has her modiste send her mounting bills to him by day. Hell hath no fury like a woman scorned…too bad this woman finds her husband nearly irresistible.

Made in the USA
Columbia, SC
29 April 2017